Also by Kylie Scott

THE LAST DAYS OF LILAH GOODLUCK
END OF STORY

For a full list of books by Kylie Scott,
please visit kyliescott.com.

THE
LAST DAYS
OF
LILAH
GOODLUCK

KYLIE SCOTT

GRAYDON
HOUSE

**GRAYDON
HOUSE®**

ISBN-13: 978-1-525-80480-9

The Last Days of Lilah Goodluck

Graydon House
22 Adelaide St. West, 41st Floor
Toronto, Ontario M5H 4E3, Canada
www.GraydonHouseBooks.com
www.BookClubbish.com

Printed in U.S.A.

THE
LAST DAYS
OF
LILAH
GOODLUCK

1

Friday

Good Witch Willow is unhappy at me for keeping her waiting. This is made obvious by the way she glares up at me through her wire-rim glasses while tugging on one of the crystal pendants around her neck. Like it is going to take help from beyond to stop her from slapping me silly or something.

"Lilah," says my best friend with much patience, "why are you like this?"

"I don't know."

"Just ask her a question already."

Rebecca (not Becca or Becky) does have a point. It's not like I haven't known this moment was coming for weeks now. She wanted to do something fun for her birthday and every other entertainer had already been booked. A lot of birthday parties in March, apparently. Guess everyone has sex in the summertime.

The private room at the back of the bespoke cocktail bar off Santa Monica Boulevard is close to capacity and a song by Hozier plays over the speakers. We stand at one of the tall round bar tables with the remains of a charcuterie board and a flickering tea light in a vintage jar. The walls are painted a bright turquoise, but the vibe is relaxed. It should be a great night. I want it to be for my friend's sake. But I am anxious and distracted and not in the mood at all, dammit.

"I honestly don't have one," I say. "I'm sorry. I told you this wasn't my thing."

Rebecca groans and downs more than a mouthful of her whiskey sour. It's her party, she can self-medicate if she wants to—and apparently, she does.

"What do people normally ask?"

Good Witch Willow is older with white skin and long gray hair in a braid. She's exactly what I imagined a witch would look like when I was a child. A dramatic long lace dress and plenty of chunky jewelry. Instead of answering me, she glances at her smartwatch and announces, "That's your two hours up. I'm out of here."

Rebecca gives me a look.

Good Witch Willow wastes no time, packing her tarot cards, a travel-size crystal ball, and a collection of brightly colored crystals back into her large velvet tote.

"I'm sorry," I say to Rebecca for the second time. "Though your work bestie hogging her for over forty minutes to ask about his fantasy football team didn't help. And your neighbor that needed that emergency love potion. I wonder if she'll actually manage to find Keanu Reeves and persuade him to drink it."

Rebecca just raises her brows.

"You have to give it to her, it's a beautiful dream," I say. "But my point is you, my friend, are popular. There are a lot of people here. The chance of Good Witch Willow getting around to everyone was always going to be low."

"Just admit you're all up in your feelings about your boyfriend again."

"I *am* worried about Josh." I take a sip from my gimlet. "He said the headache was really bad, that it was messing with his vision."

"That actually doesn't sound good," she reluctantly agrees.

"Yeah. I really think he needs to see a doctor, but you know what dudes are like."

"I don't know if you've noticed, but I've pretty much made it my life mission to not know what dudes are like." She takes another sip of her drink. "You're going to rush home to play nurse instead of going dancing with me, aren't you?"

"Rebecca, can *you* predict the future?" I fake gasp. "And you never told me... That hurts. Wait. Did you know that was going to hurt?"

She gives me an amused smile and raises the remains of her drink in a toast. We've been best friends since sharing a dorm room in college about a decade ago. She's petite with dark hair and olive skin. I, on the other hand, am more of a robust blonde. They didn't spare the tits and ass when they made me.

"Go on. Abandon me, then," she says. "But you owe me."

"How about I take you out to dinner next week? To that Japanese place you love?"

"No complaining when I eat all the salmon sashimi."

"Agreed. Happy almost birthday. Talk to you tomorrow." I set my mostly empty gimlet on the bar and give her a hug. "Don't go home with Priya. You know you'll only regret it. Again."

"But she's brilliant and beautiful and emotionally unavailable. She's exactly my type."

"Oh my God. It's like you just proved my point."

"Get out of here, loser."

I smack a kiss on her cheek. "I love you, Rebecca. Make good choices."

Despite the late hour, there are still plenty of people around. The road is glossy black from a recent storm, and puddles on the sidewalk reflect the lights from the bars and restaurants. I huddle down into my cardigan against the cold night air. There's a small convenience store open on the other side. Just perfect for picking up Tylenol since I have no idea how much we have at home, and Josh might need more. Better safe than sorry.

I join the only other person waiting at the corner to cross, and she just so happens to be Good Witch Willow. Her stereotypical pointed boot taps impatiently as she rummages through her colorful velvet tote in search of something. Being a witch must be interesting. Not that I believe in all that. Divination and spirits and so on never seemed particularly probable to me. My father is an atheist and taught us to question everything and always demand proof. I'm also a librarian, and librarians like facts. An established truth is a beautiful thing. They help to prop up society and keep us warm at night. Or they used to.

The walk light flashes, and Willow's gray braid swings as she steps off the curb. I follow with my mind wandering, thinking about what else Josh might need and whether I should buy him some soda. But out of the corner of my eye, I see it—a sleek vehicle that doesn't stop like the others. It doesn't even slow down. It is, in fact, speeding straight toward us with headlights dazzlingly bright.

There's no time to think. I grab the older woman from behind as I propel us both back toward the curb and tumble to the ground. Had she been any bigger, it might not have worked. But my years of infrequent gym attendance finally come in handy. Wheels screech and the horn blares as the sports car roars past us. It's so damn close I can feel the rush of air in its wake.

But we don't get hit.

Holy shit. My heart is hammering. Willow's elbow digs into my stomach as she rolls off me onto the pavement. Whatever. I am just honestly amazed to still be amongst the living.

"Asshole!" Good Witch Willow hollers at the fading taillights.

The cool damp ground is hard beneath me, but overhead a star twinkles in a gap between the clouds. Parts of me hurt. My hand is bloody and scraped, and my hip is bruised. There's also a tear in the tiered skirt of my new pale blue minidress, not to mention numerous stains from the wet and dirty sidewalk. Odds are also good that I just flashed my panties at the entire street.

Willow raises a brow at me. "Oh, it's you."

"You're welcome," I reply dryly.

A young man standing nearby caught the whole thing on his cell. And is still filming. A jogger stops and offers Willow his hand. He gently pulls her to her feet before doing the same for me. Which is nice of him.

Willow brushes herself off, gathering the items that fell from her tote. Breath mints, hand sanitizer, and such. "I didn't see that car coming at all."

Were I not still catching my breath, I would definitely make a smart-ass comment about her supposed prognostication abilities. Or at least give it serious consideration. But my hip is aching and my hand stings. I wince as I pick a piece of gravel out of one of my deeper scratches. What a mess.

"You're the one who wanted to know what people ask me, aren't you?" She tosses her braid over her shoulder and narrows her gaze on me. Like she's attempting to stare into my soul or something.

"Don't worry about it," I say. "Are you okay?"

She nods. "Falling on you made for a soft landing."

"Great."

"There's a lot that people would like to know," she continues. "But the most popular questions tend to revolve around love. Are they cheating on me? Will they come back to me? Who's my soulmate? Things like that."

"Makes sense, I guess."

"Then they tend to move on to more mundane issues, like if they're going to get that promotion, or are they on the right career track? Then you've got the ones who think they're funny. They like to ask me for this week's lotto numbers."

I snort. "That is kind of funny."

"Not when you're hearing it for the hundredth time, it isn't. And then there are the ones who want to know when they're going to die." She cocks her head and sighs. "That car would have hit me if you hadn't been there. Given the speed it was going, I doubt it would have ended well for me."

I don't know what to say to that, so I keep my mouth shut.

"It would seem you're owed something."

"That's not necessary."

"Be quiet and listen." Willow draws herself up to her full height, and her gaze turns hazy. As if she's staring into the middle distance. Then, in a sonorous tone, she announces, "He is cheating on you. But I think you already know that deep down. The name of your soulmate is Alistair George Arthur Lennox. What a mouthful."

My smile is bemused. "Wait a minute. You don't mean—"

"You will be passed over for the promotion. They really don't appreciate you. I have no idea why you've stayed there so long."

"It's complicated. You're actually predicting all of this, aren't you?"

"Five, eight, twelve, twenty-four, thirty-nine, and forty-three. And I'm very sorry to tell you this, but you will die next Sunday."

"What?" I shake my head. She cannot be saying what I think she is saying. Because there is not a chance in hell that this is real. "No. That's not possible."

"You might want to say goodbye to your loved ones and get your affairs in order."

My laughter is brittle with an edge of disbelief. "Are you serious? I mean, you're joking, right?"

Willow blinks several times and blows out a breath. Like she's coming back to herself or returning to her version of reality or whatever. Maybe she hit her head on the pavement. It's the only thing that makes sense. Though she believed in all the supernatural stuff to begin with. Which just goes to validate my belief that people are wild.

"Right," she says. "Good night."

"Did you mean *right* as in you were joking?"

But without another word, she heads off into the night, leaving me standing there stunned.

I ask the night at large, in a not-so-quiet voice, "What in the actual fuck?"

But no one answers. Even the dude with the cell phone

has disappeared. Despite the drama and weirdness, no one so much as spares me a glance. The world keeps turning and life goes on. Insert big sigh here.

What I need is to buy the Tylenol, go home, check on Josh, down some of the previously mentioned painkillers (for my poor sore hip and hand), have a long hot shower, and then go to bed.

By the time the Uber drops me home, the lotto ticket for Saturday night's big draw is hidden in the bottom of my cross-body bag. I think I remembered most of the numbers. I've always been more of a word person. But it's not like it matters. No one even needs to know I bought the thing. Because it's stupid. There is no way that Willow is actually psychic. Josh and I are solid. There aren't even any suitable jobs currently available in my area. And I am not dying in nine days.

The actual definitive proof with regard to all of this, however, is the name she gave me of my supposed soulmate: Alistair George Arthur Lennox. I don't need to look up who he is because I already know. I doubt there's anyone on the planet who hasn't heard of him since the paparazzi love him as much as he loathes them.

I trudge my tired self up the stairs to our second-floor apartment. All my moaning and groaning echoes up the stairwell and out into the uncaring night. The sound is neither brave nor attractive, but I don't care. If this is how it feels to be almost hit by a car, it officially sucks.

My apartment building dates back to the fifties. Two neat lines of boxlike apartments, all opening onto the central strip of garden running through the middle. It's a style typical of

LA and the times. I walk with my keys sticking out between my fingers like my mom taught me. Just in case.

Music is playing inside. Something by the Arctic Monkeys. Josh must be feeling better. When I left, he was lying in the dark with a wet facecloth covering his eyes and talking in whispers. He doesn't usually get migraines or headaches. Another reason to be concerned. But he insisted I go to my best friend's party without him. And I did want to be there for Rebecca.

I unlock the door and toss my purse and the box of painkillers on the kitchen counter. Toeing off my favorite booties has never felt better. They too are sadly scuffed from the night's drama. Hopefully they can be fixed. An antique mirror hanging on the wall confirms that my long blond hair is a bedraggled mess. So much for beach waves.

There's no response to my call of "Babe?"

The apartment has a simple layout, with an open living/kitchen/dining space and a separate bathroom and bedroom off to the side. Not particularly large but reasonably affordable and close to work. I asked Josh to move in with me on Valentine's Day. It was almost our six-month anniversary and the timing felt right. It still gives me a thrill to call it *our* apartment. I've never lived with someone who I was in a committed relationship with before. It is a whole new level of adulthood.

"You're home early," he says, stepping out of the bedroom wearing only a pair of boxer briefs. His short blond hair is in disarray, and his smile is strained. Like it won't quite stick. "Thought you were going dancing after drinks."

"I was worried about you. How are you feeling?"

"Yeah. Okay."

"You look better. There's color back in your face." I turn

to show him the tear in my skirt and the graze on my hand. "You're not going to believe what happened to me tonight. Just let me get the first aid stuff, and I'll tell you all about it."

"I'll get it. You wait there."

I ignore him and follow him into the bedroom, where the bed linens are askew. Like, seriously skew-whiff. The pillows are on the floor, and our blanket has been kicked to the end of the mattress. Only the white sheet remains. It's so rumpled that it appears as if someone was bouncing on the bed or something.

"I said I'd get it," he says with a frown. His hand is on the bathroom doorknob, but it does not turn and open the door as nature intended. Nay. It just sits there waiting.

"What's wrong, Josh?"

His frown deepens and his gaze skips around the room. Almost as if he is avoiding eye contact. "Nothing. I just…"

"You just what? Why are you being weird?"

And then I hear it…a quiet shuffling sound coming from inside the bathroom. For a moment I almost think I imagined it. Like my mind is playing tricks on me. It has been that sort of night. But the way my boyfriend reacts leaves no room for doubt. His eyes go wide, and his mouth does the same. Though there are still no words coming out. Guess he doesn't know what to say. Which would be a first.

"Is there someone in the bathroom?" I am quite proud of my voice. It is a little quiet but firm. "Josh?"

Now there's panic in his eyes.

No. This cannot be happening. But the way my heart has sunk straight through the floor says otherwise. My boyfriend really is cheating on me. He hasn't even finished unpacking, and he's already chosen to stray. *Holy shit, the witch was right.*

He finally pulls himself together enough to say, "Babe, I can explain. It's not what you think."

"It's that new girl from work, isn't it? The one you said you asked to stop messaging you because it was inappropriate. But of course, that was a lie. Because you faked being sick and invited her to my home so you could bang her in my bed." My hands start to shake, so I curl my fingers into fists. I'm not going to hit him. Not that he wouldn't deserve it. But I will deal with this like a grown-ass woman. One who doesn't want to be charged with assault.

"It was an accident," he says. Followed fast by "This is just a misunderstanding."

A loud thud comes from the bathroom. Guess his sexy-times guest disagrees.

"Babe, I swear, just let me explain. I didn't have a clue she was coming over. Don't even know how she got the address." The doorknob tries to turn beneath his hand. "Stay in there. Just give us a minute, please."

This time, there's an angry thump against the other side of the bathroom door. Fair enough.

"This is all just a horrible mistake," says Josh. "I mean, you've been working such long hours lately and—"

"Are you trying to tell me this is my fault?" I ask, incredulous. "Seriously?"

He tugs his short hair in frustration. "No. Yes. I mean... you're so busy all the—"

"Stop." I take a deep, cleansing, fortifying breath and let it out slowly. "I don't want to hear it. Just pack your shit and get out of here."

"But it's not what you think!"

"It is exactly what I think, and we both know it," I all but growl. "I want you out of my home and out of my life. Right now, Josh. You and I are through."

He stares wide-eyed at me in shock. Then his shoulders finally slump in defeat. Josh has always been a bit of a golden boy. The favorite child and so on. I don't think the idea of there being actual consequences to his behavior ever occurred to him. Life sure comes at you fast sometimes.

Finally, a woman's voice calls out through the bathroom door, "Can I come out now?"

2

Saturday

"You look awful," my boss tells me the next afternoon at the end of my shift. Patricia is tall, thin, and more than a little mean. Take for instance the way she glares at small children. Sure, they can be shouty. But it isn't easy to explain the concept of quiet in the library to a toddler. And sometimes being a book lover does mean attempting to eat them. Such is life. "Not that I don't appreciate you covering Courtney's shift. But are you certain you're not also coming down with the flu? And what on earth happened to your hands?"

The dream of enjoying a lazy weekend after dancing the night away with my best friend is long gone. I am instead at work after approximately two and a half hours of sleep, much soul-searching, and no small amount of crying. Not that Josh deserves my tears.

It took a while to remove every trace of his presence from my apartment. Then, at three a.m. when he was finally gone, I donned my emotional-support hoodie and had a much-deserved breakdown. Just got it all out. And I solemnly promised myself this would be the last time it happened.

At least for a while.

Forget dating. I am focusing on my career for the foreseeable future. I turn thirty later this year, and there are things I want to achieve by then. A committed relationship was on the list...but oh well. Turns out you can't schedule love. However, it's not too late for the others: inching my way closer to managerial level, visiting the Bodleian Library in Oxford, England, eating my way through the pastry display case at my favorite bakery on La Brea, and learning how to keep a houseplant alive.

When I still couldn't sleep, I had a stern talk with myself about Good Witch Willow. I am not superstitious, and I don't believe in the paranormal. People cheat in relationships every day. The data relating to this is of course unreliable, but estimates suggest that up to 75 percent of people have cheated in some way at one time or another. My parents are the outliers, still being happily married after over thirty years and two children. Plenty of people come from single-parent homes and split families. All my friends have struck out relationship-wise at least once. I myself have been ghosted, disappointed, dumped, and duped. Without being bitter, I think it's reasonable to acknowledge that finding *the one* is hard. If *the one* even exists. There is nothing spooky or mysterious going on in my life. Josh is just an asshole. End of story.

Despite the long night, when the request came from work to fill in for a sick colleague, I said yes. A distraction sounded great. I fortified myself with more painkillers, caffeine, and carefully applied makeup. Then I made my way back out into the world as a strong single woman.

"I had a little accident last night." I hide my hands in my pockets and give my boss my best fake smile. "But I'm fine. Just fine."

"If you say so," she sniffs. "Can you stay a bit longer? Some items are about to be dropped off for a display. If you could handle that before leaving?"

"Not a problem, Patricia."

"There was also another matter I wanted to quickly talk to you about." She looks down the length of her nose at me. "I know you applied for Program Librarian last year and were disappointed when you didn't get it. And of course, there was Acquisitions Supervisor before that."

"Right."

"Well, the position of Children's Librarian will soon become available. Ming is moving to Chicago."

"Really? That's wonderful news. Not about losing Ming, of course. But Children's Librarian…that would be perfect."

Patricia's answering smile is more of a grimace. Like positive emotions aren't really her thing. But I don't care. I could hug the woman right now. Though that would be wildly awkward for both of us.

Take that, Good Witch Willow. Talk about being validated. I didn't expect to have further proof that her late-night sidewalk prophesies were rubbish until the lotto draw tonight. But this is great. My boss has given me a heads-up, and she's supporting my bid for promotion, going directly against what Willow said. It's honestly like a weight has been taken off my shoulders. You know when you've been worrying about something in the back of your mind while telling yourself it's okay the entire time? This is exactly that.

"It would be ideal," Patricia confirms. "You tend to have

more patience with our younger patrons than some. But while you're of course welcome to apply, just quietly between you and me, I have already spoken to Brian about him taking on the role."

The smile of relief falls straight off my face. "You've already decided on Brian?"

"Not officially, of course. But I would hate for you to get your hopes up."

It's like time has slowed down. As if I can suddenly hear a clock ticking, counting down the hours left in my days. "Let me get this straight. You've already passed me over for the promotion before I even applied?"

The woman sucks on her teeth. A solid sign of irritation. "Lilah, you have to understand—"

"What, that you don't appreciate me and I shouldn't have stayed here as long as I have?" I say in a tone somewhere between stunned and surprised. "Shit. She was right about this too."

"Of course, staying or leaving is your choice to make," says Patricia in her most strident tone. "But I'll remind you that getting any sort of job in the library system in this city is extremely competitive. There are plenty of people with their Master of Library Science who have been volunteering and applying for years for positions such as yours."

The woman is speaking nothing but the truth. But she still lost me mid-rant.

How was Willow right about this too? It's impossible and improbable and fucking ridiculous. What are the odds of Josh cheating on me and me being overlooked for a promotion all within such a short time span? There are coincidences and then there are clusterfucks. Which is what my life is suddenly turning out to be.

"Lilah?" Patricia asks impatiently. "Are you listening?"

"No."

She splutters in outrage, and I ignore her.

My mind is a mess. A swirling, whirling storm of what-ifs. I can't *die* in eight days. I have things to do. Deep breaths don't help, and calm thoughts do nothing. I am sweaty and stressed out to the nth degree. This might well be my first-ever panic attack. If I could just stop the downward spiral and think things through logically, it still might be okay. I mean, it all comes down to tonight's lotto draw. Say I only get one or none of the numbers, then there's my answer. It's been nothing more than a couple of truly awful coincidences. But if I happen to get more right than that...

"You're right, Patricia. I think I am coming down with the flu," I say as I grab my bag. "I should go."

She gives me the death glare reserved for rule breakers. Patrons who write on or dog-ear pages. But, alas, I am immune.

Death isn't something I tend to dwell on. My father likes to point out that people worry about what happens after they die but don't give much thought to where they were before they were born. A philosopher named Epicurus said as much. This always seemed kind of profound to me. Like if we were fine wherever we were before we were born, odds are we'll be fine wherever we go after we're dead.

I have approximately two hours until the lotto numbers are drawn. Until I find out my fate. Of course, my rational mind refutes all this nonsense. Won't even give it the time of day despite the possible evidence starting to stack up. I sit in my old Prius in the parking lot and inspect my skull. Give it a good going-over searching for any lumps or bumps. Because if I cracked my head last night when I hit the pavement, it would explain a hell of a lot. A concussion can cause all sorts of problems and make you imagine the strangest things.

But there's nothing. All I do is mess up my hair.

Time to calm down. I should go home and fill in the spaces left by my ex. Spread my belongings back around. It might help to give me a feeling of control. I turn on the engine, buckle up my seat belt, reverse out of the parking spot, and maneuver through the lot.

Home sounds good. I'll read a book and rest my sore hip. Ooh. I could get takeout. Now there's an idea. There's nothing fajitas can't fix.

When the radio starts playing a moment later, however, it's a love song. Our song. The one that was on high rotation last summer when Josh and I met. Gah. Make it stop. Have I not suffered enough? The answer is apparently no, since stabbing hard and fast at the buttons only succeeds in cranking up the volume to a deafening level.

The thing is, taking your eyes off the road for more than a moment isn't a good idea. It's just not recommended. There's a reason why you're supposed to watch where you're going. Because despite managing to shut down the damn noise, I look up to find myself deep in the shit. In the wrong lane with a car coming toward me. We're so damn close I can see the man's brows jump high in surprise above his sunglasses.

I screech as the car sensors start blaring. The muscles in my arms strain as I turn the steering wheel sharply to the side. Just veer the vehicle the fuck on over. And it would have been fine if I'd just gone back into my lane. But no. I turn the wrong way and crash straight into a concrete post with a *bang*.

The airbag smacks me in the face, shoving me back against the car seat before deflating with a prolonged hissing noise. It almost drowns out the ringing in my ears. My nose hurts, but I don't think it's broken. All I can do is sit and stare at the crumpled hood. My poor car is ruined. Just absolutely trashed. At least I was still in the parking lot and not driving too fast. I have no new injuries—that I am aware of. It's as positive a spin I can put on such a shit show.

"Are you all right? Can you hear me?" asks a deep male voice with an accent that can only be described as posh but not. A blend of British high society and Scottish brogue. Thank you, romance movies, for teaching me which is which. Christmas rom-coms with lots of snow, and European settings in particular. It's the dude with the sunglasses who I almost ran into. He raps his knuckles on the driver's-side window to be sure he has my attention. "Miss, do you need help?"

An awful mechanical grinding sound comes from deep within the door when I try to lower the glass. Excellent. I push on the door, and he opens it wide before taking a step back and giving me space. He is tall with fair skin and dark stubble. But most of his face is hidden behind black sunglasses and a baseball cap.

"I'm fine," I say, climbing out of the remains of my car. "Thank you."

"Are you sure?"

"Yes. Are you all right?"

He just nods.

Paul from security is jogging through the parking lot toward us. How do I even explain this? A meltdown due to a music malfunction? Fuck my life. Seriously.

The man with the sunglasses wanders back to his own vehicle. He almost looks a little like... No. That would be whatever word is beyond *ridiculous*. I know I am not dealing well when I start misplacing words. Not good. The man licks his lips and turns away as if he needs a moment. "You almost hit my car."

"But I didn't."

"But you *almost* did," he says tersely. The vehicle in question is old, silver, and streamlined—a thing of beauty. Another damn sports car. Why do luxury vehicles suddenly seem to have it in for me? I can see why he would be upset at the thought of it being damaged. However, my vehicle is destroyed and my day has been awful. I am the clear winner in this situation. Or loser, as the case may be. But this doesn't stop his lips from flatlining in unhappiness. "You almost hit *me*."

"And yet the fact remains that I didn't. I missed you and hit the concrete bollard instead. Didn't I?"

Nothing from him.

"Didn't I?"

People obviously don't often contradict him. Because it takes him an overly long moment to admit, "Yes. You did."

"Thank you."

He stares at me and I stare right back at him. At least, I think that's what he's doing behind those dark glasses. It's no joke to say the man is fire. He has to be a model or an actor or something. Though almost everyone is in this town. Stubble lines a jaw that could win architectural awards. His car and clothes scream quiet luxury. A simple modern black leather jacket with matching jeans, tee, and boots. And they're all low-key, classy, and well cut.

Paul slowed down and is talking to someone on his cell phone. I hope it's not the police or Patricia. It's probably just him reporting to the security office that there's been an accident. Fingers crossed.

On the bright side, Good Witch Willow didn't see this one coming. There was no prophecy about crashing my car. It could almost be taken as a positive if you didn't look at it too closely. And right now, I need all the doubt I can rally when it comes to her and her skills of divination.

"Your vehicle doesn't look good," says the tall, dark, and handsome stranger. "It'll need to be towed."

"Yeah."

He sighs and with an air of great reluctance asks, "Do you have a safe way home?"

"I'll sort something out. Thanks."

"Right." He nods. "I should go, then."

"Okay."

He nods again, and this time I can feel his gaze on me. The weight of his regard. I have to say, the sensation is not unpleasant. Then he takes off his sunglasses.

People talk about where they were when some momentous historic event occurred. How it imprinted on them. A pristine memory unlike any other. They remember exactly where they were when they heard the news and how they felt—and they never forget. Because suddenly their life was divided into before and after. This is one of those moments for me.

Alistair George Arthur Lennox, the illegitimate son of the king of England, has eyes the same shade as the blue spring sky. The one I drove to work beneath not so long ago. Such a beautiful color. His gaze immediately turns wary. Like he's used to being recognized and it doesn't make him happy. Meanwhile, the clock inside my head is back and ticking louder than before.

"Noooo. You're not him." I take one step back and then another, until I am backed up against my car, scared and cornered with nowhere to go. "You're not. You're someone else. Because if you were him it would mean what the witch said was right and I… No. You're not you. Absolutely not."

His heavy brows draw tight together. "What are you talking about?"

"I said no."

"Are you okay?" Paul from security puffs out his chest. "Is this guy bothering you, Lilah?"

"Everything is fine," I say, diving back into my car. My insurance details are in the glove box. "Here you go. That's what you need, right?"

Paul juggles my license, car keys, and insurance paperwork. "Yeah."

"I've never been in an accident before. But no one is hurt and nothing is damaged apart from my car."

"Right. I'll, ah, call my friend who owns a tow truck. Have it taken to a garage so it can be assessed."

"That sounds great. Do I need to go with it?"

He shakes his head. "I'll send you the details so you can fill out your accident report online."

"What's your number?" I ask. "I'll text you so you have mine."

He rattles off the digits.

"Thank you so much, Paul."

He blushes. "No big deal. People have accidents here all

the time. They don't leave enough room in parking lots for people to maneuver anymore."

"They really don't. Thank you so much for understanding." I can feel the other man's eyes on me. But I refuse to spare him so much as a glance. Nope. Not happening. "I'll be at the bar in the restaurant on the corner if you need me."

"You'll be in the… Okay," Paul is saying.

But I'm already gone.

3

The restaurant on the corner has a cool modern bar. White walls, tan leather seats, and lots of hanging plants. I like the way sunlight streams in through the skylights, making the inside feel like you're outside. Our work events are often held here. Birthdays and send-offs, et cetera. The dinner crowd has yet to arrive. It is mostly those wanting to hang somewhere on a Saturday afternoon.

I take a seat at the end of the bar on a stool and stare into eternity for a moment. Of course, eternity for me is apparently up next week. My brain is an even bigger disaster than before. But everything will be all right. I just need to sit quietly and calm down. Sort this whole situation out within the quiet confines of my skull and decide what to do.

"Can I get you something?" asks the bartender, an older woman with short cropped gray hair and one of those nose piercings. The kind that hangs through the middle part. "Hello?"

"Sorry. I'll, um… You know what? I'll have a Bloody Mary."

She nods and gets busy mixing the vodka, tomato juice, and spices.

I ignore the man who slides onto the stool next to me. I ignore him with all my heart and soul and then some.

"Did you hit your head?" he asks. "You know, when you crashed the car?"

Funny how that idea keeps coming up. "No."

Turns out he's hard to ignore. The cap and sunglasses are gone. He sits facing me with his back to the rest of the world. "I've had some odd reactions to people recognizing me. But that was particularly unusual back there."

"Particularly unusual," I repeat. "Is that the best you can come up with?"

"Fucking weird?"

I nod. "Better."

"You actually ran away from me," he says with something close to wonder. "After almost hitting my car and telling me I wasn't me."

"Yep. That about sums it up."

He stares at me for a long moment while I ignore him some more. Any hope of him losing interest and going away, however, is dashed when he asks, "So what's the story?"

"Hmm?"

"You said something about a woman being right. What did you mean?"

"Do you always ask this many questions?"

The bartender places a napkin along with the impressive red concoction in front of me. It is embellished with a stick of celery and a cocktail pick loaded with an olive, a pickled onion, a gherkin, and a cube of cheese. How great is a cocktail that comes with its own snacks?

"Thank you," I say. "It looks amazing."

"I'm not staying," the stranger tells the waiting bartender when she asks if he'd like a drink.

"Then you should go." I take a sip of the drink and *holy shit*. "Whoa. That's spicy."

The corners of his eyes crinkle in amusement. "You've never had a Bloody Mary before?"

"No. But I always wanted to try one. No time like the present." Then it occurs to me. I slap the palm of my hand on the wooden bar top. "Septum. It's called a septum piercing. Gah. I hate it when I get all worked up and lose words. It is so annoying."

His mouth opens slightly but nothing comes out. The way he's watching me...it's actually closer to amusement than wonder now. His scales of judgment have definitely tipped in the wrong direction when it comes to me.

Some of the paprika dusted around the rim of the glass has fallen on me. I carefully brush off my fifties-style cream-colored short-sleeve top and navy pants. "I bet you're perfect and never get frazzled or forget anything."

His gaze jumps from my breasts to my face. So busted. "I wouldn't say that," he says.

"Whatever. You were leaving."

"I was actually waiting for you to tell me your story."

"I never agreed to that. Who says there even is a story?"

"Oh, there's definitely a story," he says. "I can feel it. And wouldn't it be great to get it off your chest?"

"Your concern for my chest has been noted. Thanks."

He has the good grace to look mildly ashamed. But not for long, and it doesn't stop him from once again demanding, "Tell me."

"No. I'd prefer not to."

"Why not?"

"Because you'll think it's stupid. *I* think it's stupid." A sigh. "Why do you even care? Where is this sudden concern for a commoner like me coming from?"

"Commoner." He snorts. "I don't know. It's not like there aren't things I should be doing. Call it curiosity. My gran always said I had an excess of the stuff."

"Great." I down more of the drink and watch him out of the corner of my eye. If I avoid direct eye contact, he might go away. A girl can hope. "The Tabasco is a lot. But there's a hint of citrus too. I think it's lime juice."

"Bartenders tend to have their own recipes. But it's usually some combination of pickle juice, horseradish, and Worcestershire sauce."

"Look at you, being all fancy and correctly pronouncing woos...wooster...whatever that sauce is called."

"Worcestershire?" He bites back a smile. "If I promise not to think your story is stupid, will you tell me?"

"Will you promise to go away if I do?"

"Sure."

He sounds sincere. But I need to see his face to know if I can trust him to keep his word. That's what I tell myself, at any rate. There is nothing wrong with his strong jawline and high forehead. His nose, however, is almost too large for his face. Nice to know he's not perfect. He has well-proportioned lips and a subtle natural sort of pout. But it's the air of rugged masculinity that pulls the whole thing together. The whole thing being him. It's clear why the press calls him Prince Charming. He definitely qualifies for dashing and dreamy.

And he sits and waits with amiable patience while I look him over.

"Well?" he asks finally.

"You're too handsome. I don't trust you."

He's not as successful at smothering his smile this time. "This from the woman who bedazzled poor Paul from security and left him to deal with her mess."

"You mean like with rhinestones?"

"No. I do not."

"I did kind of lose it back there," I say. "I'll have to buy Paul something nice to say thank you. But I object to you saying I bedazzled him."

He just raises a brow. Jerk.

"Be real. I'm a solid six. And there is nothing wrong with being a six. Now and then, when I'm in the right mood, I happen to have a great personality," I say. "But unlike you with your pretty privilege, I don't go around just... Why are you looking at me like that?"

"How should I look when you're talking rubbish?"

"It's not *rubbish*, it's *trash*. We're in America. We have trash. Get it right."

"Whatever," he says, quoting me back to me. "Just tell me the story. Why are you drinking that? You obviously don't like it. What else haven't you tried?"

"I don't know. I'm too busy spiraling to know things."

He gives me a long look. Then he picks up the drink menu. "Do you like champagne?"

"Not really."

"That just means you haven't sampled the good stuff." He gestures for the bartender and says, "A glass of... Actually, make it a bottle of Dom Pérignon for the lady, please."

I push my Bloody Mary aside and rest an elbow on the bar. "You're buying me a bottle of champagne?"

"I am," he confirms, as if surprised himself.

"Why?"

"In all honesty, you look like you need it. Badly."

I snort. "Thanks."

"And I really want that story."

"You're used to getting what you want, aren't you?"

In lieu of a response, he removes his leather jacket and lays it on the bar. Of course, his biceps are sublime, with just the right amount of bulge. The man needs to get away from me. I only just had my heart trampled last night. Though it's hard to worry about Josh and his wandering ways in the face of everything else going on.

My unwanted companion watches me as the bartender sets down two glasses and the bottle in a bucket of ice. Once she pours the champagne, he gives her a curt nod. As if he has been waited on hand and foot for the better part of his life and is comfortable with it. As if it is his due. Which makes sense since he's sort of royalty.

I pick up the glass and take a cautious sip. There's the usual faint taste of fruit and bubbles, but better. It is delicious, and the happy humming noise I make gives it away. Dammit.

"Look at you, all angry that I was right," he says with glee. *Asshole.* "Now tell me the story."

"Fine. But you're not going to believe me." I hold up my hand, showing him the cuts on my palm, half healed and covered in scabs. So gross. "My hip is also one big bruise, but you'll forgive me if I don't show you that."

"What happened?"

"Last night I saved a woman from getting hit by a car. We

started crossing the street, and I saw it coming. There was no evidence it was slowing for the red light. So I just sort of grabbed her and pulled us back toward the sidewalk. Still can't believe it worked."

"You were lucky."

"Very," I say. "This is where it gets strange. The woman was a witch hired to be the entertainment at my best friend's birthday. And when it was my turn to talk to her, I had no idea what to say. But then her two hours were up, and she wanted to go home."

"Right."

"As a thank-you for saving her from getting hit by the car, she told me some things. Made some predictions. Like how my boyfriend was cheating on me and that I would get passed over for a promotion again at work."

He cocks his head. "You don't actually believe her?"

"I didn't. Not at first. I still don't want to. But when I got home last night, my boyfriend had company. There was a naked woman hiding in my bathroom. Can you believe that shit?"

"Ouch."

"Then when I got to work today, my boss told me not to bother applying for an upcoming promotion. She had already decided to give the position to Brian."

His blue eyes are serious. "That's awful. But surely these are just—"

"Coincidences?" I finish with a bitter smile. "Yeah. That's what I thought too. The problem is, the witch also told me the name of my supposed soulmate."

"And?"

"It's you."

Laughter bursts out of him. "Good story."

"You think I'm lying?"

"I think you're extremely entertaining. Enjoy the champagne." He hands a black credit card to the bartender. And he's still smiling and shaking his head when she hands him the receipt. Then he turns to me and says, "Have a nice life."

I should shut up and let him leave. It would probably be for the best. But it feels so good to talk to someone about it. To air my anxieties. Whether I'm talking or trauma-dumping is debatable. "She mentioned something about that too. Apparently, my time is up a week from tomorrow."

He pauses. "What?"

"She said I die in eight days."

"Bullshit."

"I wholeheartedly concur. But three in a row, you know?" Nothing from him.

I hate this…feeling fragile. It's not me at all. "She also told me tonight's lotto numbers. I bought a ticket, and if I don't win, then I'll know. I'll laugh at how gullible I was and put this all behind me with a great sense of relief."

He still hasn't moved. All six feet something of him just stands there frowning. He is seriously displeased. A lesser woman would shake in her shoes, but honestly, at this point what have I got to lose? "This actually happened, didn't it?" he asks. "The witch and you almost getting hit by a car and all that?"

"Yes, it did."

"And you believe what she said."

"That's the problem. I honestly don't know what to believe. I mean, there are a lot of people in this city. What is the likelihood of us meeting? What were you even doing in the library parking lot?"

"Dropping some of my mother's first editions off for a display."

"Then we would have crossed paths either way," I say, somewhat vindicated. "My boss had asked me to meet you for the handoff. But I was upset about Brian and the promotion and walked out."

He keeps staring at me, and it is all too much. Today has been stressful enough. I turn away and, oh, this is awkward. I've changed my mind. It would be better if he left. Then I'll just sit here quietly and work on both my buzz and forgetting the many ways in which I have embarrassed myself. He must think I am a walking red flag. A stalker with a wild story or something. Nothing else makes sense.

The irony of me trying to be mindful and make careful choices throughout my adult life. To make my parents proud. And here I am in a bar with a pity bottle of Pérignon, waiting for fucking lottery balls to decide my fate.

My cell buzzes with a text. It's from Paul.

Tow truck on the way. All sorted out.

I reply: I'm so sorry I freaked out and ran. Thank you again.
Paul sends a thumbs-up emoji. He's a good person.

Meanwhile, Alistair is still standing there with his coat in hand. "Are you really just going to sit here alone until the draw?"

"That's the plan."

He swears under his breath and sits back down. Then he picks up his glass of champagne and downs it in one gulp.

"You're staying?" I ask.

"Apparently." His forehead is wrinkled to heck and back. The man is not happy. He signals the bartender and orders a coffee. "Only for a while, and for the record, I am definitely not your soulmate. I just don't like the idea of you sitting alone worrying yourself sick about this."

I ponder his words and sigh. He has a point. Being alone with all of this is a lot. But I don't want to worry any of my friends and family. Not yet, at least. "That's nice of you. Even if you are breaking your word about leaving. But I would like to point out that I didn't say we were soulmates. I just got out of a bad relationship and may or may not hate all men. I haven't quite decided yet. It was the witch who—"

"We don't need to keep talking about it," he says, cranky as can be. "Any of it."

"Fine." I pour myself another glass of champagne. "Why don't we sit here in silence, then? Let's just not talk at all."

"Sounds good to me."

4

"You cannot be serious," Alistair interrupts me. He's such an entitled prick. Though the Scottish half of his accent gets stronger when he's wound up. Which is hot.

I don't really know much about his background. The bulk of it happened before I was born and on the other side of the world. How the future king of England was dating someone deemed unsuitable. Then she disappeared from the London scene, and nothing was heard from her for years. Not until news of her (mostly) secret baby was revealed. Then the press all but badgered them out of the United Kingdom. It must have been awful for them. I remember Mom saying once that it was all anyone could talk about. Even on this side of the Atlantic.

His mother moved them from her ancestral home in the Highlands to California when he was in his teens. But there's no trace of the Golden State in his speech. "He killed his own father for no good reason. There is no coming back from that."

"But he sacrifices himself in the end."

"I don't care."

"Of course, if they got married, she'd probably keep her own surname. Otherwise, imagine having to answer the phone at work."

He just shakes his head. Even the way he sips his coffee is graceful, in a brisk, efficient sort of way. There's this confidence about him. "I can't believe you're telling me that all it takes for you to be okay with murder is for the killer to have muscles and floppy hair."

"You have muscles and floppy hair."

"I haven't killed anyone lately."

"But you also haven't been in the situation that character was in. That I'm aware of, at least."

He gives me a long look. "You're problematic."

"I am not problematic." I scoff. "Well...maybe a little bit. But that's beside the point. These are fictional characters we're talking about. Kylo Ren is not a real person, and neither is Rey. We're discussing Star Wars. An imaginary science-fiction universe, remember?"

He shakes his head and sneers. "I will never understand the allure of bad boys."

"Um. Excuse me. You just finished telling me Han Solo was your favorite."

"That's different. He's an antihero."

"I see. Do you consider yourself to be a bad boy?"

"I'm thirty-eight years old. I'm a grown man." Such indignation. He scowls and turns away. "Don't believe everything you see on the gossip sites."

"Like I follow you online. Come back when you're Beyoncé." A last lonely drop emerges from the bottle when I try to pour myself another glass of champagne. "Oh, it's empty. How sad. As I was saying, people need to be free to explore new things in a safe manner through story. To expand upon their experiences and view the world through different eyes. That's what was so remarkable about the invention of the printing press. It brought the struggles of the lower classes into the drawing rooms of the wealthy for the very first time."

"I love it when you lecture me."

I laugh and he smiles and *yikes*. The way it makes my tummy turn upside down.

"Excuse me, Your Highness?" A teenage girl is standing behind us with her cell phone in hand.

Alistair's whole demeanor changes. His shoulders stiffen and his face falls. "You don't have to call me that. I'm not, strictly speaking, one of them."

"Sorry, sir."

"Just Alistair is fine."

She blushes. "Could I take a selfie with you?"

"Sure," he says gently. Though his smile as she snaps the picture is strained at best. The girl runs off back to her table, and his fingers tap agitatedly against the top of the bar. It must be weird to be famous for just being born. "Don't you have someone you can call to come down here and wait with you?"

"It's my best friend's birthday today. I don't want to ruin it with all of this. Same goes for my family. Just let them enjoy their weekend. I don't want to tell them until I know what's going on. Maybe not even then. I don't know. I haven't thought it all through yet." I paste a smile on my face. "It was kind of you to stay. But it's okay for you to go."

"You'll be alone." This is the second time he's said this. Like it's a sticking point for him. "It's not long now until the draw."

"I don't mind my own company."

A line appears between his dark brows, but he says nothing. Not at first. "I hate that you're so worried. That you're even giving this bullshit the time of day."

"You don't even know me. I'm just a random stranger, Ali. Can I call you Ali?"

"I would very much appreciate it if you never called me that again." He signals to the bartender and says, "She needs another bottle of champagne."

"Those things are expensive. Why are you being so nice to me?"

"Why is it so surprising that someone would be nice to you?"

"Don't answer a question with a question. It's obnoxious."

He gives me an amused look. He has many of them. Though they do generally tend more toward dismay than delight. "I am curious about how all of this turns out. I like hearing about people's lives. Tell me about your boyfriend. Ex-boyfriend. The one who cheated on you."

"Ew." I scrunch up my nose. "Why?"

He tosses a peanut in the air and catches it with his mouth. The man has skills. I'm a little surprised he would do something so déclassé.

"We'd been dating since last summer," I say. "He was in sales. I thought we were ready to try living together, but apparently not."

"That's it?"

"What?"

"That dry statement of facts is how you sum up your most recent romantic relationship?"

The new bottle of champagne arrives. He was right. I do need it. I could give or take oxygen, but alcohol in this situation is a must. "Were you expecting me to cry?"

"I was expecting you to care."

"Fuck you," I say calmly and clearly. "I care very much that someone I trusted just betrayed me."

He pauses. "I apologize. Of course you do. I shouldn't have said that."

I nod and accept his apology like a gracious queen.

"But just out of curiosity, did you love him?"

"You can't ask things like that."

"Why not?"

"Aren't you people supposed to be all about good manners?" This is a fine time to dodge and evade to my heart's content. My mouth, however, won't shut up. In vino veritas. "No. I didn't love him. I liked him and I liked us as a couple, and I thought that would be enough. Like more would come given time, you know?"

He nods and picks up another peanut.

"What about you?"

His face goes blank and he's suddenly on guard. "What about me?"

It would seem I have put my foot in it. He is allowed to ask me personal questions, but it doesn't work the other way. Interesting. Though what would I know about being Alistair George Arthur Lennox, who has the whole damn world watching his every move. Despite having his back to the restaurant, he continues to draw attention. The maître d' has asked several people to stop taking pictures.

"Well?" he asks in a cranky tone of voice.

"What's your favorite book?"

"My favorite book? That's what you want to know?"

"Yes."

For a moment, he just stares at me. Then he says, "*Catcher in the Rye.*"

"Ugh. You're kidding me. No. That's so…ugh."

"You already said that."

"It bears repeating. There's just so much wrong with that choice."

"Is there now?" The corner of his mouth curves upward. "It's all right, Lilah. I'm joking. It's *The Count of Monte Cristo* or *The Martian*. They were both great."

"Oh. Okay. Thank goodness."

"So judgmental," he tsks.

"Like you're not."

Having someone so pretty smiling at you makes it hard to care about anything. A bottle of champagne in your belly doesn't hurt either.

"I shouldn't have asked about your boyfriend if I wasn't willing to share in kind," he says in a low voice.

"He's not my boyfriend anymore." I pour myself another glass and think deep thoughts. "Why do you even believe my bizarre story about the witch?"

"I've known a lot of liars," he says, taking his time and choosing his words carefully. "When you were talking about it you had this look. There was fear in your eyes."

I frown. "I don't like any of this."

"Apart from the champagne."

"I don't like any of this apart from the champagne," I correct.

"And me."

"No." I shake my head. "Just the champagne."

"Then why did you specify that you were single?" he asks

with a sly gaze. Like he's caught me or something. Men are such idiots. Seriously.

"Do you think I'm flirting with you?"

"I don't know," he says with a smirk. "Are you flirting with me?"

"Ali. Sweetie." I smile. "Let me assure you, I am not sizing you up for a rebound."

"Your loss." He shrugs. "It's sort of my specialty."

"How so?"

"I, ah…"

I wait. And then I wait some more. "You can't just throw that out there and not give me details," I finally say. "Come on."

"I don't know if I should talk about it."

"Don't be a tease."

He grimaces and groans. Like he didn't kick off the topic. "I have a tendency to be the one before the one. The penultimate partner, shall we say."

"What proof can you offer?"

"Google it if you like. Fuck knows there's been enough written about me."

I think it over. "No. I don't think so. I'd like to hear it from you."

He gazes at me out of the corner of his eye for a minute. Like those internal scales of his are busy with the judging once again. Then he checks over his shoulder to make sure no one is listening. And finally, he says, "Eleven of my, shall we say, *longer-term partners* went on to get married straight after me."

My eyes are as wide as can be. "Eleven?"

"Yes."

"You're kidding me."

"I am not."

"Wow. I feel like such a failure. I've only had four boy-friends ever, and one of those didn't even last three months. You know, I'm not even sure I have eleven friends." I stare at him in awe. Or something like that. Given the situation, I would rather not like the man, but he's not making it easy. There's the whole hotness thing, of course. But then he goes and compounds the issue by being so easy to talk to. Some of the time. Most of the time. It's like we have our own little comfortable bubble of space at the end of the bar. "What kind of time period are we talking about here? How long were you with these people?"

He blows out a breath. "I don't know. Say half a year and more. Three years at most."

"Huh. Interesting. Would you call yourself a serial mo-nogamist?"

"I don't need to—you just did."

"Do you consider yourself a good boyfriend?"

His chin jerks up. Arrogance has most definitely entered the conversation. "I am an excellent boyfriend or partner. The latter feels like a more adult term for the situation, if you don't mind."

"Have you been told that you're an excellent partner, or are you just jumping to that conclusion because…"

"Because what?"

"I don't know," I admit. "I was hoping you'd finish the sentence."

"I am not finishing that sentence."

"Okay." I lick my lips and his eyes track the movement. Which is interesting. "How many people have you dated in total?"

"I'm not answering that either." He laughs softly. "But I will note that I think I'm older than you."

"Yeah. But still…would you say that the bulk of your break-ups were brought about by your own actions?"

"No comment."

"How much downtime do you tend to have between partners? Are you actually comfortable on your own, or is that a problem for you?"

"Still no comment."

"Were these relationships largely based on sex or friendship or what exactly?"

"You're just going for broke now, aren't you?"

"Yes."

"Lilah," he says in a chiding tone, "for shame. I'm beginning to think the second bottle of champagne was a mistake. Now give me the lotto ticket so I can check the numbers."

It's like he throws cold water in my face. All levity disappears without a trace. "It's time?"

He nods somberly.

My hand is shaking as I search through my purse. Meanwhile, he pulls up the lotto website on his cell. And sure enough, it has been updated. "Read them out to me," I say, holding the ticket. And now it's shaking too.

There's no dawdling or telling me it is going to be all right. He just gets down to business. "Five, eight, twelve, twenty-four, thirty-nine, and forty-three."

The blood drains out of my face. I feel lightheaded, wooziness taking over. There is every chance I am about to vomit or faint or fuck knows what.

"Lilah?" he asks. When I don't respond, he takes the ticket

from my hand. His gaze roams over it, his face dead serious. "You got five numbers."

"Yeah. I—I knew I didn't remember them all." I sound so calm, and yet my head is spinning in circles. "She rattled them off so fast, and I was a little distracted from almost getting hit by a car and being told that my boyfriend was cheating on me and so on. But five. Huh. Not bad."

"Shit." He grabs hold of my upper arm to hold me steady. "Lilah, you're okay. It doesn't mean anything. Apart from you having won some cash. You're going to be fine. It's just…"

"What. It's just what?"

"It's just five numbers," he says in the same calm tone. "You have to be rational about this. It doesn't mean you're going to die."

"Thank you for waiting with me." I grab the bottle of champagne and hug it against my chest. Who cares about cold and damp? This baby is most definitely going to come in handy when I get home and have my second serious meltdown of the weekend. If I can just hold out until I get there. "But I think I should go now."

"Don't get a car," he says. "I'll drive you."

"Okay. Thanks."

As soon as we step outside, a bright light blinds me. It's the flash from a camera. The paparazzo is a stout figure dressed in all black. "Is this your new girl, Alistair? What's your name, sweetheart?"

I give him serious stink eye. Random endearments from strange men will never not be gross.

My companion ignores him completely and keeps his body between me and the photographer at all times. With a hand to my lower back, he ushers me along the sidewalk to where his car is parked. Guess he decided the parking lot was too dangerous. He opens the passenger-side door and I climb inside. Whatever sort of car it is, it's compact. It has leather seats and an immaculate interior. Lord knows what it's worth.

The paparazzo keeps taking shots, both visual and verbal. "Heard from your father lately? How about the Prince of Wales's engagement? Do you think you'll get an invitation to the wedding?"

The demanding voice is only drowned out when Alistair shuts the driver's-side door and starts the engine. He only had the one glass of champagne, so he is fine to drive. And he wastes no time in leaving.

"Sorry about that," he mutters.

"Not your fault."

"Where do you live?"

I give him the address, then sit and stare straight ahead and do not think. A nice calm, empty mind, that's what we want. In the small confines of the car, however, I'm suddenly overly aware of the male sitting beside me. Better I fixate on him than my apparent dire fate. Being famous doesn't seem half as much fun as I thought. It's a good thing I set aside my childhood dreams of becoming a pop star. Not being able to sing worth a damn helped cement the decision. But being stalked and harassed the way Alistair is must suck. He doesn't say a word during the drive either. Not until we arrive outside my apartment building. Home sweet home.

"Thank you," I say, opening the door and climbing out. Which is especially hard to do from a low sports car when you're clutching a bottle of champagne. But what does dignity matter in the face of imminent death?

"You're not going to die," he says.

"We all have to someday."

He gives me one of those long looks he seems to special-
ize in. No idea what he's thinking. The man is a mystery.
His blue eyes are subdued in the low lighting, and the sharp
angles and planes of his face are cast in shadow. "Take care
of yourself, Lilah."

I nod and close the car door, and that's that.

5

Sunday

There seem to be several schools of thought regarding how best to deal with death. You have your standard five-step process: denial, anger, bargaining, depression, and acceptance. Then there's the more popular boho hippie method: meditation, preparation, forgiveness, and gratitude. I myself have chosen a combination of the two.

Hanging out in the shower with my bottle of champagne until the water went cold covered denial, anger, and depression. I was, however, too tired to meditate last night and too hungover to manage it this morning. Talk about a headache. Though spending over an hour on the phone dealing with the details of the car accident and my insurers could be seen as preparation. Same goes for downloading a do-it-yourself will. I don't want to die intestate and leave a disaster for someone else to deal with. That would be rude. I seem to have skipped forgiveness and bargaining so far and am still working my way toward gratitude. Because fuck this shit.

But it's not all doom and gloom. I refuse to spend the next seven days in a downward spiral. Not a chance.

Good Witch Willow made five predictions. My boyfriend was indeed cheating on me, and I did get passed over for promotion. That's two points. But while I did meet Alistair George Arthur Lennox, we did not instantly fall in love, and I saw no definitive sign that he is my soulmate (not that I would necessarily know what I was looking for). I award this prophecy half a point. As for the lotto, since I could only remember some of the numbers, she misses out on a full point there too. I'll give her three-quarters of a point. Her total is therefore three and a quarter out of a possible five points. Let's call it 70 percent. A high enough number to demand action. But low enough to still hold out some hope. (This also counts as *acceptance*.)

Now to decide how to spend my time.

My inner child immediately takes charge. I need to see the house I grew up in and be with my parents. To smell the faint scent of lemon cleanser and home cooking. It's a small Spanish-style home in Santa Monica. Three bedrooms and a lovely garden located a good way back from the beach. Dad used to teach at UCLA while Mom managed a local café. But now they're both retired and doing their own thing.

I have so many memories of this place. It's always been a safe space for me, and I know I am lucky. As often as my mother and I disagree—which is often—I never doubted that I was loved. My brother moved to Boston years ago for work. We're not close. But I know if I called, he would answer.

"Hello there." Mom is packing the dishwasher when I wander into their kitchen in the afternoon. Just being here calms me down some. Coming here was a good choice. I inherited the buxom and blond from Mom. She was born in Denmark; her family moved to America when she was five. Just old enough to remember the harsh winter weather. The worry line instantly appears between her brows at the sight of me. We have that in common. "I didn't hear your car in the driveway, Lilah."

I lower the cold brew from my lips. "My car was in a slight accident yesterday."

"How slight? Are you hurt?"

"I'm fine." I press a kiss to her cheek. "You didn't hear the car because I'm Ubering around at present. The Prius won't get assessed until Wednesday. But I doubt the news will be good."

"Honey," says my dad, coming in from the front room. "I thought I heard your voice."

"Hey, Dad."

There didn't used to be a whole lot of hugging and kissing in my family. Neither of my parents are touchy-feely people. Once my brother and I moved out and got on with our own lives, however, that started to change. It's funny how family cultures evolve. How certain practices get passed down often without any real thought. None of my grandparents were especially affectionate either. I don't know if they felt it was awkward or unnecessary or what. But I like that we've started being more demonstrative.

"What's this I hear about a car accident?" he asks.

"It's a long story, but basically, I was distracted and drove into a concrete bollard. I'm fine, but my car is not."

While Mom has her worry line, Dad has his sigh. Both are effective in their own ways.

"But wait," I say. "I have two more announcements to make."

Dad leans his hip against the kitchen island. "We're all ears."

"Josh and I broke up."

Mom and Dad exchange a look. One of those loaded parental glances. Like there's a lot they could say on the subject, but they're debating the wisdom of sharing their true thoughts and feelings.

"He was never good enough for you," says Dad, making his mind up fast. "You know those people that talk fast but say nothing?"

"Babe," says Mom in a wary tone.

Dad throws up his hands. "It's the truth."

"How are you feeling about it, Lilah?" asks Mom, wiping her hands on a cloth.

I down more of my cold brew and think it over. "I was upset at the time. But now I think I'm actually okay."

"That means it was the right choice," says Dad.

Mom nods wisely. "He was too normal for you, to be honest. A bit boring. You know what I mean?"

"No, I do not know what you mean." I laugh. "How was he too normal? Does that make me abnormal? Please explain it to me, Mother."

"What's the other news?" asks Dad, coming in with a diversion. He obviously has no interest in watching a girl fight. As much as he enjoys a good debate, he hates to see us disagree.

"Oh. Um. I won the lotto," I say. "Not the top prize, but not a shabby amount either. I got five numbers."

"Five? Wow. How about that!"

Mom cocks her head. "That's amazing. But you don't gamble. You always said you couldn't afford another bad habit, with what you spend on books and shoes."

"That's true." I take another sip of coffee to buy myself time. "It was just... The thing is..."

"Yes?"

I hesitate and prevaricate and all the rest. Telling them just doesn't seem like a good idea.

"Who cares? Call it a random stroke of luck," proclaims my father with a grin. "Congratulations, honey. What are you going to do with the money?"

"It's about a quarter of a million after tax. I'm not sure yet. I think I'm still in shock."

"Lilah! That's incredible!" gushes Mom with wide eyes.

"Yeah."

"Possibly life-changing. It might not feel real until you see it in your account. I could make you an appointment with our financial planner," Dad says. "You let me know if you're interested."

"As long as you're not going to spend all your time hanging out at casinos from now on," says Mom. "I had an uncle like that. He would set his alarm to wake him at two in the morning. He had this theory that less people in the casino meant more luck to go around. It was sad to see him throw his life away. You're not going to start doing that sort of thing, are you?"

It's possible that I also get the penchant for randomness and drama from my mother. "No, Mom. I can honestly say the thought has never crossed my mind. Though I am taking the week off. I was due a break from work anyway."

Cue another round of hugging. Then Dad is off to hang out in his office and work on his book about ethical theory, and I am left alone with the family matriarch.

There was always a solid chance I wouldn't be able to bring

myself to tell them about the predictions. For so many reasons. The key one being, my time might be limited, and I'd rather focus on making good memories. But I also want to relive the best bits of my life. The everyday things I took for granted. "Mom, if I make a sad face, will you bake me your chocolate chip cookies?"

"I don't know." She gives me a long look. "I just cleaned up. It would need to be truly wretched."

"I'm talking profoundly pathetic. Like lost Dickensian orphan pressing her nose against your kitchen window on Christmas Eve."

"Hmm. You'd need to squeeze out a tear or two. Do you think you're up to it?"

I laugh. And then I stop laughing because this is serious. This might well be the last time I see my parents. I have no idea what the next week will bring. A lump is lodged in my throat, making it impossible to swallow. "I'm sorry I was such a pain in the ass growing up. You know I appreciate you, right?"

Mom cocks her head. "You weren't a pain in the ass."

"What about when I was a teenager? All the sneaking off to parties and skipping class?"

"To my knowledge, you snuck off to exactly two parties and skipped class once in a blue moon." Her gaze is full of confusion. "Lilah, where is all of this coming from?"

"Nowhere. It's nothing." I pull up my metaphorical brave big-girl panties and paste on a smile. "You were going to make me cookies."

For a moment she says nothing. Then she nods. "All right. I'll make you a batch. But don't smudge the glass pressing your nose against it. I don't need a demonstration."

"I won't smudge the glass. Thank you, Mom."

"You're welcome," she says in a soft voice. "Are you sure you're okay?"

"Yeah. I'm making a plan for what to do with my free week."

She turns on the oven and starts assembling the ingredients and utensils. "What have you got in mind?"

"I want to make the most of my time. Do all the experiences and events and whatever that I should have done by now." I pull out my cell and bring up the note app. "The things I hoped to achieve before thirty but delayed due to time or money or laziness."

"It's not like you don't still have plenty of time. But that could be fun. What have you got so far?"

"Not much. Care to brainstorm with me?"

Mom smiles. We have the same smile too. "I would love that."

"Well, well, well," says Rebecca, dramatically sweeping into my apartment. "If it isn't the mystery woman herself."

"What are you talking about, and do you want a glass of wine?"

"Of course I want a glass of wine. What kind of question is that?"

The makings of my bucket list are spread across the small dining table. Mom and I came up with a long list, and there are lots of ideas on the internet. Now I need to eliminate and prioritize. Visiting my parents helped calm me down. But this situation, the whole "Will I or won't I die?" thing, makes me anxious as heck. I am taking deep breaths and thinking calm thoughts on the regular. It's almost working. The list could well come in handy for distracting me from my possible imminent death in the days ahead.

"Do you really not know what I'm talking about?" asks Rebecca, dumping her purse on the kitchen island. "Ooh. Cookies."

"Mom made them. Help yourself. Do I really not know what you're talking about with regard to what?" I retake my seat at the table. "How did things go with Priya?"

"Really good!" says Rebecca. "We have plans for tonight. I'm cautiously optimistic. She really seems open to the idea of seeing where this thing between us could go this time."

"That's great news. What changed?"

"I don't know," she says. "I'm just glad it did."

My best friend works in accounting at one of the big film studios. She makes up for spending her days crunching numbers by wearing the brightest clothes she can find. This evening, she's sporting a fuchsia pantsuit with gold jewelry. Her dark hair is styled in its usual chin-length bob. The woman is fire.

With a glass of wine in hand and a whole cookie in her mouth, Rebecca thrusts her cell at me and points at the screen.

And there on-screen is a shot of Alistair ushering me into his Aston Martin. *Shit.* I completely forgot about the paparazzo. My face is in profile but still definitely me. "I was in a bar and, um, he was just being kind and gave me a lift home."

She just blinks. "Wait a minute. You actually met Alistair Lennox, and he drove you home in his ridiculously sexy sports car?"

"Yes."

"I thought it was a doppelgänger and we'd laugh about it. But you're telling me that's really you in the picture?"

"It is indeed me."

"Whoa," she says, the whites of her eyes shining bright. "How the hell did this happen?"

"Yeah. Some things occurred after I left your party..."

I've thought about it at great length and the same reasons I have for not telling my family about the predictions and my possible dire fate also apply to friends. Even my best friend. I mean, they may not agree with my assessment of the situation. Which would be fine. But whatever they believe, I don't want to be watched or worried over for the next week. My goal is to enjoy whatever time I have left.

Prevarication ahoy!

"It's kind of a long story. First, Josh and I broke up. There was a naked woman hiding in the bathroom when I got home Friday night."

Her eyes grow wide as can be. "No! Holy shit. Why didn't you call me?"

"I didn't want to ruin your birthday."

"You should have called me," she insists sympathetically. "Did you throw him out?"

"I did indeed."

"That duplicitous fuck. I'm so sorry. Are you all right?"

"I'm actually dealing with it better than I thought I would. Which is telling." I frown. "Then on Saturday I had a disagreement with my boss."

"Boo. That woman is the worst."

"She really is. But it gets better, because then I had a car accident in the parking lot at work and probably killed the Prius. It was Alistair's car that I swerved to avoid. Totally my fault since I was distracted and in the wrong damn lane."

"Are you okay?"

"My neck is a bit sore today but otherwise all good."

"You've been busy." Rebecca's lips skew to the side, and she gives me a look of commiseration. "That would be a lot for anyone to deal with. I can see why you were in a bar in need of the kindness of hot royal strangers."

"I went to that restaurant on the corner from work and had a few drinks and felt sorry for myself, and we got to talking."

"Did you get his number?"

"No."

She winces and sips her wine. "That's a shame. Talk about a once-in-a-lifetime opportunity. I'm sorry your weekend turned out to be so awful. But what was he like, just out of curiosity?"

"He was nice. Though he could also be cranky. I don't know. We just chatted for a while. It's not like we bared our souls to each other or anything."

She ponders this for a moment. Then she picks up her cell and swipes several times. "Did I mention that you also broke the heart of America's sweetheart?"

"I did what?"

She turns her screen toward me, showing a tear-stricken woman in designer apparel. Her beautiful face is familiar. As it should be, seeing as she was in *the* blockbuster movie from last summer. Josh took me to see it on our first date. I flick through a series of photos and articles in amazement. And more than a little horror. The headlines read "Betrayed by Prince Charming" and "Daria Gets Dumped." Ouch.

"'Charming Cheats' is my personal favorite," says Rebecca, lowering her phone. "Clear. Concise. It says it all."

"'Insiders say the king is furious with the illegitimate playboy prince over this latest scandal,'" I read. "Do you think these so-called insiders ever actually exist?"

"I highly doubt it."

"Me too. I didn't even realize he was dating Daria Moore. Wasn't he with that singer?"

"They broke up a while back. She's engaged to some nepo baby now."

"Huh." Guess he's the one before the one after all. "This is… Yeah. I honestly don't know what to say. But I definitely didn't steal anyone's man. I didn't even make a pass at him."

"I believe you." She sets her empty glass of wine on the kitchen counter and picks up her cell. "I have to go. But we need to schedule time to talk smack about your ex and rehash all of this. Just in case you forgot any important details. And don't forget, you promised me sashimi. Though, given your run of bad luck, maybe I should be buying."

"Oh. I also won some money on the lottery last night."

She just blinks.

"It's a lot. I know. I'm taking the week off work, so let me know what day suits."

"Will do."

I follow her to the front door to relock it after she's gone. Outside, the night is as quiet and still as it ever gets in LA. March is jeans-and-cardigan weather, and I am dressed accordingly. A cool breeze is making the palm fronds wave in the wind. My elderly neighbor two doors over, Mr. Pérez, is standing on his doorstep talking to someone. Someone who is tall and broad with dark hair. Someone vaguely familiar. *No way.* It can't be.

"Yes, sir," says the man with a familiar Scottish accent. The warmth that rushes through me at the sound is wild. He is here. How amazing. "You're absolutely right. I should have asked her for her apartment number when I was with her. But I am not harassing her, I promise."

Mr. Pérez answers in Spanish, and he is not happy. I don't understand enough to know what he's saying. Not at the speed at which he's talking. Though Alistair has no such problems, switching languages with ease.

"Excuse me," I say. The conversation pauses and I raise my hand. "Gracias, Mr. Pérez. I do know him. It's okay. Sorry to disturb you."

Mr. Pérez nods and wanders back into his apartment without another word. He probably has soccer waiting. It's his favorite. For Christmas, his daughter installed a huge flat-screen TV so Mr. Pérez could watch his games in high definition. I helped to lift it into place and was rewarded with a couple of pieces of tres leches cake for my efforts.

"Lilah," says Alistair, heading my way. I couldn't take my eyes off him if I tried. He really is like a modern-day Prince Charming. The man has such presence.

"How many doors did you knock on trying to find me?"

"That was my third. No answer at the first, and the second was slammed shut in my face."

This is wild. I honestly never thought I would see him again. But here he is, standing right in front of me. He is neither smiling nor frowning. The sharp lines of his face are set in this careful blank, though I detect a hint of apprehension in his beautiful eyes. My heart is now beating much harder for some reason. My anxiety changing focus from worrying over my dire fate to freaking out about him and his sudden presence in my everyday life. If only I could turn off my feelings and take a break. It would be so helpful right now.

"What are you doing here, just out of interest?" I ask.

"I wanted to make sure the press wasn't bothering you."

"No. No sign of them so far. But doesn't you being here increase the odds? Not that it isn't nice to see you and all."

He stuffs his hands in his jeans pockets. "I made sure I wasn't followed."

"Right." I nod. "Well, it was just my profile in the pictures. I don't think anyone really expects me to be in a photo with someone like you, so…yeah."

We stand there in silence that is not comfortable in the least. Amazing how his stiff posture lends his jeans and Henley the air of formal wear. His gaze takes in my face before returning to the garden. This couldn't be more awkward. I don't have a clue what to say. He does not, however, make any move to leave.

I take a deep breath. "Would you like to come in?"

"Yes," he answers with zero hesitation.

Huh. "Okay, then."

6

He walks into my small apartment, gaze constantly moving, taking in everything. It can't be anything like what he's used to at home. Being a librarian isn't the best-paying job, especially at the lower levels, and rent in this city is astounding. I also love vintage stores. Therefore, my decorating style is best summed up as "I found it discounted or for free and thought it was cool."

In my living room, there's a charcoal sofa (half price) with an array of colorful throw pillows (also bought on sale). A chunky wood coffee table a friend gifted me (the scars give it character). A cracked antique mirror I found on the sidewalk (definitely neither cursed nor possessed). And an assortment of pillar candles and houseplants. There's always at least one on its deathbed in need of replacement.

But it's my big old bookshelf that holds his interest. He bends down, and the way the denim molds to his behind is something else. The thirst is real. Not that I have any business looking. I still have no idea what he's doing here. While we were outside, we established that the press hasn't bothered me. But here he is, inspecting my habitat just the same.

"A lot of Nora Roberts," he says.

"La Nora is queen."

"Three different editions of *Frankenstein*?"

"Mary Shelley is life." I shrug. "Or life after death. At any rate, they keep putting out great new hardcover editions. What's a girl to do?"

Then he spies my battered copy of *Wuthering Heights* and decides to examine it. "Did you steal this from your high school library?"

"As if I would do such a thing."

He does the solo eyebrow-raise thing. It's definitely one of his go-to facial expressions.

"It was on the verge of falling apart, and no one had borrowed it since before I was born," I confess. "I felt bad for it sitting there all unloved and unwanted."

"There's a reason that happened. Heathcliff is a dick."

"This is more of your 'I hate bad boys' shtick, isn't it? I was sixteen. What do you want from me? I said I lost it and paid the fine, so it wasn't really stealing, thank you very much."

He shakes his head sadly. "What shocking behavior. I am shocked."

"Oh, shut up."

"Now you're abusing me. A fine hostess you are. Are you even going to offer me a glass of wine?"

"Would you like a glass of wine, Ali?"

"I'd prefer a beer if you have it," he says, cool as can be. "And I believe I asked you not to call me that."

"It's good to want things. I love that for you. Keep it up."

He grunts.

There just so happens to be a couple of bottles of Blue Moon in the back of the fridge, cunningly hidden behind a bag of out-of-date salad mix. I twist the cap off one and hand it over.

"Thank you." He heads toward the mess on my dining table. "What's all this?"

"The makings of my list. Things I want to do before… you know."

His frown returns with a vengeance. "Have you told anyone else about that? Your friends and family?"

"I decided not to."

He waits patiently, but I have no more to say on the subject. "As ridiculous as it is, I know it's still weighing on your mind," he says finally. "You shouldn't have to deal with it alone."

"I'm not. You're here now. Hooray!"

He narrows his eyes on me. Like he's not entirely certain I am joking. Messing with this man just might be my new favorite thing.

"So I made a Hollywood star cry," I say. "That's something that happened."

"Please." He snorts. "Daria's an actress with a film to promote. Her marketing team must be loving this."

I am not convinced. Given I just got cheated on, the idea I might have inadvertently hurt someone in a similar manner is not nice. Though nothing happened between him and me.

"Lilah," he says in a gentler tone. "Daria and I aren't together. Any moment now, there'll be exclusive photos of her being comforted by her costar."

"If you say so."

He takes a seat at the table, setting his ankle on the opposite knee, making himself comfortable. "You were about to tell me why you haven't talked to anyone else about this Witchy Wanda situation."

"Good Witch Willow," I correct, taking the seat across from him. "The thing is, I've decided to embrace toxic positivity. This whole dying-next-week thing doesn't make me want to vomit at all. Everything is fine."

His grunt is full of disbelief.

"I mean, think about it, Ali."

"You really do need to stop calling me that," he mumbles.

"What would even be the point in freaking out? We all die sometime. It's an irrefutable fact of life," I say, doing my best to convince us both. "What does it matter if my time is up sooner rather than later?"

"Is that so?"

"Yes. Good vibes only."

"Good vibes only," he repeats in that accent, sounding not the least bit convinced. "Great."

"I have a plan. I'm going to spend the next week working through items on my wish list. The idea is to enjoy myself so much that the threat of an early demise hanging over me won't even matter."

"What's a wish list?"

"I am so glad you asked. It's like a bucket list, but better," I explain. "No negative death connotations. Nothing to do with domestic cleaning supplies either. It's all happiness and sparkles from start to finish."

"Right."

"The thing is, I ran the numbers. You'll be delighted to hear that I now believe the situation could go either way. I may or may not die next Sunday. But whatever happens, I've taken the next week off work, and I'm going to have fun."

"All right," he says, as if he's considering giving me his grudging approval. As if I even need it. This one has some alpha tendencies. "What's on the list? Skydiving and bungee jumping and so on?"

"No. None of those things. Yikes." I take a sip of wine. "I do not feel the need to test gravity. There's a delicate balance between experiences that make you feel alive and ones that actually increase your chances of an early death. I intend to stick with the first."

"What have you got, then?" Now he's on his feet again. He takes a cookie off the plate on the kitchen island and takes a bite. After he's finished his mouthful he says, "These are great."

"My mom made them. She can bake like nobody's business."

Head cocked and beer in hand, he starts reading the papers on the table. Guess I took too long to answer his question. There's a lot of paperwork to see. Mom printed off numerous articles about best bucket-list ideas and top things to do before turning thirty, along with several versions of my list. Lots of ideas were added before later being discarded.

"'Drive along the coast in a convertible,'" he reads aloud.

"I will of course be wearing a scarf that will dramatically fly away on a gust of wind. Just like Grace Kelly in *To Catch a Thief.* My gran used to love that film. And I mean, where would we be without metaphors regarding the fragility of life and the importance of living in the moment?"

The frown he gives me is lukewarm at best. Like he disapproves of the idea but doesn't see any actual harm in it. "'Eat at a Michelin star restaurant.' Any in particular?"

"I imagine it will largely depend on what I can get into on such short notice."

He looks up. "You crossed out 'Cut own bangs and dye hair blue'?"

"Yeah," I say. "I just don't know how it would look. If I do die and they decide to have an open casket, it could be a disaster."

He says nothing for a time. Just stares at me.

"If you're going to be judgmental, you can leave," I say, legs crossed and glass of wine in hand.

"Sorry. 'Axe throwing' has a question mark next to it?"

"I'm not sure about that one. I can be a little clumsy."

He picks up a pen and crosses the idea out. Fair enough. "'Stay up all night with someone special until the sun rises. Go skinny-dipping. Wear a ball gown to the opera. Attend a polo match. Designer shopping spree.'"

"I'm open to re-creating any scene from *Pretty Woman*. It's one of my mom's favorites. The women in my family have great taste in films."

"What's yours?"

"What's my what?"

"Your favorite movie," he says. "You've told me your gran's and mom's. But you haven't told me yours."

"*The Shape of Water*. It's so romantic but weird too, you know?"

"I don't like your chances of finding a fish man to woo in the next week."

"Me neither."

He just nods. "The rest of these all seem reasonably do-able, however."

"For someone with your resources perhaps. It might prove

a little trickier for me. I have no car and the lotto check won't clear for five days."

He selects another handwritten document from the table. "'Drink absinthe and dance in the rain.'"

"Of course, those two aren't mutually exclusive. I checked the weather report. It doesn't look promising, but you never know."

"'Milk a cow' has also been crossed out."

"Time constraints. I can't do everything."

"Right," he says. Then his brows start to rise. "What have we got here?"

"I don't know. What have we got where?"

"'Have great sex.' Interesting. Very interesting."

"You just had to pick up the piece of paper with that on it, didn't you?" I scramble out of my seat and attempt to rip the piece of paper out of his hand. Of course, he holds it high over his head. The smirk on the bastard's face makes me want to growl. "Give it to me, Alistair."

"Now you say my name properly. Though I'm saddened to see you forgot your manners. Where's the 'please'?"

Given the chance to climb a ridiculously hot and hard-bodied man, I always thought I would be more than happy to rise to the challenge. But it is in fact more difficult than it looks. My poor sore hip doesn't appreciate it, for one. And this T-shirt bra is simply not up to all my jumping around. As much as I try tugging on his arm, it doesn't move an inch. Trust him and his stupid bulging biceps to ruin everything.

"Fine. Have it." I retake my seat with a sniff of disdain. Salty suits me. "I don't care. I am an adult. You will not shame me for having a healthy sex life. Or attempting to have one, anyway."

A moment later he sits too. "Where are you intending to find this great sex, if you don't mind me asking?"

"I mind."

"Your ex wasn't up to the job, I take it?"

I pick up my glass and swirl the remaining wine around and around. Class and sophistication—that's me. "Do you remember when we were at the bar last night and I started asking personal questions and you refused to answer?"

"I remember you saying answering a question with a question is obnoxious."

"Look at you, dancing so skillfully on my last nerve. Bravo."

His smile is fleeting. There and gone in an instant. "My mother made me take lessons."

"What? Dancing?"

He nods. "Along with etiquette and some other nonsense."

"Did you enjoy them?"

"Not particularly. It was a lot of memorizing forks and waltzing." He downs a mouthful of beer. "I preferred being outside playing rugby." And that is when his guard goes back up. You can see it in his eyes. He sits up straight and frowns. "I should be going. I only wanted to check that you were okay. Thank you for the beer."

I hate the idea of him leaving. Let's not examine why. But I have a sneaking suspicion that if he walks out now, I won't see him again in this life. Which would be sad. "I, um, used to work after school in the café my mom managed. It didn't leave much time for sports or other stuff. But I got free cake."

"Free cake is good."

"That's what I thought." I smile. "Mostly I'd hang out at the library or the Santa Monica Pier or the mall with my friends."

"You grew up near the beach?"

"In the general vicinity."

"We moved to Malibu when I was thirteen. It was a hell of a change from home. Not much sunshine in Scotland." His fingers tap against the table. "What's the plan for tomorrow?"

"With the wish list?"

"Yeah."

"Well, first I have to organize all of this and come up with a clean copy of my top twelve most desired things to do. A dozen feels like a doable number. Along with a backup selection in case some don't work out. That's going to take a little while. But it's best to be prepared, right? I don't want to rush and leave out something that could be great, you know? A ranking system out of ten might be useful. How excited I am about the idea versus how far it will push me out of my comfort zone versus viability, time, and money. I've got my Post-its and my favorite ink gel pens and one of my keep-for-a-special-occasion notebooks here," I say and pause. "You're frowning at me. Why are you frowning at me?"

"The week will be gone, and you'll still be sitting here playing with your stationery."

"That's not necessarily true."

He just looks at me.

"Fine," I say. "What would you do?"

He downs the rest of his beer and stands. "I should be able to get my hands on a convertible for tomorrow. I've got some business in the morning. Meet you here at around three?"

My mouth hangs open for a moment. "Uh. Okay."

"Give me your number," he says, pulling his cell out of his back pocket.

I enter my number into his phone and hand it back. A moment later, my phone vibrates with an incoming text. This is all happening very fast. At least for me. "I'm confused. Are we becoming friends? Is that what's happening here?"

"Do not misuse my number," he says in a particularly stern voice with a very serious expression on his face. A combo that hits me right between my legs.

"As if I would misuse your number." I am shocked and stunned that he's sharing it with me. Given his general distrust of people and his need to keep things private. It's a huge act of faith on his part. "What am I going to do, Ali, text you pictures of my feet?"

"And don't make a big deal out of this. It's a onetime thing," he says, heading for the door. "You need help. I happen to know someone with a convertible. That's all."

"Of course. I appreciate you putting yourself out like this. Thank you."

He gives me a stiff nod.

"It does kind of feel like we're becoming friends, though."

"So long as you don't think we're soulmates, I don't much care what you call it." He opens the door. "Come and lock this behind me."

I set down my glass and stand. "I know basic home security. You'll note that I didn't even bring up the soulmates thing this time. That was all you."

"See you tomorrow. Don't forget your scarf," he says and shuts my front door in my face. As one does.

7

Monday

After an hour of working on the wish list, I curl up in my preferred spot (a surprisingly comfortable old black leather armchair I found in a vintage store) with *Slave to Sensation* by Nalini Singh. New adventures over the next week sound great, but so does visiting with old favorites. The books, music, and movies that helped make me.

There are many reasons for rereading a story. To remind us of special times. To revisit characters who feel like best friends. To wander again through worlds that thrill and delight. Fiction has always been an escape from reality. When you know what's coming, however, books also become a place of absolute safety and comfort.

I read until the early hours. It's easy to forget how quiet it gets when the night's slipping away but it's not yet morning. How silent and still everything is once the world goes to sleep. Feeling like you might be the only one awake is a small and curious sort of magic. Until some drunk down the block starts yelling and kills the vibe. That's when I know it's time for bed.

Much later that morning, I walk to my favorite local café for the best breakfast burrito. Scrambled eggs, black beans, ham, Monterey Jack cheese, guacamole, and salsa on a white-flour tortilla. With strong coffee, of course. The joy this breakfast brings to my mouth and belly cannot be underestimated. It truly is the simple things in life sometimes. I follow it with some online snooping into Alistair Lennox.

I could lie and say it's purely educational. Knowing what topics to avoid would be useful when dealing with him. But let's be honest, it's just me being nosy. But also, when your life is out of control, you look for ways to cope. And research is an old and proven coping mechanism of mine.

The monarchy isn't my thing, and I was too young to remember the scandal when Alistair was born. However, I do know the basics of the story due to Mom. She loves a good scandal.

Lady Helena was a staple of the London scene in the eighties. A socialite who worked as model and muse for a major fashion label, she dominated the social pages and gossip columns for years. *And* she was often seen in the company of a certain bachelor prince. Then one day she disappeared. Of course, the rumors flew. But nothing was known about her or her secret baby, not for a long time.

Over a decade later, an anonymous tip to the gossip rags turned her and her child's world upside down. Suddenly everyone knew the now happily married heir to the throne had an illegitimate son. Public interest in the story was intense. The British press hounded them day and night. That's when

Alistair and his mother left her family estate in Scotland and escaped to America.

How fucking awful. No wonder the man has issues.

The more recent information about him isn't as clear. After college, he served for two years as a marine before being wounded in combat. Guess he became an American citizen at some point. But after he was discharged, he and some friends formed a tech company. They're involved in game development and have apparently been successful.

He's dated a wide variety of women. Both famous and not. It seems his father disapproved of each and every one to varying degrees. Though little is known about their actual relationship. The king has never publicly discussed him. Never confirmed that Alistair is his son. But the rest of the world has plenty to say on the subject.

There are dozens of photos of Alistair at parties and events with lots of beautiful people. He's even smiling occasionally. Some of the pictures are him striding about looking serious, taken by paparazzi as he was just going about his life. And then there's the selection of shots taken with long-range lenses. Such as him in his bathing suit on a beach or relaxing on a hotel balcony with a drink. He is, of course, disgustingly handsome in all of them. Shame on him.

None of this offers any clues to why he's spending time with me. Not to be hard on myself, but I am an anomaly in this picture. When it comes to Alistair, I think Good Witch Willow was wrong. Which is both good and bad. Good that I might live past Sunday. Bad that I won't get the boy. Not that I ever really thought I would. Guys like him don't choose girls like me. It is a fact of life.

There have been no further news items in the Daria Moore

situation. Guess they're waiting for someone more famous to do something newsworthy. The gossip sites are mostly regurgitating yesterday's articles and shots about us, along with a few new theories about who the mystery woman might be. One article claims we've eloped to the Caribbean. Another posits that Daria is pregnant. They all declare that the king is furious at Alistair for his reckless bachelor ways. Again. Stress would have done the king in years ago if he actually did all the raging about the palace that the media claim.

By the time three o'clock approaches, I am ready to roll in gray plaid high-waist trousers with a pair of flat black booties and a fitted pale blue tee. My hair is tied back in a low ponytail and my makeup is immaculate. Definite main-character energy.

My phone buzzes with a text from Ali.

Outside.

I reply: Coming.

I grab my sunglasses and purse and head out. There's a humming in my blood. A mixture of nerves and the sensation you get when you just know something is going to be good. And Alistair does not disappoint. I doubt he even knows how to. A beyond beautiful shiny black convertible with a white leather interior is parked at the curb. He leans against it like he's in a movie, and the whole scene makes my heart beat faster. But I'm sure that's just because he's making a dream come true. Growing actual feelings for this man would be a bad idea. I might die in six days; I don't have time for a crush on Prince Charming.

When he sees me walking down the cracked concrete pathway, he gives me a brief smile. As if his happiness is only meted out in small doses. "Got your scarf?"

"Yes, I do," I say with a giddy smile. There will come a day when his accent will no longer thrill me. When I will learn to gird my loins against him. Today, however, is not that day. "Nice car."

"Ferrari GTO California Spyder Revival." He opens the passenger-side door for me. "Glad you approve."

"Thank you for this."

He gives me one of his signature stiff nods.

"No photographers?" I ask, looking both ways down the street.

"There were a couple, but I lost them on the way."

"Guess you're good at that sort of thing."

We don't talk as he drives through the city and toward the coast. Not at first. He keeps giving me these side glances with a faint frown. As if he can't quite believe he is here in this car doing this with me. Which makes two of us. But eventually I can stand the silence no more.

"I got some good work done on my wish list after you left last night," I say. "Then I read a book for a while."

He nods.

"And this morning I went out for the best breakfast in existence."

"What exactly is that?"

"It's this breakfast burrito from a local café. Eggs, black beans, ham, Monterey Jack cheese, guacamole, and salsa on a white-flour tortilla."

He raises a brow. "Sounds interesting. But you can't tell me it beats a good old brown-sugar Pop-Tart."

"Are you being serious right now?"

"I am always serious about breakfast."

"A Pop-Tart." I give him a long look. No idea if he is winding me up or what. "Please."

He takes his eyes from the road for a moment to shoot me another one of those glances. Though this time, it seems more curious in nature. "Your choice of cheese also gives me pause. Would you really willingly choose Monterey Jack over mozzarella?"

"What do you have against Monterey Jack?"

"It's fine, I suppose," he says with a faint air of disdain. "If you like that sort of thing."

"By 'that sort of thing,' do you mean *cheese*? Because I like cheese."

He lifts the fingers of one hand from the wheel. As if he's waving the subject adieu.

"There's nothing wrong with Monterey Jack. It's a wonderful cheese."

"Whatever you say, Lilah."

There's something in the way the Santa Ana wind tousles his dark hair that works for me. Makes it hard to look away. Though he is alluring with or without the weather.

"You're staring at me," he mumbles.

"I want to commit what a Monterey Jack hater looks like to memory. That way, I can avoid your kind in future."

His smile is a split-second sort of thing. Like it escaped him for a moment. "Bold words from a Pop-Tart-phobe."

"I never said I hated Pop-Tarts. Just that there is no way they compare to a breakfast burrito." I wait for a while. "What's up, Ali? Nothing to say in your defense?"

"I just thought I'd let you sit over there and dwell in your wrongness for a while. You seem like a bright enough lass. I am sure you'll come to your senses eventually."

I snort.

We're heading northwest, and there's little to see until we join the Pacific Coast Highway at Santa Monica. The gods of traffic smile on us and we make good time. A handsome man in a sedan tries to catch Alistair's eye at a red light, along with several women in an SUV. Who can blame them?

"What?" asks he of the dark tousled hair and chiseled jaw-line.

"Hmm?"

"You're still staring."

"No, I'm not."

"Yes, you are. What's on your mind, Lilah?"

I sigh. "I was just thinking…"

"About?"

"How wonderful this is. The sun is shining, music is playing, and this car is a dream. Thank you."

"You already thanked me."

"And now I'm thanking you again. You put yourself out for me. A veritable stranger in a sticky situation," I say. "You're a good man, Alistair Lennox. Even with the whole cheese thing."

He grunts.

"What else would you like to argue about?"

"I suppose we could move on to lunch. I grabbed a burger. What about you?"

"Brunch was late, so I didn't bother."

He just nods.

It is a spectacular day for a drive. The endless blue of the ocean disappears in the distance. There are gorgeous beaches with expanses of sand, rugged cliffs, and rock formations. But it's the cool salty air rushing past that makes it sublime. My scarf is wound around my neck, and the ends flutter in the wind. I want to imprint this moment in my memory so I can play it back at will whenever I need a hit of happy.

I clear my throat and announce, "Back to my wish list. I decided not to attempt riding a mechanical bull."

"Probably for the best."

"I also started working on a second wish list, which—"

"Did you finish the first one?" he asks.

"No. Not quite."

"What does the second one cover?"

"Things I want to revisit, like my favorite books and so on."

He thinks it over for a moment. "That makes sense. What's on the list?"

"The paranormal romance I read last night and season one of *The Vampire Diaries*. Except it's twenty-two episodes, so I don't know how feasible a rewatch is given time constraints and the other things I hope to do. But those two choices kind of sum up my teenage years."

"Maybe you could just watch your favorite couple of episodes."

"That would work."

"What else have you been doing?"

"Not much." I stare out at the ocean and try to convince myself that everything is fine.

"What are you frowning about?" he asks. "What's wrong now?"

"I looked you up online, and I feel a little weird about it."

"Did you?" he asks in an unhappy tone of voice. "Weird how?"

"Guilty, I guess."

His lips thin, and he shoots me a look out of the corner of his eye. "You could have just not told me."

"I don't want to lie to you. It doesn't feel like a good time for me to be adding to my karmic debt. But I did want to know more about you since we're spending time together, and you're touchy about being asked anything. Which is, of course, your right." I swallow. "That excuse sounded more plausible in my head."

Nothing from him.

"I should point out that I already knew most of it due to living on the same planet as you for the past twenty-nine years. And wanting to know more about the person you're spending time with isn't exactly nefarious. Though I can also see how you might feel it's ever so slightly an invasion of your privacy since you're sensitive about that sort of thing."

His jaw is set in stone. It would take a chisel to move the thing. "I just wish you hadn't done that, Lilah."

"But don't you think maybe you're being a little overly sensitive?"

"Are you deliberately trying to start a fight with me?"

"No. Just thinking things through."

His frown turns contemplative, but he says no more.

The cell attached to the dashboard vibrates with an incoming call, and Helena flashes on the screen. He dismisses the call, and a moment later, the cell starts vibrating once again. He punches the button with his finger and says, "I'm about to walk into a meeting."

"No, you're not," says a woman with an upper-crust English accent. "You're driving on the highway a few minutes from home."

"Mother—"

"Carlos just passed you. He's heading into Beverly Hills to visit his brother. He texted to tell me you were on your way."

"He did, did he?" asks Alistair in a defeated tone.

"I'll see you and your blonde friend shortly. I'm very excited. Such a wonderful surprise, darling!"

His previous unhappiness has been doubled at least. It's obvious in the stark line of his jaw. "I'm sorry. We're going to have to go."

"Of course," I say quickly. "Does she really think you were on your way to visit, or was she just pretending so she could guilt-trip you?"

"With my mother, you never know."

He doesn't offer any further explanation. Just slows the car and turns at the next exit, taking us toward the beach. Lots of big, impressive homes. I doubt I can even afford to breathe the air around here. His mother was right—we were indeed only minutes from her place. Alistair's grip on the wheel tightens with each mile while I feel smaller and more insignificant. Facing down this sort of wealth is intimidating. Multimillion-dollar properties and cars that cost more than all my worldly possessions. It just reinforces how he and I have nothing in common. Not really. Our budding friendship was probably bound to crash and burn.

We pull up outside a tall iron fence and wait for it to slowly open. A hedge guards the property from prying eyes. Spiky cabbage palmettos and olive trees with branches twisted from the harsh coastal winds line the driveway. We pass two smaller buildings and pull up behind a sprawling midcentury modern house. A five-car garage sits to the side. I think this is what they call a compound.

And the man beside me continues to be one big ball of tension. He takes off his Ray-Bans and says, "I'll try to keep it brief. Then we can get back to our plans."

"Sure."

A pale woman wearing a voluminous pastel dress with her gray-tinged dark hair piled messily on top of her head emerges from the house. She is nothing less than spectacular. "Darling!" she calls.

"Hello, Mother," Alistair says, climbing out of the car with the air of someone submitting to some sort of horrible fate.

"It's so good to see you." She throws her arms around him and squeezes him tight. "My beautiful little baby boy."

Meanwhile, his expression is pure stoicism. "Brave words from someone who doesn't even reach my chin."

"Introduce me to your friend."

"This is Lilah" is all he says.

I climb out of the car and give her my best non-awkward smile. "Hello, Lady Helena."

"She's nervous, darling. Isn't that sweet?"

"Mmm" is all he says.

"It's been too long since I've seen you."

He scoffs. "A month at most."

"Try three, my darling child. You're always so busy." She beams up at him. "But you're here now and you've brought a friend. You never introduce your friends to me. Not since... Well, we won't talk about that. But Lilah must be special indeed."

Alistair frowns. "Mom, we're not—"

"Welcome to the beach shack." She sweeps forward and grasps hold of my hand. "Come inside, come inside. It's too windy for drinks on the patio. But they'll taste just as good in the parlor."

Beach shack, my butt. The place is a mansion. All glass walls and beamed ceilings. Despite her colorful clothing, the decor seems sedate. Lots of cream and dark wood. And the moment we walk inside, Lady Helena bellows, "Dougal, they're here. Where are you? We need drinks."

"I'm coming," yells back someone with a heavy Scottish accent. Dougal appears to be around the same age as Lady Helena. In his sixties, if I had to guess. He's fit and tall with a bald head and bushy gray beard. And after giving Alistair a hug, he heads immediately to the well-stocked bar in the corner of the living room. "What's your lass's name?"

"My name is Lilah and we're just friends," I say. "Nice to meet you."

The older man laughs. "The lad's always been a friendly sort. Hasn't he, Your Ladyship?"

"Oh, yes," she says. "Wait. Is that the right answer? Should I have lied? We don't want to scare her off."

"You've forgotten your glasses, old man," says Alistair. "Need me to come back there and pour?"

Lady Helena reclines on a cream armchair. "You better, or half of the good whiskey is going to end up on the floor."

"I heard that," says Dougal.

"Of course you did. We never said there was anything wrong with your hearing." Lady Helena turns to me with a smile. "Dougal is my gardener, butler, chauffeur, and so on. He grew up on the family estate in Scotland and then went on to work there like his father."

"Did you grow up there too?" I ask.

"No. I was mostly in London or away at school. Mother hated that drafty old castle. But we visited now and then."

Alistair and Dougal continue to argue good-naturedly behind the bar. It might be the first time I've seen him remotely relaxed. Smiling and laughing. Whatever hesitation he shows with his mother, there's none when it comes to this man.

"Talisker, thirty-year-old single malt, from the Isle of Skye," announces Dougal, serving first Lady Helena and then me. There are several fingers of amber liquid in the heavy crystal glass. "In honor of our new friend Lilah."

"Thank you."

He stands beside my chair, waiting until I taste it. Talk about putting on the pressure. "What do you think?" he asks. "Nice and peaty, isn't it?"

I swallow it down and smile super convincingly. "It's very good."

"Just admit that you don't like it." Alistair sits on the sofa opposite me. "Lilah is apparently not a scotch drinker."

Dougal's face falls. The man is heartbroken. How could I have done such a thing? He then shrugs and swiftly takes my glass from me. "We won't waste it, then."

"Oh, no," cries Lady Helena. "What *do* you drink? Darling, what does she drink?"

"I'm fine," I say. "Really."

Alistair taking a seat on the opposite side of the room from me seems like a statement. Though I am a grown-up who doesn't need her hand held. But there's a distinct distance between us now.

"How long have you two known each other?" asks Dougal.

"Since Saturday," says Alistair.

Dougal's brows rise. "Not long at all."

"When you know, you know." Lady Helena sighs wistfully. "I once got engaged to a total stranger while on a bender in Paris for Fashion Week. These things happen. The sheer awkwardness of waking up with the most exquisite hangover and not being able to remember my fiancé's name."

Alistair blinks. "So, you didn't in fact know."

"She left the ring on the nightstand and got on the first plane back to Heathrow," says Dougal. "Never saw him again."

Lady Helena pouts. "My point is that you can fall at first sight. There's no set allotment of time that must pass before love is allowed. Isn't that right, Lilah?"

"Time is just a construct," I say.

"Suck-up," mumbles Alistair.

"But we're only friends, as previously mentioned."

"Oh." Lady Helena's smile doesn't stay down for long. "But you must have a good feeling about where things are heading, though, darling. Otherwise, you wouldn't have brought a woman you've only known for two days home to meet me."

Alistair's brow furrows like never before.

"Just friends," I repeat with a smile.

She turns to her son and asks, "You spend time with women who are just friends?"

"Yes, Mother."

"Well done, darling. You certainly didn't get that from his side of the family."

"I always wanted to drive the coastal ride in a convertible," I explain. "It's on my wish list. Your son was kind enough to offer. Of course, it would have been rude not to stop since we happened to be passing."

He nods. "What she said."

"How did you meet?" asks Dougal.

"She almost crashed into my car."

Dougal gasps dramatically. "Not your grandfather's Aston Martin!"

Alistair confirms this with a nod, and I am most definitely in Dougal's bad books. The man is outraged.

"But I didn't in fact hit your car, did I?" I ask. "I swerved and hit a concrete bollard instead."

"Are you all right, Lilah?" asks Lady Helena.

"The muscles in my neck are a little stiff. But otherwise fine. Thank you."

"You didn't tell me your neck was sore," says Alistair, suddenly looking concerned.

"It's nothing." I stand and wander over to the front of the house with its view of the Pacific Ocean. "What a great outlook."

"We're right on the beach," confirms Lady Helena. "If you like sand. Which I don't."

"You live at the beach, but you don't like the beach?"

"I like looking at it from a suitable distance with a drink in my hand. Much more civilized."

"Are you still seeing that medium, Mother?" asks Alistair.

"Colin? Yes. But he prefers to be called an intuitive." She pauses to sip her scotch. "He's been so helpful. We've been dealing with a lot of my issues around self-love. He actually had a message for me to pass on to you the last time I visited. He said, 'Beware the color blue.' It all sounded rather ominous, actually. Make of that what you will."

Alistair's gaze slips from my face to my pale blue tee and back again. Then he says, "Very interesting. Tell Colin I said thank you."

As juvenile as it is to scratch your cheek with your middle finger, it still happens from time to time. Such is life.

"Betty White is one of his spirit guides," continues Lady Helena. "Isn't that brilliant?"

"I would take advice from Betty White," I say.

Dougal nods. "You'd be a fool not to."

"Remind me, Mother," says Alistair. "What happened to that last psychic you were seeing?"

Lady Helena sighs and flops back in her chair. "It's hardly Gabi's fault that she's in jail for grand larceny. Communing with the dead is complicated. Messages are bound to get jumbled every now and then. It's also not like everyone is ready to hear the truth, let alone have the wisdom to apply it to their life in a beneficial manner. It's so sad the way people harbor resentment in their hearts."

"That is sad," I agree, turning to her son. "It's not like we don't all do things now and then that we regret. And to forgive is divine."

Alistair's gaze is as cranky as can be. Due to my research or this visit with his mother or a combination of both, I do not know. But it would greatly ease my mind if he could be less hot while behaving ever so slightly like a dick.

Lady Helena points her glass of scotch in my general direction. "Exactly right, Lilah. We can only move forward by releasing the past and embracing the future."

"What nonsense," grumbles Alistair. "All your psychics and spirit guides. You know I don't believe in any of it. What happened to science and reason?"

"Well, my darling boy, I believe we should all be free to live our truth."

"I'm well aware."

"That's enough," says Dougal sternly.

"Imagine him daring to disparage my spiritual beliefs. And just like that—" Lady Helena snaps her fingers "—he's out of the will."

"Again," says Alistair in a lighter tone.

She laughs. "Again. I don't know how many times that is now. Just as well—I can't be bothered to contact my solicitor and make any actual changes."

"Phew," says her son with a small smile. His gaze lingers on me as he sips his scotch. Then, out of nowhere, a sly sort of smile appears on his lips. "Actually, Mother," he says. "You asked what Lilah drinks? I just remembered, she mentioned wanting to try absinthe. It's another item on her list."

Lady Helena bursts out of her seat. "What a wonderful idea!"

"No. Absolutely not. I'm putting my foot down," says Dougal, who does indeed put his foot down. "The last time you opened a bottle of that stuff, you rang you-know-who and told him to kiss your ass."

"That was years ago, and he deserved it. You know he did." Lady Helena sweeps over to the bar and reaches for the top shelf. Several sparkling diamond bracelets slide up her arm as she stretches and strains. "I won't be the one drinking it, anyway. It's for Lilah. Alistair. Darling. Please help. I'll need the fountain too if we're to do this properly. I think it's on the bottom shelf of the cupboard here."

Alistair rises to his feet. "Coming, Mother."

"Well—" Dougal sighs heavily "—I hope you have a stout constitution, lass."

"Me too," I say, with no small amount of fear.

"Your mother is a creature of pure chaos."

"You're not wrong," says Alistair. "Are you sure you don't need ibuprofen or something for your neck?"

"I'm fine."

Malibu is magic. It reminds me of hanging out at the beach when I was younger. The sun is setting, and the play of colors across the sky is sublime—hues of orange and terra-cotta fade to peach and pink before melting into lavender and mauve. There's something soothing about watching the water. Having an unimpeded view of this dreamlike vista from Helena's living room. And yet my sigh is the heaviest known to womankind.

Alistair's face is blank. The same as it's been for the last hour. "What was that for?"

"The burden of big thoughts."

"Such as?"

I do my best to gather said thoughts into a straight line. It doesn't work. "Please take into consideration that there's a small chance I am somewhat inebriated."

"You don't say," he replies in a dry tone.

"You also make me nervous, so don't expect this to be eloquent."

He frowns. "I make you nervous?"

I just shrug.

"Why would I make you nervous?"

"Hush. I'm talking now," I say, moving right along. "You see, this whole situation with the predictions has been making me take stock. I always thought I would travel and do all the kinds of things that are on my list. But then routine takes over, and it's all work and bills. I want to try to live with joy and notice the little things."

"It's a nice idea," he says.

"I am going to try to be more present and live in a more… Shit. What's the word? What kind of manner?"

"Mindful?"

"Yes! Thank you. Live in a more mindful manner."

There's definite amusement in his gaze. "Good work."

"You're mocking me because I'm under the influence, but I don't care." I am almost finished with my second glass of the green-colored cocktail Helena made me. It tastes of aniseed, apple juice, lime, and mint. And is poured from an ornate antique glass-and-silver fountain, which is basically an orb full of booze on a stand with a little tap on the front. "My lips are numb, and my head is light."

"I told you to go easy. Absinthe is strong."

"Doesn't it frustrate you?"

"Beyond belief," he says. "What are we talking about, Lilah?"

"We're so programmed to worry about what other people think all the time. But the fact is, no one's sitting at home mulling over some stupid shit I said last week. Or last year. Or a decade ago. There's no need to spend my life second-guessing everything I say or do."

He cocks his head and just listens.

"We waste so much time that way. Worrying. I wouldn't have rushed to ask my ex to move in with me if I hadn't been trying to meet some idiotic… Shit. It's happening again. What's the word I'm after?"

"Plan? Schedule? Ideal?"

"Any of those will do," I say. "Don't underestimate how embarrassing it was to admit that about my ex either. It's stupid the way society still pushes people to conform in subtle ways. My life won't be bereft if I don't partner up and have children. It'll just be different, and that's okay. How ridiculous is it that I still feel the need to tell myself that in this day and age."

He nods. "Fuck the patriarchy."

"I couldn't have said it better myself."

"Are you happy, Lilah?"

"What?" I frown in confusion. "Right now?"

"No. I mean in general, with your life."

"Some of the time. Happy is hard," I say. "What about you?"

"I would say I'm content."

We sit in silence for a moment. Then I ask, "You're still cranky at me, aren't you?"

He looks away and sighs. "No."

"Really? That's great. Though it might have been wiser of me to keep my mouth shut and not say anything about looking you up online. I'll have to think about that when I'm sober. When does honesty kick you in the pants, and is it really worth it?"

"Oh, no!" cries Lady Helena, illustrating my earlier point about her being pure chaos. A moment ago, she was on the other side of the living room dancing to disco music from the seventies. "What happened? You looked him up?"

Alistair rises and walks away.

Lady Helena winces. "The press is a particularly delicate topic. You have to understand, Lilah. He's had no control over the narrative they spin about him since he was twelve. They've invaded his life at every possible opportunity and made money off their lies. It's not something you can appreciate until you've actually experienced it. Not that I would wish it on anyone. I invited them in a long time ago and have to live with that decision. But my son never had a choice."

I nod.

"He was such a happy child before all of that. Everywhere we went, he made friends. You couldn't stop to buy gas with-out him getting into a conversation with someone. People fascinated him. He always wanted to know the story of everyone's life. Then he became so sad and withdrawn." She sighs and pats my shoulder. "There, there, dear."

"Now, then, Your Ladyship," says Dougal. "Alistair is quite capable of handling his own affairs. Why don't we talk about something else?"

"What a good idea. Drink this." Alistair returns and pushes a glass of water at me while removing the remains of the absinthe cocktail. "That's enough of that."

I down the water.

With an expression of relief, he announces, "It's time for us to go."

The drive back home is a quiet one. Though the rush of the cold night air helps to clear my head. I don't know if we're going to continue being friends, but we're definitely not in love with each other. The truth of the matter is Alistair Lennox is a field full of land mines that I lack the skills to navigate. Time for more toxic positivity. Good Witch Willow couldn't have been more wrong about us. Therefore, after deducting the half a point I had awarded the prediction, the chance of me dying next week is down to 55 percent.

Not bad.

He pulls up at the curb outside my apartment, and I climb out of the convertible and close the door. It is a truly beautiful car. The sounds of the city fade away, and there is only this horrible silence between us. It's like the whole world is holding its breath. Or maybe that's just me.

"Alistair—"

"Drink some more water before you go to bed," he says in a no-nonsense tone.

"Thank you again for doing this. It was great."

"You're welcome." He nods. "Thank you for going along with visiting my mother. She enjoyed meeting you."

"Sure."

I search for something meaningful to say. Something to prolong this moment with him or to check on the heartbeat of our burgeoning friendship. However, not enough sleep last night and a full day with absinthe have caught up with me, and my mind is a mess. What I really want to ask is if I will see him again, but instead, I just stand there and dither. Given everything going on, I should be braver and put my heart on the line. But what if I say the wrong thing? What if he gets all up in his feelings again?

Fuck it. "This was fun today. I was wondering did you want to maybe—"

"I'm busy," he says, frowning at the steering wheel. Like it personally did him wrong.

"Oh. Okay."

"You should head on inside. I have to go." And that's exactly what he does.

8

Tuesday

The first thing I decide the next morning is to be more daring (after popping some Advil for yet another hangover). My wish list is too staid. Too boring. There must be a balance between *What a stupid thing to do* and *Whoa!* but in a good way. It takes some calling around to various businesses, but I manage to line up two new and interesting experiences. And the first one happens at midday in a nearby park.

"Talk it through," says my skateboarding instructor, Booker. He has short braids and is cooler than I could ever hope to be. He also has much better balance. Though that isn't hard.

"My foot goes over the front hardware, positioned at a slight angle."

"That's right."

"Are you sure there isn't a rule about which foot goes where?"

"Nope. Left or right is fine. Just use whichever feels the most comfortable."

"That's a shame. I kind of like rules," I say. "Okay. Lining up my back foot with the back hardware on the board. But my foot is on the ground, of course."

We're in a skate park in West LA. I have already mastered the art of standing on the board while it is stationary. My balance isn't too bad. The children on the other side of the park are laughing at me and calling me a noob. Little jerks. But everyone has to start somewhere. On the plus side, we've been at this for almost an hour, and I haven't broken a bone or landed on my ass once. Which I count as a win. High school phys ed classes can convince you of all sorts of things, like how much I suck at sports. But this skateboarding class has kind of been cathartic. It also makes for a great distraction from pining over a certain Scotsman.

"Push with my back foot while shifting my weight to the front foot." And forward I go for about five or six feet. I won't be taking home any titles or performing tricks in the near future. But having never been particularly athletic or coordinated, this effort is fine with me. "That wasn't bad."

"You're doing good," says Booker, who is a man of much enthusiasm and great patience. "That's our time. How are you feeling? Did you enjoy it?"

"I did. Thank you."

"That's great. You've got my number if you want to book another lesson." He smiles and I smile back at him. It takes me a minute to remove the hand, elbow, and knee guards. Then I give all of them back, along with the helmet and board. And I tip him well because the man is doing God's work out here in the half-pipes.

My cell vibrates in my back pocket. Rebecca is texting me a series of screenshots from a leading gossip site. The headline is "Prince Charming Breaks Another Heart." I can feel my soul leave my body. It's just me and my sense of impending doom sitting on a park bench. And sure enough, there's a photo of us in the convertible. Me climbing out. And him driving away.

The expression on my face as I stare after him is pathetic. Just fucking awful. To think all of this is out there in the universe and anyone can see it. But this also means I've been identified. My name is in the article, and they knew exactly where to be to get these shots. *Ugh.*

My cell vibrates again, and I answer the call on the first ring. "Hey."

"What are you going to do?" asks Rebecca. "These photos are spreading like a virus. You can't go home. They'll probably be there, right? The paparazzi and so on?"

"Yeah."

"Come stay with me."

"No. I don't want to dump this mess on anyone."

"Where, then?" she asks. "A hotel?"

"I think so. Something with security and room service." I take a deep breath. "It should only be for a day or two."

"They'll see that you're boring and go back to chasing pop stars and actors around town in no time," she jokes. "Lilah, are you okay? Your face in that photo… You look so sad."

"It was nothing. Just weird lighting or something."

"That's the excuse you're going with?"

I sigh. "The truth is, I hardly know the man, and I doubt I'll be hearing from him again. It's not worth worrying about."

"I didn't realize you'd been in touch with him again. You really don't want to talk about it?"

"No," I confirm. "Not right now. But thanks. I have an appointment to get to."

"Okay. Let me know if you change your mind. Or if you want some company in your hotel room."

"Will do."

My phone chimes, and a text message appears on-screen.

Josh: How could you do this to me?

Josh: I was giving you time to calm down and you fucking cheat on me? You're such a bitch!

What an entitled prick. Kicking Josh out is fast becoming the best choice I've ever made.

"Stay in a haunted hotel" wasn't on my wish list before, but what the heck? The Hollywood Roosevelt is a Spanish-style building from the 1920s. The first Oscars ceremony was held here, and the ghosts of Marilyn Monroe, Montgomery Clift, and Lucille Ball have been sighted on the premises. My loft suite has a modern king-size four-poster bed, a big comfy armchair, and a desk. It is both cool and comfortable, and only a few blocks' walk from my second appointment of the day.

But more about that later.

Booking into a hotel in the middle of Hollywood might not seem smart for someone on the down-low. However, it's not like I plan on leaving my room for the next twenty-four hours. It sucks to lose a day, but this will blow over. In the meantime, the bathtub is calling my name. My apartment doesn't have one, and hot water and bubbles are sublime. The heat is particularly great on my neck and hip. Though I make sure to keep the new bandage on my wrist from my afternoon's adventure out of the water.

Now is the time to wrangle my cell. I block Josh for both being a dickhead and a hypocrite. My bad I hadn't already blocked him after I caught him cheating. But the feeling of liberation is immense. Just pure freedom. The amount of energy I exerted when we were together telling myself that we worked is embarassing. Live and learn.

Now might be the time to get a new phone number. I delete over a dozen messages from curious contacts who've seen my picture in the paper: an acquaintance from work, someone I knew in college, a roommate from way back when. They all have questions, none of which I have any interest in answering. Most of these people I haven't heard from in years. Making friends as an adult is hard, though I also might just not be any good at it. I always had books to keep me company.

I do answer a message from Mr. Pérez with an apology. He found a photographer standing in the front garden. Staying away from home for now is the right choice.

Next is an email from my insurers confirming they're writing off the Prius. The repairs would cost more than the vehicle is worth, apparently. I call Mom and Dad and update them on my whereabouts. Mom's cousin had texted her about my situation. But I manage to explain things without too much trouble. Sort of. After the lotto win, they seem open to almost anything happening when it comes to me. Then I nuke anything and everything from the media. Including the offer of a stupid amount of money for a tell-all interview about you-know-who. Like I even know him that well.

I don't mean to google myself. My fingers must have slipped, as wrinkled and waterlogged as they are. The moment it's done,

I know it's a mistake. Dread sits heavy in my stomach. People always say, "Don't read the comments." But when you accidentally go viral, "Don't read anything" would be better advice.

The body positivity movement has claimed me. Which is cool. However, most monarchists think me fat and common. Same goes for many of Alistair's stans. The few that are shipping us are being buried under the avalanche of online hate. Anonymous sources say the king is horrified. Again. (You would think he had better things to do.) There has been no sign of Alistair himself, so they make his absence a statement. He is embarrassed. He is heartbroken. He is in an emergency meeting with his people. And my personal favorite, he and I have made up and eloped to Mexico. How exciting. Nothing new to report about Daria Moore. Though of course there is plenty of speculation. And Lady Helena declined to comment, but she did flip the bird at a photographer from her front patio. What a woman.

She was right about how understanding what parasites the paparazzi are requires firsthand experience. There's nothing like having your life reduced to clickbait. Let alone the whole damn world having an opinion about you. So gross and weird.

I have to convince myself to get out of the bath. Staying in it feels safe, though my skin is going to shit. I climb out and wrap myself up in a fluffy white robe. It's been a while since I stayed at a hotel. All I have with me are the contents of my purse. I washed my panties, bra, socks, and tee with soap in the basin and hung them on towel racks. Happily, local stores can deliver whatever else I need.

This is not so bad. No sign of any ghosts yet. However, if I were a deceased Hollywood star, I wouldn't show up until after midnight. It would almost be common to haunt the

halls before then. Make people work for the scares by staying up late. I am determined to give my poor liver a day off.
But I can still order room service and read a book on my cell.
I am perfectly fine dealing with this all on my own. No one
else needs to be bothered by this bullshit. I'll do the sensible
thing and hide away for a day or two, then get on with my
wish list. All good.

"Yes! Success."

Two whole bowling pins topple noisily onto the wooden
lane, and I do a dance in my borrowed shoes. It's important
to celebrate your own small triumphs. The bartender said
the speakeasy is usually busy, but not tonight. Lucky for me.
Though it is past eleven on a weeknight, and this is LA, and
some people will party any time of the day or night.

The Hollywood Roosevelt has several bars and restaurants.
This one is an old gaming room on the mezzanine level. Lots
of polished wood and a wealth of liquor bottles lined up on
the shelves behind the bar. And two bowling lanes, which is
great. I have never bowled before. As demonstrated by my
current performance.

The truth is, I got lonely in my room. A good book is usually more than enough to keep me company, but my mind kept
wandering. Being stuck in a hotel room, no matter how nice,
got old fast. Down here, however, the vibe is good, and the
music is loud. The pins are set up again, and I stretch my neck,
pick up the bowling ball, and do my thing. Such style and
grace. The ball unfortunately heads straight into the gutter.

"That was close," says a familiar voice behind me. And it's
accompanied by clapping.

I spin to face him with wide eyes. "Ali. Hi."

Alistair's arms fall back to his sides, and we stare warily at one another. He's wearing a black suit and a white shirt with the top two buttons open. Which should be illegal. On the right man, tailoring is such a turn-on. The way the suit jacket frames the breadth of his shoulders. The general air of formality, capability, and control. I have a boss kink now, apparently.

I don't think I realized how much I wanted to see him again. Not until this moment. He makes my heart do a weird fluttery thing. It can't be healthy.

"Wasn't easy to find you," he says. "A journalist friend helped me out."

I sit down on a nearby chair and start unlacing my bowling shoes. "You're friends with one of them?"

"They're not all bad."

"If they know where I am, where are they?" I ask. "Or am I no longer of interest?"

"You chose a good hotel. Security has been sending any press or lurkers on their way."

"Hmm." I give him a long look. The butterflies in my stomach need to get better taste. It's a pity you can't turn off your libido. Have some downtime now and then from any feelings in the heart and/or pants. "I thought you said you were busy. Why are you here, Ali?"

"I need to talk to you about something."

I keep on gazing up at him. Dark stubble lines his jaw, and there are lines beside his eyes and bracketing his mouth. He seems tired. Like he should probably be napping, not standing here with me. "You could have texted."

"I did. You didn't answer."

"Right. I turned off my phone," I say. "Didn't expect to hear from you again."

"No," he agrees, giving me a shifty glance. "My, ah, friend the journalist. She said you were offered a lot of money for an interview. Are you going to do it?"

I stuff my feet back into my sneakers and stand. "Go away, Alistair."

"I have to know. Yes or no, Lilah?"

I hand over the shoes and nod good-night to the bartender. She gives my companion a curious look but says nothing. All I have to do is make it to the elevator and return to hiding in my room. I hit the button and wait with my shoulders up around my ears. As if I am in need of protection. A woman farther down the hallway is waiting on something, but she doesn't pay us any mind.

"Lilah?" he asks, standing behind me.

"The answer is no."

"You're not going to do the interview? It's a lot of money."

"So you said. The answer is still no."

"Are you absolutely sure?" He gives the closed elevator doors a scowl. It seems the whole world is annoying him to-night. "They need to know."

"They? Who is *they*? Is that your father or...?"

His lips slam shut, and he says no more. Which says more than enough.

"Might be best to make everyone you meet sign an NDA. Less stress. Just make it a part of your everyday life. Get a coffee— ask the barista to sign away their rights. Say hi to someone at a bar—see if they'll give you a quick signature. I know it sounds awkward at first, but I have every faith in you making it work. And then you'll never need to have a shitty conversation like this one ever again." The elevator chimes and the doors slide open.

I step inside and press the button for my floor. "I've answered your question. You can go away now."

He just stands there watching me with his inscrutable blue eyes.

My shoulders sink as the doors start to slide closed. The truth is, the sight of him hurts my heart. That and the fact that he actually thinks I'm the sort of asshole who would sell him out. Though I'm sure his past played a part in making him believe I'd do this. Trust seems so hard for him.

But before the doors can close, he thrusts his hand between them. With an irritated noise, they pause, before sliding back open. A muscle jumps in his jawline as he steps into the elevator and glares down at me. Like this is all my fault somehow.

"What are you doing?"

"I don't know," he growls back at me.

9

"I won't do any interviews, Alistair," I say. "You're safe. Go home."

A shadow crosses his face when I say his full name. Not sure what that's about. But then, he seems wound up and upset at everything right now. "I heard you."

"What? Do you think I'm lying?"

"Yes," he says, looming over me in the confines of the elevator. Then he grimaces and says, "No."

Surprised laughter bursts out of me. "Holy shit. I knew you didn't trust me, but wow. Which is it, yes or no?"

"I don't know you well enough to trust you. But no, you're not lying. I can see that. Fuck," he says, the brogue as thick as can be. He takes a step closer, gets all up in my face, and asks in an accusing tone of voice, "Were you in that hotel bar hoping to find your great sex?"

I wrinkle my nose in confusion. "Was I *what*?"

"You heard me."

"Because nothing says looking for a hookup like bowling shoes. Why do you even care?"

"I don't," he says bluntly. "But it's not safe picking up some stranger in a bar."

"Like no one's ever done that in the history of time and space."

"Lilah…"

The elevator chimes and the doors slide open to my floor. I head down the hallway to my room and swipe the door card. The prince is hot on my heels. *Oh, man.* I kind of want to hit something. His handsome face would do. But I don't, because unlike some people, I am an adult who can handle her feelings. Most of the time.

"Being concerned about my safety sort of qualifies as caring," I point out. "But moving right along. We've reached the part of the conversation where you explain how my sex life is any of your business."

His mouth opens, but no words come out.

"That's what I thought."

"So you won't do the interview?"

"For the third time…no. No interviews. No comments. Nothing."

"Thank you," he says in a slightly more subdued voice.

"You're welcome. Was that all?"

He nods slowly but still shows no sign of leaving. So much brooding, with his rigid shoulders and set jaw. Like he's feeling a lot and is not the least bit happy about it. Which is when he notices the small bandage on my wrist and scowls some more. "What happened there?"

We'll be spending the night in the hallway, at this rate. Just us and the ghosts. I don't answer him, but I do hold the door to my room open. It feels like kicking myself, letting him back into my life. If that's what's happening. I am such a sucker for this man. My idiocy knows no bounds. He follows me into the room and stands at the end of the bed. He truly broods like no other. It's such a talent. And in the low light, the shadows beneath his eyes are like bruises.

"When was the last time you slept?" I ask.

"Had an early start this morning."

With my sneakers off, I climb onto the bed. It really is comfortable. I pick up the remote off the bedside table and turn on *The Vampire Diaries*. Oh so carefully, I pick at the tape securing the bandage on my left wrist. It doesn't take long for the black ink lines and irritated pink skin beneath to be revealed.

He takes a step toward me for a closer look. "You got a tattoo?"

"After my skateboarding lesson. Don't worry. I went to a studio with a stellar reputation." I hold up my hand to show him the simple outline of a book and its ruffled pages on my wrist. It's about an inch and a half square all around. Not too big.

"You had a skateboarding lesson? Lilah, you're still recovering from a car accident. Was that really a good idea?"

"Are you aware that you're a worrier?" I ask. "It was fine. I had fun. And it's still safer than bungee jumping or skydiving."

He sighs. "What's next on the list?"

"I don't know. My decision to be more daring is shaking things up."

A moment of silence passes. Guess neither of us knows what to say.

"I'm sorry if you feel that I was being unreasonable just now," he says.

"Is that your idea of an apology?"

He grips the back of his neck and frowns his heart out. "It was never my intention for your feelings to get hurt, but I—"

"No. Stop. That's not it either. You're seriously bad at this, aren't you?"

This time he simply says, "I'm sorry."

"You can stay and watch TV if you want. This is the episode where Caroline just got turned into a vampire. It's one of my favorites. She throws Damon down a hallway, and boy, does he deserve it."

For a minute, he just stands there. Then slowly, warily, he walks around to the other side of the bed. A wild animal would be less cagey. Such a shame I wasn't a Girl Scout, because I have earned my badge for dealing with grumpy bears. Alistair toes off his shoes and removes his coat. Then he unbuttons the cuffs of his shirt and folds them back. That he feels safe enough to let his guard down and relax is like Christmas to me. Though his exposed forearms shouldn't affect me so much. He's only getting comfortable. But everything low in my belly draws tight. The scattering of dark hair and lines of his muscles. How efficient he is with those big, strong hands.

He catches me staring and happily jumps to the wrong conclusion. "I had meetings today."

"It's a nice suit."

"I can only stay for one episode."

"Okay."

"I don't like you being alone," he says, as if I demanded he justify his actions.

"Me being alone seems to bother you more than it does me. Have you noticed that?"

Nothing from him.

"I was alone a lot when I was younger. Guess I got used to

it. My brother always had sports practice or something after school. Until I was old enough to work in the café, I was home on my own most afternoons and evenings." As much as I want to ask how much of his life he's spent alone, I keep my mouth shut.

He sits down, extends his legs, and shoves a cushion behind his head. It's just me and him and a TV. And that is fine and dandy—friends hang out, it's what they do. Though I don't want to get my hopes up too high for us actually having a friendship. He might change his mind again.

"I take it you're here because the press are hassling you?" he asks. "That's why you're in a hotel?"

"I have it on good authority that there are some hiding in the bushes at home."

He nods.

"Who's the *they* you referred to?" I ask, treading on dangerous ground. Damn my curiosity. "You said *they* needed to know if I was doing the interview."

For the longest time, he says nothing. So long I think he's not going to answer. But then he does. "The people around him can be pedantic. They're used to controlling things."

"The people around the king?"

"Yes," he says, his jaw cracking on a yawn. "Sorry. Long day. They called me at two in the fucking morning in a furor about the pictures."

"Seems excessive. There are photos of you online all the time. Both of us were keeping our hands to ourselves and wearing pants in all the shots."

He just grunts. Guess he's not ready to see the humor in the situation. "Their reaction to things can depend on what else is going on at the time. It's complicated."

"Try me."

"Lilah…" he starts and then falls silent for a while. "If they're setting up some positive press with, say, a charity visit or whatever and something I do eclipses that reporting, then they have a tendency to get upset."

I wrinkle my nose in both distaste and confusion. "Are you just not supposed to live your life? Is that what they're telling you?"

Nothing from him.

What I really want to know is why these people have a say in his life at all. But it's none of my business and pushing for further answers might push him away.

"Let's talk about something else," I say. "What do you feel like talking about?"

"I don't know."

"Hmm. Me neither."

He stays silent. But I can feel his side of the bed relax some.

"Thanks for explaining the situation to me."

He just grunts.

The Vampire Diaries is not his thing. That much is obvious when he falls asleep approximately four minutes into the episode. Imagine being able to just go to sleep like that. It usually takes me at least an hour to quiet my mind.

I lower the volume on the TV and listen to the deep and even sound of him breathing. The hard lines of his face soften when he sleeps. It's a king-size mattress, but still. I am hyperaware of his presence. Of the heat of his big body and the cedar of his cologne. Friends don't stare at friends while they sleep. It's bad manners to the extreme. He didn't affect me in this way when we first met. At least, I don't think he did. There was a lot going on that day. But now his presence hits me in the heart and the loins, and I don't know what to do.

"Stop staring at me," he mumbles without opening his eyes.

"Shut up and go to sleep."

Wednesday

It takes a moment for me to figure out where I am when I wake up. And then another to understand why I'm so toasty warm. Josh didn't spoon without cause. Any spooning always preceded an attempt at morning sex. It was fake affection to the extreme. I never found the position comfortable either. Sleeping peacefully requires space. I am not at my best in the a.m. The only thing I usually want first thing in the morning is coffee and quiet. Being conscious is hard-core. But here I am, with a body pressed to my back and an arm thrown over my middle and another under my neck. Alistair is smooshed up against me and I don't hate it. And what's more, the hard-on pressing against my butt cheek definitely has me wide-awake and aching in a good way.

"I know you're awake," he murmurs, his voice husky from sleep. "I have to be honest—this is slightly awkward."

"Whatever do you mean?"

"You're going with denial?"

"Sure, why not? I can ignore it if you can. How did you sleep?"

"Great," he says with some surprise. "Though I'm not sure you ignoring my dick is a compliment. Let me just state for the record that this situation is not my fault. You're soft and you smell good. But we're still not soulmates."

"You don't think morning wood means it's true love?" I press my thighs together oh so subtly. The way he's making me wet is worrisome. "That's disappointing. Serious question. Are we actually attempting friendship here?"

"I don't know."

"Because if there's a high likelihood you're going to turn around and tell me you're busy again and drive off into the distance, then maybe we shouldn't. That kind of hurt."

He sighs.

"Also, total honesty here. For a big burly dude, you're kind of sensitive. Which is not necessarily a bad thing. It makes total sense, given your background and all. But you and your situation are way outside my field of experience, and you have to know I am going to say or do the wrong thing sometimes."

"You've given this a lot of thought."

"I have."

"As for you saying or doing the wrong thing sometimes... I'm sure this will shock you, but I'm far from perfect myself." He stretches his neck and rolls his shoulders. Then he glances back at me. "What's this? Nothing clever to say?"

"No."

"Wonders will never cease." He's busily slipping on his shoes and tying the laces. "I think we should give being friends a chance."

"Really?"

He nods.

"I'd like that." *Like* would be an understatement. "Very much."

He looks up and says, "What's that look on your face?"

"I don't know, good sir. What look is on my face?"

"Sort of pleased crossed with confused. Though you might just have gas. It's hard to say."

I groan and stretch. "Ha."

"Well?"

There's a small chance I lay awake until one in the morning constructing an overly long speech to woo him back. It was quite good. There was a heavy focus on the joy I could bring to his life, such as my penchant for witty dialogue, excellent taste in reading materials, and access to my mother's chocolate chip cookies. A shame it won't be needed.

"Not to sound needy or insecure, but when it comes to you, I do occasionally have a 'Why me?' moment. I mean, you're who you are and I am me."

He frowns. "Why not you?"

"I don't know." I sit up cross-legged on the bed and tie back my hair. Which has to be resembling a bird's nest right about now. Coffee is required. Stat. "Because I'm not one of the beautiful people. Whoever the hell they are."

He scoffs.

"I'm being serious."

"I could ask you 'Why me?' since you have no interest in the fame or infamy or any of that other shit." He stands and glances at the watch on his wrist. It's probably platinum. "I can only assume it's my charming personality. Right. I have to get a move on. Hopefully you'll be able to go home today. The paparazzi just need their attention diverted to something new. Save Thursday afternoon for me. I have an idea for your list."

"You do?"

He picks up his suit jacket and heads for the door. "Yes."

Then he's gone, leaving me with a wealth of warm, fuzzy feelings. Just a whole heaping lot of them. My cheeks hurt from being happy, and my brain is operating way beyond a safe speed. So many thoughts and emotions. I see to the essentials in the bathroom and wash my hands. Brush my teeth and hair and so on.

A lot has happened. There's much to overthink. His morning wood is best ignored. I doubt I'll ever encounter his hard-on again. Metaphorically speaking, we were just two ships passing in the night. Same goes for him saying I was soft and smelled good. He was being kind or something. Alistair and I are just friends. Emphasis on the *just*. But there's a definite fun edge of flirt to our friendship. I am not imagining it. Not even a little.

Time to order breakfast and caffeine. While waiting for my buttermilk pancakes with strawberries to arrive, a bad thing occurs to me. Our return to friendship status increases the likelihood of me dying on Sunday. I can't discount the way the other predictions came true. Though having lived with a due date for my death for a while now, the threat doesn't seem as sharp. It's more of a nagging ongoing anxiety causing concern. And if it is true, if I am doomed to die, there isn't anything I can do to assuage the situation. Or is there?

"I was expecting you days ago," Good Witch Willow greets me.

"You say things like that, and it makes me wonder how precise your predictions really are." I take a seat on a nearby bench. Thanks to social media, it wasn't hard to track her down. We're in a community garden located off Hollywood Boulevard. "I didn't even know this place existed." LA is a big-ass city. It's good to see some green amongst the concrete. All sorts of people are working in the garden. Young and old and everything in between.

"It's been here since before you were born. You should pay better attention." She kneels in a garden bed full of leafy greens, tomatoes, and cucumbers. Bushes of parsley, basil, and dill grow nearby, scenting the air. Her braid of silver hair hangs down her back as she digs with a small spade. "How are things with your boyfriend?"

"He was cheating."

"And your job?"

"They passed me over for promotion."

She sits back on her heels. "I don't suppose you happened to catch the lotto numbers?"

"I won a quarter of a million."

"Couldn't you remember all of them?"

I shake my head. "No."

"Shame" is all she says, and goes back to digging.

"I have some questions."

"What a surprise."

I slide my sunglasses to the top of my head. The sun is warm, and it is a beautiful day. A dragonfly lands near my hand, its body a shimmering metallic green in the sunlight. It's like everyday magic. Fall was always my favorite season. But maybe I was wrong. Maybe it should be spring. Those cooler days before boob-sweat season kicks in. "If you can see these things, why don't you use them for yourself?"

"My ability is a gift. It is not to be misused for personal gain."

"Do you know when you'll die?"

"No," she says. "But I never wanted to know."

"Maybe I didn't either. Did that ever occur to you?"

"You get what you're given. Sometimes you have to take the good with the bad." She nudges her wire-rim glasses farther up her nose. "How's the prince?"

"He's not really a prince."

"The right blood flows through his veins." She shrugs. "I never understood all the nonsense about being born out of wedlock. The supposed shame of it. It's good that society has moved on from such bullshit."

"Yeah."

"Of course, they're counting on their blue blood to elevate them above the rest of us," she says. "If the old rules don't apply, then there's nothing saying they're any better. Just their money and everything else they stole over the years and refuse to return."

"Not a fan of the monarchy?"

"Never saw the point." She takes a swig from her nearby water bottle. "What do you want?"

"Not to die."

She laughs. "We all want that. Well…most of us."

"I want not to die on Sunday."

"Mmm." Her gaze softens. "Can't help you, sorry. I am not all-powerful, I just deliver the message."

I sit forward, choosing my words with care. "If I were to stay away from him, have nothing to do with him, would that stop the last two predictions from coming true? Would it put a stop to it all?"

"Do you really want to do that?"

"No. Of course not. I like him."

"There's your problem. He's already in your heart."

I snort. "I'm not in love with him. Sheesh."

"I didn't say you were. But you're not immune to him either. You two are already on your way to becoming." She pulls off a gardening glove and takes one of the crystals hanging around her neck in hand. Her gaze goes hazy as she stares off into the middle distance. "I'm not unsympathetic to your plight. But I can't help you."

"Can't or won't?"

She just sighs.

"There's nothing I can do?" I ask.

"You can make the most of the time you have left."

I let my head fall back and stare at the endless sky. High overhead, a crow passes, a blot of darkness against the blue. I should be thankful it doesn't shit on me. Things can always be worse. Though Italians believe being crapped on by a bird is a sign of good luck. Guess it's all about perception. "I still can't believe this is happening."

"Then ignore it and go live your normal life. There can be great comfort in routines," she says. "Who knows, maybe I'm wrong?"

"Wait, are you?"

"What do you think?"

"What you're basically saying is that the only thing I have control over is how I react to the situation, huh?"

"Got it in one," she says, pulling her glove back on. "Now go away. I'm busy."

I slide my sunglasses back on and wander out of the community garden. I remember hearing a quote about how aging is a privilege denied to many that feels particularly relevant now. I would have made a great grumpy old lady with sparkling silver hair. People talk about how your fucks fall away with age. How freeing it can be. Good Witch Willow certainly doesn't suffer fools gladly. It sucks that I might not get to experience the same.

I order an Uber and stand on the sidewalk waiting. Every week or so, I stop at a nearby thrift store that donates their profits to charity. I help them with their books, sorting the new stock into categories and keeping the display looking great. It's where I'm heading now. A car drives slowly past before parking halfway down the block from me. The person in the driver's seat doesn't pull out a camera or anything. Not that I can see, at least.

It turns out the lure of the internet is not one I can ignore after all. What can I say? I am weak.

There's no sign of my name on the latest offerings from the gossip sites when I check on my cell. What a relief. A rock star and their model/actor partner had been seen shopping for baby gear. And a popular comedian had cheated on his wife. The text messages were cringey. An Olympic gymnast had announced her engagement to a celebrity chef. The photos of the two women were gorgeous, their beaming smiles and adoring gazes. Talk about showing that love is real. Alistair's half brother, the Prince of Wales, also rates a mention due to rumors his recent big royal engagement is on rocky ground.

Some people love the fame monster. They crave it and chase it and make it their own. Having been briefly on the receiving end, however, made me wonder. How many of these people would choose to keep their private lives private? If they could do their job without the public scrutiny, would they? I know their position comes with immense privilege. But the pressure of the public gaze and being subject to so many opinions is a lot.

I don't know.

I saved my least favorite site for last. The one that had speculated on my dress size with horrified glee. *Assholes.* At the top of the page are new photos of Alistair with a lingerie model at a charity luncheon at the Beverly Wilshire Hotel. He's wearing another suit and, Lord, does he look dapper. The close-ups of his warm smile and very friendly gaze were... Yeah. It's great that he's having a good time. Though I could have done without the paparazzo catching the moment his hand lowered from the small of her back to the curve of his date's ass. Not that any of this is my business. We're just friends.

10

News of Alistair's lunch date means the paparazzi have lost interest in me. My brush with fame is officially over. There's no one hiding in the front garden when I return home that evening. No suspicious people lurking in the street. Though there's still a lingering feeling of being watched. It's probably just my imagination. I do my best to shake it off as I head up the stairs. It's good to be back. I owe my neighbors an apology. Maybe I can talk Mom into baking a few batches of cookies with my help.

When I reach my door, however, the quiet hum of conversation comes from within. *What the fuck?*

I drop my shopping bag and fumble in my purse for the small can of Mace. With pepper spray in hand, I slowly turn the doorknob. The door is unlocked, with no sign of forced entry. Curiouser and curiouser. No sign of any criminals engaging in nefarious activity. Just two women drinking my wine, kicking back on my couch, and reading my notebook. My very private notebook.

"Lilah!" Lady Helena cries in her posh accent. Her long

dark hair is messily piled atop her head. She's in another long flowy pastel dress paired with a cream tweed jacket and several strands of pearls. But it's the combat boots that pull her outfit together. She gets up to greet me. "How wonderful to see you again!"

"It's nice to see you too. This is a surprise. I didn't notice the Rolls-Royce outside."

"Dougal dropped me off. He had some errands to run."

"Thought I'd come over early and check on the press situation," says Rebecca, who has a key to the apartment for emergencies. "Look who I found knocking on your door."

"Wow" is all I can think to say. As good as it is to see her, I have no idea why Her Ladyship is here. Her son was out today on a date making it obvious that he and I aren't together. Maybe she wants to be friends too.

"Her Ladyship and I have been talking, and we have some questions." Rebecca holds up the notebook. "Such as why are you drafting your will and researching green burials?"

"I think being buried in a woven willow casket is lovely," says Lady Helena. "It reminds me of a picnic basket. Like you're eternally out to lunch."

"Yeah." I take a deep breath. "It was actually private...the contents of my notebook."

Lady Helena smiles. "I swear we weren't snooping, sweetheart. We just happened to see it. It was right over there on the table. Underneath those papers and some junk mail and a book or two."

"You've been acting weird, and I'm worried," says Rebecca. "What's this sudden interest in death? I know you had a hard time last weekend with the ex and work and your car. But there's more, I can feel it. What's going on with you?"

Having Lady Helena here for this conversation isn't ideal. Though she is sort of a part of things. At any rate, it was one thing to keep Rebecca in the dark to save us both some stress, but if she's stressing anyway...

"I'm going to need you to keep an open mind," I begin. "Please hold all questions and comments until the end."

Rebecca nods.

"Go ahead, sweetheart," says Lady Helena. "We're listening."

And I open my mouth and tell them almost everything.

"Goodness," says Lady Helena when I'm done, her delicate brows drawn tight together. "I can certainly see why you'd be upset."

"Yeah," I say, taking a seat. "It's been a lot to deal with."

"We don't actually know if you've been cursed or hexed or what, do we?"

"You think Good Witch Willow cursed her?" asks Rebecca with some serious side-eye.

Lady Helena taps a finger pensively against her chin. "It's times like this I wish I could see auras. Because it could have been anyone, really. Or a buildup of negative energy from your own psyche. Or even bad karma spilling over from past lives. Many things can sour a life force. A spiritual cleanse would be the safest thing."

"Guess it couldn't hurt," I say with much dubiousness. "It would definitely be a new experience."

"Don't panic," says Lady Helena, pulling a cell from the pocket of her designer jacket. "I know exactly what to do."

"You do?"

There's no reply. She's already striding into my bedroom and shutting the door. Her phone call requires privacy, apparently.

Rebecca sticks up her hand. "Hang on. I have questions. Lots of questions."

"Okay."

"The first is more of a statement," she says. "You get that I hired Good Witch Willow as entertainment for my party and that you're not actually going to die, right?"

"Well…"

"I understand how the predictions coming true rattled you. Your ex cheating and the promotion and the lotto. I mean, the lotto in particular is— Wow. But, babe, they're just coincidences. They have to be." Rebecca rises and comes toward me with arms outstretched. "We're hugging now."

"That's nice," I say, hugging her back.

"One day you're going to realize that you don't have to handle everything on your own. In the meantime, I think using this as the impetus to get out there and try new and exciting things is a great idea."

I smile. "Thanks."

"What are you going to do with the money?"

"Not a clue."

"I'm sure you'll think of something," she says. "Josh is definitely gone and out of the picture?"

My nod is one of much resolution.

"Good. So you and Prince Charming are friends now, huh? I assume as much, what with his mother being here."

"I think so," I say. "Yeah."

"Lady Helena is wild."

"So wild. You have no idea."

She turns my hand over and studies the new book tattoo. "This is cute. Did it hurt?"

"Like a bitch. But there's one more prediction," I say in a

quiet voice. "One I didn't want to mention in front of Her Ladyship because I don't think her son would approve. He's supposedly my soulmate."

"No shit?"

"Nope."

She cocks her head. "Are you two involved in a more than friendly way, by any chance, and you forgot to tell me?"

"Still just friends."

"But you almost crashed into him the day after Willow told you about being soulmates. The timing is amazing." Rebecca blows out a breath. "Though I refuse to believe that any of it's real. That these predictions are anything more than uncanny nonsense. It's important to keep a grip on reality."

"I honestly have no idea anymore."

"Which of the wish-list items can I do with you?"

I instantly perk up. "Which ones would you like to do?"

The bedroom door swings open, and Lady Helena appears with her cell pressed to her ear. "Sweetheart, I'm guessing you're probably not comfortable with casual nudity?"

"Um. No. Not really."

"You don't know what you're missing until you've had your tits out on a beach in Europe. Such a feeling of liberation. Just don't forget the sunscreen. I suppose whatever swimwear you have will do for tonight," she says before returning to her call. "We're going to need lavender for purity, rosemary for cleansing, lemon balm for healing, and cedar for protection. And I want a big-ass chunk of clear quartz, Dougal. The biggest you can get." She disappears back into my bedroom and slams the door closed. What is it with this family and slamming doors?

"This should be interesting," says Rebecca. "Are you sure you're up for being spiritually cleansed by Her Ladyship?"

"That's a really good question."

A hint of a smile curves the corner of her mouth. "I asked her earlier if I could call her Helena. You should have seen the look on her face. She was horrified."

No idea which of us started giggling first. And I'm not even entirely sure what we're giggling about. But neither of us stop for a good long time.

When I tried to envision what Lady Helena might be planning, standing in my shower in a bikini while Her Ladyship used a pump-action water pistol to spray me with a combination of essential oils wasn't one of them. Not even close. Same goes for having Himalayan salt thrown at me intermittently. The way it stings when she accidentally gets me in the eye. I don't start to lose my temper, however, until I stub my toe for the third time on the boulder-size chunk of quartz sitting on the shower floor.

"Motherfucker," I cry.

"Focus, sweetheart. You've got to say the mantra," says Lady Helena. "Repeat after me: I am whole. I am healthy. I am calm. Or reasonably calm, at least."

Rebecca leans against the bathroom counter. "I'm pretty sure calm left the building a while back."

"Aye. So did common sense," mutters Dougal, standing in the bathroom doorway. Like I need an audience for this event. He scratches at his gray beard and says, "Perhaps I should give the lad a call."

"Absolutely not, Dougal." Lady Helena turns the Super Soaker on the man with a warning look. "You know Alistair doesn't believe in any of this. He'll just be in the way. I know what's best for Lilah in this particular situation."

Dougal mutters something beneath his breath.

Lady Helena turns back to me and lets loose with a jet of liquid. It gets me right in the left breast and hurts like hell. Trusting Her Ladyship with such a powerful water pistol was a mistake. One of several I may have made regarding her tonight.

I cover my chest with my arms. "Ouch. Not the boobs."

"Sorry, sweetie. Turn around and I'll do your back."

"I think we're finished," I say, pushing my damp and oily hair out of my face. My eyes are still stinging and watering and yeah. "Thank you for trying to help, but I've had enough."

"Oh." Lady Helena's face falls. "Are you sure?"

"Yes. Thank you. I really appreciate you going to so much trouble. But yes."

"All right, then."

"Eighteen minutes of water torture isn't bad," says Dougal. "Good effort, lass."

I give him a thumbs-up.

There's a chance I've done something stranger in my lifetime. But I can't remember what or when. Once my audience is gone and the bathroom door is closed, I strip off the bikini and wash myself from head to toe—not once, not twice, but three times. It takes about half a bottle of shampoo to get the salt and oil out of my hair. Nothing is going to get rid of the various scents clinging to me. My smell could most neatly be summed up as vaguely pleasant mass confusion.

I dress in wide-leg jeans and a white tee and socks. Pure comfort. My wet hair is tied up in a bun and my face is clean. Food has been delivered by the time I head back out. I didn't know we were ordering, but I could definitely eat. A sentiment seconded by my growling stomach.

Rebecca is oohing and aahing over the assortment of dishes spread out on the coffee table. It's a beautiful display of sashimi, tempura, gyoza, edamame, and more. "Look at this! Have you ever seen such a perfect piece of sushi in all your life? It's a goddamn work of art."

"No," I agree. "This is amazing."

"I noticed you had 'Michelin star restaurant' on your list," says Lady Helena with a pleased little smile. "Dougal and I eat at Hara as often as we can. They were happy to put together something for you."

This time when I tear up, it isn't due to the salt. I mean, Uber Eats is great, but this is food delivery on a whole other level. Candles light the room and music plays at a low volume. After the drama and action in the bathroom, it is a balm to my soul. And another check off my wish list. Which makes me think about the countdown to my death day, but no, I won't ruin this lovely moment by stressing out about that. Not when it wouldn't even do any good. "This is beautiful. Thank you. But there's so much. You're not staying?"

"No." She smiles. "It's time for us to be heading home. I need my rest, what with a certain idiot who shall remain nameless calling at odd hours carrying on about absolute bollocks. I swear, one of these days, I am going to shove that crown right up his—"

Dougal loudly clears his throat.

"Thank you again," I say. "I really appreciate it."

"You're very welcome." She pats me on the cheek. "Don't forget to use your mantra. It also wouldn't be a bad idea to sleep with the crystal. Close contact can help."

"I'll keep that in mind."

"We can go over how to put a hex on someone next time

if you like. You know. Just in case you ever need it. Basic life skills and so on."

"That's enough now, Your Ladyship." Dougal holds open the door, and Lady Helena sweeps out into the night. Then he gives us a parting nod. "Nice to meet you, Rebecca. Come and lock this door, Lilah."

"Bye, Dougal," I say, closing the door behind him. Now I know where Alistair learned his security-conscious ways and general bossiness.

"Getting back to your wish list." Rebecca pours sake from the bottle into the two small matching cups. "I don't have any major meetings tomorrow. How do you feel about me being your someone special to stay up all night and watch the sunrise with?"

"You'd do that?" I ask with a grin.

"Of course." She smiles back at me. "If I qualify as a special person, that is. It might have been meant romantically."

I am not going to get teary again. People being kind shouldn't make me want to bawl. But for some reason these days, it definitely does. All the big feelings are bouncing around inside of me. Guess you appreciate moments on a different level when your time might be limited. Ticking items off my wish list sure has a special significance. "You are most definitely a special nonromantic person to me, and I would love to sit up all night with you."

"Let's talk nonsense all night, Lilah," she says. "It'll be fun."

And that's exactly what we do.

11

Thursday

A knock on the door wakes me at midday. It's a delivery person with a package containing a black leather jacket and a matching helmet, the kind without a visor that leaves the face exposed. At the bottom of the package is a note, *See you at four. Alistair.*

Just seeing his name makes me smile. The jacket is a sturdy and smooth leather in a simple racer style from a brand I could never afford. The way these people throw money around is something else. I was on a motorcycle once when I was a child. Just around a pasture on a farm owned by my uncle. I'm excited to experience it again as an adult, and for the opportunity to spend time with my purely platonic friend. Knowing your end date makes you bulletproof in a way. For instance, it's highly unlikely I'll be involved in a horrible traffic accident today. Unless such an accident were to happen and it put me in a coma and they turned my life support off on Sunday. How fucking macabre. I am going to stop thinking about this now.

Rebecca and I sat up all night. We watched *The Vampire Diaries*, ate some edibles, and talked about anything and everything.

At six in the morning, we crowded out onto my apartment's tiny balcony. The last star disappeared as the sky changed colors with the morning light. I can't remember the last time I saw the dawn, but it was wonderful. Even LA is sort of peaceful at that time of day. Then we crashed. By the time the delivery person woke me, Rebecca had left for home to sleep in her own bed.

What a week. Given the wish-list idea only occurred to me on Sunday, I've covered some ground. I got a tattoo, went skateboarding, drove the Pacific Coast Highway in a convertible, tried bowling, drank absinthe, ate food from a Michelin star restaurant, and stayed up all night to watch the sunrise with someone special. On the off chance I die soon, at least I can say I've lived.

It's an overcast afternoon. I've always thought clouds are kind of amazing. Their colors and shapes and general moodiness. The way they hang in thin air. When we were little, my brother and I used to lie on the back lawn and search for animals and faces in the clouds. I haven't thought about that in ages. No idea why it occurs to me now. I need to call him and reminisce.

By the time Alistair arrives, my stomach has been topsy-turvy for over an hour. Being in denial about him hasn't helped. Therefore, I've decided to embrace how big it feels to be seeing him again. As mentioned before, I am having a big-feelings kind of week. But I can and will keep my emotions under control. Something I believe right up until the moment I walk outside to meet him.

Huh. I have a motorcycle fetish now too. Though I have a sneaking suspicion it's more specific. More Alistair-oriented.

He is at the curb, sitting on a big matte black Triumph motorcycle. Despite its retro design, it's clearly modern. Alistair is wearing a helmet, and he's struck a pose that makes the most of his muscular jean-clad thighs. Thank goodness sunglasses hide my ogling eyes. I have no shame when it comes to this man. Still no sign of any paparazzi on the street. No telling how long our luck will hold out. We need to enjoy our time together while we can.

"The jacket looks good," he remarks with a small smile. "Put the helmet on so I can check the fit."

I slide it onto my head, and he fusses with the chin strap. "How does that feel, Lilah?"

"Good."

"Good. Ready to go for a ride?"

I lick my lips and nod. My nerves have obviously not abated. About him or the bike or both—who can tell?

"What's wrong?" he asks in an amused tone. "Don't you trust me?"

"I could ask you the same question. Though I have, haven't I?"

For a moment, there's nothing but silence between us. Then he holds my chin and stares deep into my eyes. Like he can read the secrets of the universe in my gaze or something. Having his undivided attention remains a hell of a rush. Then, finally, he says with all due seriousness, "Yes, Lilah, I trust you."

I smile. "Thank you. I trust you too."

"Hop on," he says and holds out a hand to me. I swing a leg over the machine and carefully climb on. This is obviously what had me worked up. This moment right here. Because riding on a bike with him means all the bodily contact. We could hardly get closer with our clothes on. The hard line of his back and the breadth of his shoulders. How big and solid his body feels. It's a wonder I don't drool.

"Right up against me," he says. "Hands nice and tight around my waist."

"Okay."

He starts the engine, and smooth as can be, the motorcycle comes to life beneath me. It's a heck of a vibration. I say this as someone who's made it a mission to test an array of such things. As is good and right.

"Nice and tight," he repeats, drawing my hands around him. I remind myself he is not in fact talking dirty to me. Just issuing safety instructions. Only this doesn't feel safe. Not for me and my messy emotions.

I press my front to his back and cling to his waist. It isn't fair how deep and rough his voice is. Same goes for his hot accent. Add the giant vibrator I am currently sitting on top of, and I never stood a chance.

"Lilah," he says. "Who's that?"

"Huh?" I look up.

And standing there on the sidewalk staring at us is Josh holding a single red rose. Cheating on someone and then abusing them via text seems more of a whole bouquet kind of situation. Though he always was cheap. He stares at us, his mouth open and brows high. You would think kicking someone out and blocking them would send a message. I know he read the articles about me and the almost-prince, but seeing me with another man has him stunned. Which is ridiculous.

"It's my ex," I say. "Josh."

Alistair's body tenses. "The one who cheated on you? Do you want to talk to him?"

"No."

"Can I talk to him?"

"And say what, exactly?"

He grunts. "Actually, I was just going to punch him in the face. I don't suppose you'd be okay with that?"

"Hmm. That's another no."

"Let's get the fuck out of here, then."

He revs the engine, and we take off down the street, leaving my sordid past behind. Which is exactly where it belongs.

We ride a circuit—Laurel Canyon, Mulholland Drive, and Cahuenga Boulevard—with great views of LA and the Valley. My butt goes numb about halfway, but I could happily cling to Alistair all day. What was fun in the convertible is even better on the back of a bike. The rush of the wind and the feeling of freedom as you watch the world go by. It's little wonder people get addicted. This absolutely qualifies as a daring exercise, racing through the Hollywood Hills with a royal rebel.

We don't stop or speak—we just ride.

When we're done in the hills, he doesn't head back to my place. He takes us west through town toward The Flats at the base of Beverly Hills. We pull up at a large gray metal gate and wait for it to slide open. Tall walls of the same color surround the property with trees reaching high above. A gravel driveway deposits us in a courtyard, surrounded by a tall stone building, which is also gray. It stands two stories high, and there are no windows on the street side. Just the large glass front doors and an abundance of wisteria vines.

If a modern-day fairy-tale prince turned grumpy beast were looking to relocate, this would be the place. No questions asked.

He turns off the engine and takes off his helmet. The sudden quiet seems to match this mansion looming over me. It's a mood.

"Quite a fortress," I say in a small voice. "Where are we?"

"My home."

"Okay."

"Why are we whispering?"

"I have no idea."

He holds out a hand to help me dismount. Gravel crunches beneath my black ankle boots, breaking the silence. Then an insect chirps and a bird sings. Soon this is followed by the distant hum of traffic. We are, after all, still in the city.

"What did you think of the ride?" he asks, climbing off the bike.

"I loved it." I grin. "Though I think I swallowed a bug."

"Extra protein. Good work."

"Thanks."

"Come inside," he says, nodding to the large glass door surrounded by a cool aged steel frame.

"You're inviting me into your sanctuary?"

"You don't want us being seen together by the press. Eating here seemed like a good idea."

"It's a great idea."

He flashes me a smile. There and gone in an instant. One day he's going to smile for long enough to get used to the feel of the thing. What a day that will be. Showing me his home seems to suggest a new level of trust between us, which is nice. He unlocks the front door and disables the security system of the huge and silent house. It's an interesting mix of industrial and luxe, with gray concrete walls and dark wood floors. The only sound is the echo of our footsteps.

"Can I take your jacket?" he asks.

"Thanks."

He doesn't hesitate. I undo the zipper and his hands are there, reaching around from behind me. The backs of his fingers graze against the thin material of my tee, sending a shiver through me. Everything low in me clenches. This is ridiculous, what with all the time spent on the bike pressed up against him. I wouldn't blame his new lady friend if she hated me. I get so messy around this man. He makes every moment feel momentous. It sure puts my average attraction and affection for Josh in its place. Which would be the trash. No one should settle when it comes to love or lust.

Alistair takes the jacket and hangs it on a rack beside his own. I can only hope he didn't feel my reaction. My body needs to calm the hell down.

"How high are these ceilings?" I ask, to distract myself.

"Sixteen feet."

"Wow."

He hangs back, watching my face with interest as I look around, obviously proud of the place. Which he should be. Him wanting me to like his home makes all the warm feelings rush to the surface. The non-horny ones for a change.

The entryway opens onto a sprawling combined living-and-dining space. Floor-to-ceiling windows look onto a back patio with more wisteria wrapped around pillars, the green of a lawn, and the blue of a pool beyond. In the seating area, a flat-screen the size of California hangs above a large fireplace. There's not much furniture—just a long white sofa (always a brave color) and an antique wood dining table with a dozen or so seats. A couple of boxes sit in a corner, along with several large un-framed paintings. The only real hint of personality is a gaming unit sitting on the floor beneath the TV. It feels like more than a strict dedication to a minimal decorating style. Alistair just is this buttoned-down and hidden from view.

"It was built in the sixties by a gallery owner," he says. "She wanted to be close to everything but still be able to lock out the world and have total privacy."

"I can see how that would appeal to you. This place must have been beautiful when it was full of pictures."

"I have some pieces I keep meaning to hang," he says, nodding to the collection of boxes in the corner. "Just haven't gotten around to it yet."

"I didn't mean... The house is great. Can I check it out?"

"Make yourself at home."

The house has two levels and is shaped like a C, surrounding the backyard with its pool, firepit, and hot tub. It's no wonder it feels like a fortress. There's a chef's kitchen with stainless-steel appliances, gray stone countertops, and a smaller dining table seating eight. And more of those packing boxes shoved off to the side. Given how immaculate the rest of the house is, those boxes are an oddity.

Since he already knows I'm nosy and has accepted that about me, I open the stainless-steel double-door fridge. In the freezer, there's a bottle of vodka and some ice. In the fridge is a half-empty six-pack of beer, a quart of milk, and an unopened bottle of champagne. No food. He's a breatharian, apparently. Good on him for giving alternate lifestyles a go.

"Are you judging me?" he asks in an amused tone.

"I would never."

"Of course not. You do realize your nose twitches when you lie."

"It does not," I say, reaching up to touch it just in case.

"Would you like a drink?"

"Not yet."

Beyond the kitchen, the hallway runs off at an angle while a set of stairs leads to the second story. This house is a rich man's hobbit hole. A sprawling aboveground bunker for those with a taste for luxury. There's a distinct subterranean feel to the place. Standing inside these gray walls, the rest of the world might as well have disappeared.

"Down there are the three guest bedrooms," he says, pointing down the hall. "Upstairs is my bedroom, an office, sitting room, and outdoor area."

"What's down the other end on this level?"

"Home gym, library, and a media room," he says. *Library* is no sooner out of his mouth than I am racing in that direction. Because books. "Lilah, wait. You're going to be disappointed."

As promised, exercise machines and weights occupy the first room. There's even a towel slung over the seat of an elliptical. It's the most lived-in space I've seen so far. Across the hall is a bathroom with gray stone tiling and copper pipes. Very cool. Then at last I find it—the library. He's right about being disappointed. Dark wood shelving to match the floor lines two whole walls reaching up to the high ceiling. But apart from the mountain of boxes stacked in one corner, all of it is empty. Though there is one of those cool ladders on wheels. I wonder if he'd push me back and forth if I asked nicely.

Imagine having your own library and not even using it. This is a travesty. A disgrace. It also makes absolutely no damn sense.

"This room is beautiful. Or it could be," I say. "How long have you lived here?"

"A while."

"Narrow it down for me."

He leans against the door frame with his arms crossed. "I don't know. Not quite five years."

"Five years?" My eyes are as wide as can be. "Fuck me."

"I was going to ask how you were doing with the 'great sex' thing," he deadpans.

"Don't change the subject." I point a finger at him. "You do realize you bring that up every time we talk?"

"What do you want for dinner?" he asks, most definitely attempting another change of topic. He likes living dangerously. He should take me more seriously when books are at stake. I might joke about a lot of things, but never the printed word.

I rip the tape off the nearest box and peer inside. Just as expected...books. All these boxes are full of books. He obviously loves reading, and yet his library is in shambles.

He scratches at the dark stubble lining his jaw. "Feel free to just go ahead and open those."

"Is there furniture in the guest bedrooms?"

"No. If a friend crashes, they just sleep on the couch. Unless they're a special friend."

"What about upstairs?"

"There's my bed, of course. And a desk and table in the office."

"Anything in the sitting room?"

He shakes his head. "It's not a space I use."

"What about the media room next door?"

"Got the screen set up in the main room, so..."

I stare at him in wonder. "You've been living here for half a decade, don't use the bulk of the house, and haven't bothered to finish unpacking. Does that basically sum up the situation?"

"Yeah. Basically. I've been busy."

There have been many times in my life when I wished men

came with a manual. But none so much as now. I run a finger along a shelf, and it comes away dust free. Meaning I can move straight into unpacking the boxes and getting the books in order. "I'll have that drink when you're ready."

"You're going to set up my library?"

"I am."

"That's a big job."

"Oh. I meant to tell you, your mother visited me last night," I say, piling books from the first box onto the floor.

All amusement falls from his face. "Helena visited you? At your apartment?"

"Yeah. It was fine. Don't panic." I pull out my hair tie and redo my ponytail. Wearing the helmet has left it feeling lopsided. "But she and my friend Rebecca were snooping and found my wish list, along with other clues, such as information on green burials."

"You're not going to die," he growls. "I wish you'd stop worrying about that."

"At any rate, questions were asked, and I wound up telling them about Good Witch Willow and the predictions. But don't worry. I made sure not to mention the one about us being soulmates within your mother's hearing."

His frown amps up to eleven. "All right."

"Her Ladyship decided I needed spiritual cleansing."

"Of course she did. You didn't actually let her do it, though, did you?"

"Your belief in me being sensible is beautiful but unwarranted," I report. "She filled up a Super Soaker with essential oils, and I stood in the shower wearing my bikini, and... yeah. She fired it at me."

His mouth hangs open in wonder.

"Say something, Ali."

"You let my mother fire a water pistol full of scented oil at you?"

"Yes."

He just blinks.

"She threw Himalayan crystal salt at me too. Big handfuls of the stuff. A huge chunk of quartz was also involved. I forget what that was for. But she didn't throw that at me. It just sat on the shower floor, where I kept accidentally kicking it. There was some chanting involved too. A mantra or something."

"Right." This is about when he starts to massage either side of the bridge of his nose. Like he's in actual physical pain. "I don't even know what to say."

"You don't have to say anything. I am just telling you because I thought you would want to know."

"Lilah, be careful with my mother," he says, his voice slow and deliberate. Like he's choosing his words with care. "She doesn't always make good choices."

"What do you mean?"

"Just be careful," he repeats. "Please."

"Okay. About that drink?"

Without a word, he turns and disappears. It seems I am sorting books on my own.

Alistair reads a fair amount of fantasy. I've no idea why, but this surprises me. Terry Pratchett and J. R. R. Tolkien and N. K. Jemisin are all here. I went through a fantasy phase in my mid-twenties, but it doesn't appeal as much to me right now. Guess the idea of a world with a system of magic was more enticing before these predictions bit me on the ass. Though being told you're going to die next week will suck the sparkle out of anything.

Alistair returns with the bottle of champagne in a bucket of ice, along with a single champagne flute and a beer for him. He pours me a glass of bubbles before starting in on one of the boxes alongside me. We're going to work on the library together. I like being close to him, so this is a good thing. Though I am a little surprised he didn't object to me going through his books and taking charge. Maybe he is starting to trust me after all.

"Am I allowed to ask how your lunch date went on Wednesday?" I say oh so casually. "Friends ask each other things like that, right?"

"Do they?"

"I just happened to see the photos on a gossip site."

"You just *happened* to see them?"

I nod and sip my drink. "I was actually checking to see if there were any updates on me, if you must know."

He unpacks books and doesn't answer my question.

Undeterred, I ask, "How does the fame thing affect you dating?"

"Was that the first time you've seen your ex since the night you threw him out?" he asks in return.

"If I answer your question, will you answer mine?"

He narrows his gaze on me and says nothing. And I keep my mouth shut and wait. Finally, he says, "Yes."

"That was the first time I've seen Josh since that night. Though he did text me when the photos of you and me were everywhere. Called me a cheating bitch, if you can believe it."

"Are you fucking kidding me?" he says in a low and deliberate voice. The vibes coming off him are beyond intense.

I don't know what to say. No one has ever been quite this angry on my behalf.

"You should have let me punch the little shit."

"He isn't worth an assault charge. Though I appreciate you being willing to go there for me."

"Did it upset you? Seeing him?"

"No. That part of my life, being with him, it feels a weirdly long way away. Like it was years ago. Guess a lot has happened in the meantime. Or maybe this week and the predictions and so on have just weirded out my emotions." I take a sip of the champagne and think calm thoughts. "This is good."

He sighs and allows me to move the conversation in a different direction. "It's a vintage Krug Brut," he says. "I thought you might like it."

"You were right." I smile. "Thank you."

"It's well-known for being great at washing down bugs."

"Answer my question now."

"I usually date people who know what they're getting into. Professionals in the entertainment industry and such. They're under similar pressures and know how to keep their mouths shut. Often, they have just as much to lose if the wrong thing goes public."

"Makes sense."

He pushes his dark hair out of his face and looks me over. From my sensible flat black boots to my dark blue jeans and white tee. "You look nice. I meant to tell you earlier. You always look lovely."

"Thank you. So do you." The way heat rushes to my face. I gesture to the boxes. "Have you read all these books?"

"Some. Others I bought and stored here for later."

"You didn't want your housekeeper or cleaner or someone unpacking the boxes for you?"

He shakes his head. "I don't like the idea of someone going through my things."

"I'm going through your things."

"That's different."

"Is it? But what stopped you from doing it?" I ask. "Not just from setting up in here, but the rest of the house too?"

"I told you. I was busy."

"For five years?"

"I don't know, Lilah. It doesn't matter."

I just nod and let it go.

"You were going to tell me how you were doing with the great sex." His expression is perfectly blank. Like he's just making casual conversation. *Jerk.*

No way will I be shamed. "You know, you keep asking me that question like I don't know how to work a vibrator or use a showerhead or my own hand. But I assure you I am quite proficient at all three."

It takes him a moment to respond. "Fair enough."

"As for bringing other people into the equation, I found a couple of reputable male escort agencies in the area. Meeting at a midrange hotel is apparently the way to go. Then when he arrives, you assess if there's chemistry, and if you feel comfortable before—"

"Absolutely not," he says adamantly, his accent thicker than normal.

"What?"

"You can't have thought this through."

"I assure you I have." I just wait. And wait some more. Given his cranky gaze, he dislikes me using his own silence tactic. Sucks to be him.

"I just… There's no need for you to be having sex with strangers."

"Why not?"

"It's not safe, Lilah."

"It'll be as safe as I can make it."

"I don't like it."

I scoff. "You don't need to like it. Signing off on my sex life is not your job."

He stares at me, and I stare at him, and apparently no one is going to win this competition. Not anytime soon.

"Let's talk about something else," he says. "It's your turn to ask a question."

"Fine. Do you grill your other friends about their sex lives?"

"I'm not answering that. Ask me something else." He drops some books on the floor. Poor books. "You wanted to know about my lunch yesterday. The best way to get the paparazzi off your back was to be seen with someone else. Constance has retired from modeling and is about to announce her new line of athletic wear. She was happy to have the press shadowing her to help get her name trending."

"Wait." My face is pure confusion. "You went out with her to…"

"To divert attention from you."

"It wasn't really a date?"

"No. She's just a friend."

"Is she just a friend like I'm just a friend, or is she a special friend?"

He just looks at me.

"Ignore the last question. It's none of my business. Thank you for doing that for me." I lick my suddenly dry lips. "I am a little surprised, is all. It's just that some of the photos looked a bit… What's the word?"

"Intimate?" he asks. "I never touched her ass. I know it looked like it in the photo, but that was just the angle."

The conversation has turned awkward. Awkwarder. It's all his fault for bringing up sex again. I thought we were just friends. We agreed we were just friends. Now I don't know what's going on.

A low, sonorous chiming sound fills the house.

I wipe my sweaty palms on my jeans. "Guess that's the food. That was fast."

"Can't be," he says with a frown. "I haven't ordered yet."

Next comes the distant sound of fists banging and someone yelling. And what they're saying is "Open this damn door. It's time for Thursday-night drinks, you fucker."

Said fucker just sighs.

12

Alistair is not impressed. "What are you doing here?"

Two men carrying brown paper bags push past him. They both look me over with interest. Not in a checking-me-out way. More of a curious friends thing.

"Lilah," says Alistair. "These are my business partners, Gael and Shane. They won't be staying."

"Hello, Lilah. It's such a pleasure to meet you." Gael is a charmer. It's obvious in the very warm smile on his handsome face. Business is obviously good, because he's dressed head to toe in designer wear. It's in the name on his sneakers and the cut of his jeans and button-down shirt. "To think I brought you my grandmother's tamales, you ungrateful ass."

"I do like your grandmother's cooking," concedes Alistair. "What did you bring?" he asks Shane.

"Beer," says Shane simply.

"I like that too. But you're still not staying. Neither of you."

"There's been a proposed update we want your opinion on. It won't take long."

"Bullshit."

Shane has dimples and curly blond hair and uses a mobility aid. He's also dressed casually in jeans and a Henley. "Hey, Lilah."

"Hello," I say. Not nervous at all. Much.

"Come sit with me." Shane ushers me through to the couch, collecting the gaming system as he goes. "Do you play?"

"I used to love *Minecraft*. Then my much younger cousin kept filling my house with chickens."

"Children can be brutal." He rests his cane against the chair and gets the game started. "The aim of *The Collective* is to establish a postapocalyptic community. You scavenge for supplies to house, feed, clothe, and provide medical aid for your people. While fighting off bad guys, of course."

"I've heard of this. It's really popular."

"We've worked on a couple of games. But this one in particular has done well for us."

"Yeah. I read an interesting article about how the themes of found family and social justice are incorporated into the narrative."

"Alistair handles the bulk of that side of things," says Gael, unpacking containers of food onto the dining table.

"You do?" I ask, looking at Alistair, who's sitting on the end of the couch with a bottle of beer in hand.

"Where's Nari?" he asks, ignoring me. "Why didn't your wife stop you idiots from inviting yourselves over?"

Shane has serious golden retriever energy. He seems to be constantly smiling. "She's out with her sisters. I wasn't invited."

Alistair softly laughs. "Sounds about right."

"But it did give me the opportunity to come meet your new friend. Nari dated his sorry ass for a while," Shane explains to me. "Then she realized I was superior in every way and dumped him. Sad for him. Great for me."

"True story." Gael wanders through, carrying plates and silverware from the kitchen. "Alistair has a reputation as an accidental matchmaker."

"I heard something about this too," I say.

"He finds amazing people, fails at having a relationship, and his friends benefit. So, what with me being single, when he started talking about you, I thought we should meet." Gael gives me a wink.

"Makes sense."

"Don't flirt with her," grumbles Alistair. "Lilah's had enough of fuck boys. She's off the market."

"You wound me," says Gael, clutching at his chest. "Fuck boy...as if. I'm a fuck man, thank you very much."

"Ali," I say chidingly, "I don't recall saying I was done with dating."

He blinks. "My mistake. Do as you please."

"He lets you call him Ali?" Shane's gaze is wide with surprise. "And he actually answers?"

"*Let* is the wrong word," says Alistair.

"I called you Al for all of basic training. Couldn't make it stick."

"It concerns me that this still torments you all these years later," says Alistair. "Have you considered therapy?"

Shane picks up his cell. "I'm telling my wife you're being mean to me."

"Your wife adores me. She won't believe a word you say."

"Is that what you tell yourself?" asks Shane. "Interesting."

Alistair grunts.

"We don't get to meet Alistair's special friends until after he's been dating them for a while," says Shane. "Usually about a month. It's one of his rules."

"Lilah and I are just friends," says Alistair. "We're not dating."

"But he's been talking about you so much we couldn't wait."

I smile and nod. "This is all very fascinating. Tell me more about these rules."

"He has so many of them," says Shane. "Where to even begin?"

"Not another word," Alistair warns.

Shane gives me a wink.

Gael clears his throat. "Back to what I was saying. I've given it some thought, and I believe it's his rigid life view that tanks his relationships."

"Nari said he was so serious all the time," adds Shane. "But I made her laugh."

"Yes," says Alistair. "I can see her laughing at you. That makes sense."

Shane smiles. "He messed up and I got a chance with the woman of my dreams. But Nari and I aren't the only ones he's brought together under the banner of true love."

"Lilah already knows about the matchmaker bullshit," says Alistair. He cracks his neck and scowls his heart out. Never has a man been treated so badly. Not even Sisyphus with his boulder had to tolerate this shit.

"Yeah, but just out of interest. How many weddings have you been to where you not only dated the bride but were directly responsible for introducing the couple?" asks Gael. "I know you have at least two or three godchildren because of just this sort of situation."

"I have nothing further to add to the topic." At which point Alistair rises and makes for the nearest exit.

Gael grins in victory.

As nice as it is seeing Alistair with his friends, there's something on my mind. "What did he, um, tell you about me? Just out of curiosity."

"That you almost hit his Aston Martin," says Gael, filling a plate with food.

Shane nods in agreement. "We heard a lot about that."

"And also about the witch, the predictions, and everything else. We might have been a little worried you were messing with him," says Gael. "You can see how we would think that, right?"

I wince. "Yeah."

"But you didn't sell him out." Shane shrugs. "You had the opportunity, and you didn't take it."

I have the distinct feeling they've discussed all of this in depth. Of course, I'm glad they care about their friend. But it can be awkward when you know you've been the topic of debate. Or maybe that's just me and my delicate feelings.

"You forgot your drink." Alistair returns with my glass of champagne.

I smile. "Thank you."

"Here you go, Lilah," says Gael, handing me a plate heaped high with food. Tamales, rice, guacamole, corn, and salsa too.

"Whoa." My mouth is watering. "It smells amazing."

Alistair's brows draw together. "What are you doing?"

"Hmm?" asks Gael.

"You know what I mean."

"What are you talking about?" Gael is the picture of innocence. "I'm just trying to make our guest feel welcome."

"My guest."

"Right. Your guest. That's what I said."

If Alistair had death rays for eyes, Gael would most definitely be singed. Which would be a pity. He's both a handsome and charming man who knows how to put a plate of food together. Three things I appreciate.

"You're sort of intense about this one, aren't you?" asks Gael. "This friend, I mean."

Nothing from Alistair.

"These assholes are always competing. Just ignore them like I do." Shane takes the game control to free up my hands for food. He sinks back against the couch with an easygoing smile. "What do you think of the place, Lilah?"

"The house?" I ask. "I think it's great."

"Sure," says Gael. "If you enjoy a sterile gray stone environment more suited to being a supervillain's secret hideout than a home."

I manage not to laugh. But only just.

"She already gave me shit about not having finished unpacking, then started sorting the library." Alistair sits beside me and steals a tamale off my plate. So rude. Though, to be fair, there's a lot of food.

"I did not give you shit," I say with a disdainful sniff. "I just ever so slightly questioned some of your life choices."

"Is that what you call it?"

"He let you touch his stuff?" Shane picks up his cell and shoots off another text. "Nari needs to know about this. What else happened, Lilah?"

Filling your mouth with food is an excellent stall tactic when you don't know what to say. Don't let anyone tell you differently.

Shane's cell chimes and he smiles. "Nari's reminding me of the interior decorator you dated. The one who tried to get you to fix this place."

"There's nothing wrong with my house," says Alistair. "It doesn't need fixing."

"I've always admired you for your inflexibility." Gael waves his fork in the air. "Have I ever mentioned that?"

"What was their name?" asks Shane. "The decorator?"

"Rowan," says Alistair.

Gael takes a seat with his own plate. "I remember Rowan. They were great. What happened between you two?"

"None of your business," says Alistair.

At the same time as Shane says, "Didn't they go back to their ex?"

"Their ex probably listened when they gave good advice. They probably now share a happy home that is filled with love while being both warm and welcoming. Don't you wonder what that would be like?" Gael turns to me. "How's your wish list going, Lilah?"

I swallow my food and take a sip of champagne to wash it down. "He told you about that too, huh?"

Alistair's gaze holds a hint of confusion or worry. No idea which. "Should I not have? Lilah?"

Gael and Shane watch us with interest.

"It's fine," I say. "It wasn't a secret. You're just usually so closemouthed about things. But I'm happy to see you have friends that you talk to, and I'm happy to say I'm making progress on the list."

"I know someone who does tandem paragliding," says Gael. "If you're interested, I could introduce you."

There's no time for me to get a word out. Nor is there any need, apparently.

"No," says Alistair, his tone absolute. "She doesn't feel the need to test gravity."

"Fair enough," answers Gael. "How do you feel about burlesque dancing?"

I get as far as opening my mouth this time. "I—"

"There's no way she's getting on a stage in her underwear." Alistair shakes his head. "And she doesn't want to be the mermaid in the tank at your friend's bar either. So don't even ask."

"Oh, c'mon. Who doesn't love a clamshell bra? They look so supportive!"

I take a moment to ponder the idea. "You know, Ali, your mom mentioned last night how liberating baring one's breasts in public can be."

"She's met your mom?" Shane's eyes are as wide as can be. "He introduced you to Lady Helena?"

Meanwhile, Alistair's mouth opens, but he says nothing. He just stares at me. Then he finally comes out with "I can't tell if you're being serious or not."

Shane snorts.

"If you want company in the tank, Lilah, I am there," says Gael, giving me two thumbs up. "Being a merman always looked like fun to me. The outfits are so sparkly."

"You would really like to do that?" asks Alistair, ignoring both of his friends. "The dancing and the swimming?"

I shrug. "I don't know."

"It's your choice, of course. I shouldn't have…"

"You shouldn't have what?"

He gives me his most serious look and says, "I'm sure you'd be wonderful at either."

"Thank you, Ali," I say. "Though I think it's more likely I'd fall off the stage or accidentally drown. Neither dancing nor staying underwater for prolonged periods are my strong suits. I'll stick to the existing wish list for now."

Those broad shoulders slump ever so slightly in obvious relief. Which is kind of hilarious.

"This is incredible." Shane is texting once more. "It's like he's evolving and growing into a better boyfriend right before our eyes."

"Except we're not together," I remind them. And myself.

"What else was on the list?" asks Gael, tapping a finger against his chin. "Oh. I know. How about the *Pretty Woman* moment? I know a costume designer who has great connections in the industry."

"Back off, Gael," says Alistair in a more subdued tone. "I'll handle the *Pretty Woman*."

The way my heart dies just a little at the words.

Gael does a dramatic sigh. "But—"

"I repeat, I have her very much in hand and do not need your help," states Alistair.

"You have me very much in hand?" I ask with a curious sort of smile. "Is that so?"

"Lilah…" says Alistair, visibly flustered. Again. "You know what I mean."

"Do I?"

His jaw shifts. "Yes."

"We all know what you mean," confirms Gael.

Shane nods. "That's true. We do. Even if you don't."

"I mean she's my friend and I'm taking care of it. All of it."

My hopes do not plummet. They were never that high to begin with. There's nothing like hanging out with an actual

Prince Charming to teach you to keep your feet on the ground and your head out of the clouds.

Meanwhile, there is a definite ever so slightly evil twinkle in Gael's eyes, and his smile is huge. Like he's absolutely having the time of his life. "Alistair tells us you're a librarian," says Gael. "Any other hobbies or interests besides books?"

"Like anyone actually needs a hobby besides books." I load my fork up with food. "But movies, music…those sorts of things."

"Great," he says with much enthusiasm. About ten times more than is strictly speaking necessary. And the way this annoys Alistair is clear to one and all. Though he can't actually be jealous. This is just more of their competitive friend thing. No need to blow it out of proportion. "What's your favorite movie, Lilah?"

"It's hard to narrow it down to just one."

"Give it a go."

"Um. I thought *Hunt for the Wilderpeople* was great."

"I haven't seen that one," says Gael. "We should get together and watch it sometime."

Alistair shuts his eyelids tight for a moment. Like he's searching for peace and patience deep inside and failing. The only problem with these shenanigans is how my heart keeps acting like it's poised on the cusp of something. Every action of his spurs a reaction in me. It all fuels my foolish hope that Alistair has feelings for me too. Ones that maybe go beyond the occasional bout of lust. All I can do is self-medicate with champagne and tamales. This too shall pass.

"You free at all this weekend?" Gael asks me.

"No. She's busy. And I told you to stop flirting with her," says Alistair, cranky as can be. The thrill that goes through me at the sound of his growling brogue. Some of the noises he makes ought to be illegal. Or at least confined to the bedroom.

I keep my legs shut tight and my smile serene. This is fine. Everything is fine.

Gael laughs. "I mean all of us. We'll all get together and watch it. Why are you being so uptight?"

Alistair is not convinced.

And with good cause. Because the next words to me out of Gael's mouth are: "So, Lilah, what would you say you're looking for in a relationship? Just out of interest?"

I don't mean to choke on the champagne. It just happens.

Alistair rubs my back. Guess he also gives his friend another foul glance, because Gael says, "What did I do now? Lilah, babe, you okay?"

"Do *not* call her *babe*," rumbles Alistair.

"Why? You got dibs on that endearment? Were you planning on calling her *babe*?"

Alistair frowns at me before saying, "That's none of your business."

"Shane," I say, a little louder than intended. All the back-and-forth was cute for a while, but now I am done. Hoping I mean something to him is starting to hurt. A diversion is needed. "Would you mind showing me the game now?"

Shane gives his two friends a chastising look. "Sure thing."

"What are you doing?" asks Alistair.

His friends have just left. Things calmed down after Shane and I modeled appropriate adult behavior. Not being fought over by a pair of dueling idiots improved my night tenfold. We played the game for hours. Or rather, I played it while three men shouted advice at me and gestured wildly at the screen.

Then they started discussing different technical aspects of the game. Notes were taken on new ideas for updates and extensions. It was interesting seeing them work together as a team.

But back to the here and now. My cell is in my hands. "Ordering a car."

"I'll drive you home."

"It's fine. Thanks."

"Lilah," he says, stepping closer, "look at me."

"Hmm?"

His blue gaze takes me in, and he sighs. "You're still upset about earlier. I'm sorry about Gael. He doesn't mean any harm, but he gets carried away sometimes."

"It's fine," I repeat. "Gael apologized for the shenanigans when he kissed me good-night."

His brows descend. "He kissed you?"

"On the cheek. Shane did too. Your friends are nice. I like them."

The frown remains in place. "If it's about me telling them about you, I—"

"I have chosen to take you talking to your friends about me as a compliment. Though it does sort of feed into the larger issue."

And the frown still remains. "Which is?"

"This here," I say, pointing at the deep line embedded between his dark brows. "This is the problem, Ali."

"What do you mean?"

"You just... I am *so* confused."

"About what?"

I take a deep breath and let it out slowly. Needing a moment to get my thoughts in order. Being brave isn't necessarily my thing. But it's not like I have time to waste these days.

I push my shoulders back and thrust out my tits and say, "You know, for just a friend, you sure do get upset when someone flirts with me."

It's obvious the instant his walls go up. How the sharp lines of his face are suddenly set in stone. Not an iota of emotion can escape.

"You're right—Gael was just playing," I say. "But that doesn't explain why you were reacting as strongly as you did."

He scoffs and shakes his head and says nothing.

"And while we're discussing it, the idea of me having sex with someone doesn't exactly thrill you either, does it?"

"That's me being concerned with your safety," he says, the brogue thickening. "We talked about this. I made my position perfectly clear."

"Changing the topic of conversation doesn't make your position clear. Kind of the opposite."

"You're deliberately being obtuse," he says, talking to some fixed point past my shoulder. "You and I are friends, Lilah. That's all."

"So, what, I'm imagining all of this?"

He jerks his chin, which is answer enough. Ouch.

"Okay." Sometimes you've got to let go of things for your own sanity. Such as this conversation. "Thank you for the motorbike ride. I really enjoyed it. I'll order a car and wait outside."

He follows me with a frown. "I said I'd drive you."

"I think it would be best if I found my own way home."

"What? Why?" he asks in outrage.

"We sort of just covered the why. Let's talk tomorrow and—"

"No."

I just blink. "Excuse me?"

"No."

"Yeah, I heard that. I was just wondering if you could expand on the response a little."

"No to whatever you're talking about. I'm driving you home after we talk this through. Now." He stares down his nose at me and *holy shit*. It's like he's handing down the law. The man couldn't be more of a pompous asshole if he were standing in a palace and wearing a crown.

"We're pretty much done talking about it. But why is you driving me home such a big deal, Ali?"

"I could ask you the same question."

"Okay. I, um, I'm tired," I say. "Good night."

When I reach for my jacket, however, he grabs hold of it too. And he doesn't let go. We're having wrestling competitions over clothing now. Which is a totally normal thing that friends do.

"Leaving during a disagreement is juvenile, Lilah."

"Or, and hear me out here, it's a chance for both of us to calm down and rethink things."

"What we're going to do," he says, ignoring me completely, "is go back to the living room, sit down, and work this out like two calm, rational adults. Whatever it is you're upset about."

"That would be a no from me. And now would be a great time for you to stop telling me what to do."

"Then why don't you try listening?"

"Fuck you, Alistair."

His brows descend and his gaze goes nuclear. But it's the way he gets all up in my face that is truly special. "Don't you dare call me by my full name."

"I thought you preferred it. I thought me calling you *Ali*

annoyed you. Keep the jacket. Maybe you can return it and get your money back."

"What's wrong with us being just friends?" he asks, emphasizing the *F* word by tossing the offending item of clothing into the corner. "Tell me."

"Nothing. Not a single thing. If you behaved like just a friend."

"You're misreading things. I was only looking out for you. This isn't to do with that bullshit prediction about us being soulmates, is it?"

"No," I say, loud and clear. "This is me simply reacting to your behavior."

"Nothing about you is simple."

"Straight back at you, buddy."

I grasp the door handle, but he's there, pushing against the front door and holding it closed. While kneeing someone in the groin isn't on the wish list, it would be a daring, new, and interesting experience. I am not ruling it out. Because, boy, is he asking for it right now.

"If this is what you learned at your dancing and deportment classes, something went very wrong somewhere along the way," I say.

"With all due respect, you're being fucking unreasonable. You know that, right?"

My laughter is wholly without humor. "*I'm* the one being unreasonable? Are you serious? You're not letting me leave, you asshole!"

"Because if you leave when you're still angry, you might not want to see me again!"

And I have nothing. Nada. Not a damn thing. I stand there and stare at him while he proves my point. Whatever is going on between us is more than just friendship. I have no idea how or when, but feelings have been caught by both sides. It might only be lust. Something we can learn to ignore. But he's lying when he says it doesn't exist, and now he knows it too. The evidence is right there on his somewhat startled face.

He hangs his head and stares at the hardwood floor. His shoulders rise and fall and the sides of his chest expand with his breathing. "Say something."

"I honestly don't know what to say."

"Yes, you do." He stands tall and moves toward me. He takes a step forward and I take a step back. We keep moving like this until I am backed into the closest corner. With a hand to the wall on either side of me, I am caged, and he is right the hell there. Both of us breathing heavier than normal. My heart is beating so hard it's about to break right out of my chest. Being this pissed off and turned on at the same time is a lot. "Go on."

"I don't want to keep arguing with you," I say. "I also feel like I've won, so it's probably best to quit while I'm ahead."

"You've won, huh?"

I just shrug.

His gaze drops to my mouth and stays there. Is he going to kiss me? I have no idea how we went from arguing to this, but I am not complaining. I lick my lips and his dark gaze tracks the movement. Fuck. This is actually going to happen. But then he takes a step back and my heart sinks to my toes. I am not surprised. Though I am disappointed.

"So," I say.

"So," he replies.

"It would seem that one of us has some abandonment and intimacy issues that could do with a little work."

"I'm happy to find you a good therapist if that would help."

Patience is a great virtue. A pity I'm currently out of the stuff. "Okay. I better—"

"My pool is heated," he says out of nowhere. "I don't think I mentioned that."

"What?"

"My pool is heated," he repeats.

"Your pool is heated?"

"Yes."

"Ah, no, you didn't mention that before."

He just looks at me.

"That's nice," I continue. "I can see how it would come in handy during the cooler weather."

Without another word, he bends at the waist and tugs off his boots. First one, then the other. Same goes for his socks. Then he straightens and removes his T-shirt. Just takes a handful of the fabric covering his back and drags it off over his head. It's amazing I don't swallow my tongue. My fingers itch to touch. From his pecs to his neat brown nipples and the trail of dark hair leading down from his belly button to the waistband of his jeans. He's giving me a heart attack with this show of skin. Perhaps this is how I die. It's a few days early. But not a bad way to go.

"Ali, what are you doing?"

He crosses his arms over his perfect chest. "You had 'skinny-dipping' on your wish list."

13

"You want us to go swimming?" I ask. "Now? With no clothes on?"

"It's where this is heading, isn't it?"

"I actually thought we were moving more toward me leaving as opposed to us undertaking any naked aquatic adventures."

He grimaces. "Maybe I wasn't clear, but I don't want you to leave. Especially not when you're upset at me."

"Um. Yeah. You're not exactly subtle."

In lieu of a response, his fingers go to the top button on his jeans and *damn*. He needs to stop it with the striptease. Now.

I grab his hands and hold fast. "I would take it as a personal favor if you would please stop taking your clothes off."

He peers down at me, and the side of his mouth kicks up. Oh, good. He's happy again. My distress at his bare chest pleases him, apparently. And the moment I attempt to remove my hands from his, he starts back in on the zipper. His smirk is sly as fuck. *Jerk.* The backs of my fingers brush against his bare stomach and warm skin. A shiver runs through both of us. It's like we're connected. I can feel the heat radiating from him. With all of this on show, it's also hard to know where to look. I settle for a freckle on his left shoulder. It's lopsided and kind of cute. Like a little wonky smile.

"No one's said that to me before," he says. "Told me to stop taking my clothes off."

"Correct me if I'm wrong—"

"You're wrong."

"Ha. You're not funny."

He lifts one thick shoulder in a half-assed shrug. "Matter of opinion."

"Enough with the nonsense," I say, gripping the waistband of his jeans and holding it together for dear life. "As I was about to say when you so rudely interrupted. Are you taking your clothes off because you lost the argument? Is this you trying to reassert control of the situation by wantonly flaunting yourself?"

"Of course not," he says with much scoffing. "Why would you even think that?"

I just wait.

"Fine," he concedes. "Maybe a little. But it's more to do with what the argument was about."

"Please explain."

After a heavy sigh, he says, "You were right. I was jealous. You win, Lilah. We're not *just friends.* Therefore, this is the direction we're heading in, right?"

"As in both of us taking our clothes off? I don't know."

"You don't know?" he asks with much doubt. "Seriously?"

"That's what I said."

At this, he snorts. "Let me guess. You'd prefer we take

things slow, overthink it for a while, throw in some mutual pining, and see what happens."

"No. I just think stepping back from this just for tonight might not be a bad idea."

"It's not a good one either."

"Would it mean anything, us having sex?"

"Does it have to mean anything?"

"I don't know. I'm obviously not averse to hookups, but this feels different," I say. "Why don't we give ourselves tonight to think this over? Circle back to the subject tomorrow over lunch or drinks or something?"

"Did you actually just suggest we circle back to the subject of us having sex?"

"Yeah…"

"Tell me you're not working on a list in your mind entitled 'Reasons Lilah and Alistair Shouldn't Bang.'"

"That wasn't the title I was going with, but there's nothing wrong with a nice clear bullet-point presentation of the facts. And it was more of a pros-and-cons thing."

"Right. Well, I think we should just fuck and get it out of the way," he says wisely. Or so the sage expression on his face seems to suggest. "I'll give you the great sex you're after. You can tick another item off your wish list. Then we can go back to being just friends."

"Get it out of the way… I don't know."

"I didn't hear a yes. Did you mean to insert a yes in there?"

I pin my lips shut with my teeth for a moment. "Just to double-check. You're offering me sex followed by a swift return to platonic friendship?"

"Great sex. That's right."

"The ego on you. I'm trusting you to keep your pants on,"

I say, taking a step back. It's nice to hear he finds me attractive and wants to play naked with me. Given the whole "I might be dead soon" issue, I should probably jump on both the opportunity and the man. It's the only reasonable response to such an offer in such a situation. And yet I am hesitating.

"Well?" He puts his hands on his hips and stares down at me. "Are you done overthinking it?"

"For now. Things feel weird between us, and I don't want to compound the situation." My polite smile is small and set. "Therefore, my decision is we have sex tomorrow. This would also give us both time to anticipate the act, which I think would be pleasant."

By the positioning of his dark brows, I am able to see that the man is both put out and surprised. Being denied things is not his norm. "Why not tonight?"

"Tomorrow is really not that far away."

"Or, and hear me out here, you could just take off your clothes now."

"That's another issue. I need a minute to get used to the idea of being naked in front of you," I say. My face feels hot again. There's a chance I might be allergic to all this honesty, particularly in one night.

His eyebrows rise in surprise. "Why?"

"No. We're not discussing this. It's personal and messy. But I'm also not always great with surprises, and honestly, this coming from you has been quite surprising."

"What are you worried about, Lilah?"

It is absolutely my turn to ignore a question. Getting into my relationship with my own body and a lifetime's worth of negative messaging from the media about the same is a no.

Then there's me wanting time to shave and wax and primp some. "What time suits you tomorrow?"

But the cranky and still-half-naked man didn't seem to get the message. He takes a step toward me and says, "You're not delaying because you're worried I'll be shit in bed, are you?"

I wrinkle my nose in both distaste and confusion. "Are you serious?"

"You heard me."

My mouth opens, but holy hell. "That's what you took away from what I said, huh? That me needing a minute is all about you? That I'm doubting your prowess?"

"Answer the question, please."

"Now that you mention it, I do only have your lofty opinion of yourself to go by. I don't suppose you've made any home movies or have an ex you'd be comfortable with me having a chat with? A dick pic or two also wouldn't go amiss. If you don't mind, of course."

We stand there and frown at each other. It's a beautiful moment. Not.

"We're not going to fuck tonight," he says finally, his shoulders drooping with disappointment. Which is actually kind of gratifying.

"That's right. We aren't," I agree, reaching for the door handle. "I'm seeing my mom in the morning. But I'm free after that. Let me know what time suits you."

"Right. I'll schedule you in," he says dryly. "You still won't let me drive you home?"

"No. Thank you."

"Wait," he says. "One more thing. You let Gael and Shane kiss you good-night. Don't you think I should get the same consideration?"

"You want to kiss me on the cheek like them?"

He nods.

"As just friends."

"Right," he agrees. "Just friends. Who you are going to fuck tomorrow."

"All right," I say with a smile.

He steps closer and leans in, his lips brushing against my cheek. They're warm as is his breath on my skin. I hold myself perfectly still, waiting to see what will happen. Anticipation might just kill me. Every hair on my body stands on end. He brushes the tip of his nose against mine before going in for another cheek kiss. Only it's not really a kiss. It's him lightly dragging his lips along my jawline and up to my ear. My very sensitive ear. He gives my lobe a gentle nudge with the tip of his nose as well. Like he's just experimenting. Finding out the ways in which we can get close.

"You're so soft," he whispers.

"Mmm."

"And you always smell so good."

"It's just soap," I manage to say. "And perfume, a couple of face creams, and deodorant, of course. Guess you could include my shampoo and conditioner on the list too."

"That's good to know. But you're overthinking it again."

This is all very friendly and flirty. But he hasn't yet strayed into straight-out seduction territory. Not yet. My stomach is already topsy-turvy. I'm standing in the open doorway, and my back is to the door frame, and he's right in front of me. So close. And still only half dressed despite my very reasonable request for him to put on his shirt. I scrunch up my fingers into fists and touch nothing. Letting him set the pace. Though he goes no further and seems to be finished.

"Okay," I say. "Good night."

He pulls back a little and blinks. *Oh, fuck.* His eyes are such a hypnotizing shade of blue in this low light. The man and his intensity dazzle me. There's no other word for it. And the expression on his face, like how dare I. "I'm not finished yet, Lilah."

"Well, did you want to move it along a—"

"No."

"I swear, you're just like a toddler sometimes. *No* seems to be the only word you know tonight." I sigh. "When Shane kissed me on the cheek, it really was more of a there-and-gone sort of thing."

"What about Gael?"

"He may have lingered a little."

Alistair just grunts. Then he stops playing and angles his head and covers his lips with mine. Giving me a firm and insistent closed-mouth kiss. Chaste, but not really. His eyes are closed, and his dark lashes are so long. A vein of tension seems to be running through him, stringing him out from head to toe. Because his hands are curled into fists and hanging by his sides too. Just like mine.

He doesn't stop or take a step back or any such thing. He just keeps kissing me. And this kiss is asking me a question. No. It is pleading with me. I open my mouth the smallest amount, and I can feel his smile rather than see it. His hands cup my face and his tongue traces over my bottom lip and *whoa*. Off we go. My eyelids slide closed and my mind spins in dizzy circles. We have most definitely moved beyond friendly kissing.

His tongue sweeps into my mouth and toys with mine. Teasing and inviting and turning me on. It is all so hot and good. He tastes faintly of beer and mostly of warmth. Not a flavor I would have recognized before, but here we are. I can't explain it, but he's everything. He's just everything. I don't know when my hands went rogue. They are, however, pawing at him like there's no tomorrow. How shameful. The thrill of running my fingertips over his warm skin. Over his stomach and around his sides and up the strong lines of his back. I want to mark him with my nails just a little. Just enough to leave a reminder that I was there.

A sound of pure need comes from deep in his throat and the hairs on the back of my neck stand on end. My skin is electric and alive. Everything low in me squeezes tight in want. My vagina is a total traitor. Catching my breath seems to take forever.

"You lied, Ali. That was not a simple kiss on the cheek. Not even a little."

He rests his forehead against mine and says, "We could still fuck tonight. Now. Right now."

"No. I want to do this right. It matters to me." My heart is galloping inside my chest. Just running right out of control. I push him back and pull myself together. "I'm leaving. I'm going home. I mean it this time."

"Just to check I have made myself absolutely clear. I don't want you to have sex with someone else. Let me give you what you want. Okay?"

"Okay."

"You're really leaving?"

I nod.

His face is now a careful blank. As if he's reined in his hunger. But his lips are swollen and damp from me. Then he says these words like a promise: "Stay near the light by the gate where I can see you. We'll continue this tomorrow."

14

Friday

My grandma Inge rests in a cemetery half an hour from my parents' house. Mom visits regularly to share the tea. I was young when Grandma passed, and I don't really have many memories of her. Just of the scent of lavender from her perfume. But she and Mom were close. Mom still likes to talk to her as if she were here.

"You explain the photos of you with the prince," says Mom, arranging the bouquet of wildflowers I bought in the stone vase attached to the headstone. "I wouldn't know where to start."

I sit on the grass beneath another clear blue California sky. Last night with Alistair shook me. I can't even think about what comes next on my wish list. There are bruises from lack of sleep beneath my eyes. If lying awake making up imaginary conversations that will most likely never happen were an Olympic sport, I would be representing the country in no time. My state of mind is also evident from my outfit—safe and comfortable old clothes. Like the oversize hoodie from senior year. It's seen me through it all: relationship breakups, series binges, and everything in between. But beneath my homely clothing, my legs and pits are freshly shaved, and every inch of me has been lotioned. "He's not a prince. Though I don't see that it's anybody's business what his parents' relationship was exactly."

"She's talking about Alistair Lennox," Mom explains to Grandma's grave. "You remember the scandal. That poor boy. He was so young." Then she turns to me. "Inge was a royalist. But she preferred the Danish royal family over the English, of course. She threw such a party for Margrethe's coronation."

"What about you?" I ask. "Do you have any interest in royalty?"

"I don't mind the occasional funeral or wedding. All the pomp and pageantry, the pretty dresses and hats."

"Yeah, but the king always seems like such a miserable ass."

Mom clicks her tongue. "And yet he's still your friend's father. Though, to be honest, I never liked the man either. I detested him for his behavior. For not publicly claiming Alistair as his son or acknowledging him in some way. It was obvious the boy was his. His affair with Lady Helena was common enough knowledge. They were pictured together in the gossip magazines all the time. Inge used to buy them. She lived and breathed all that nonsense. Said she bought them for the crosswords, but we all knew better. Of course, I told her they were trash and then read them when she wasn't looking."

I laugh.

"They caught him coming and going from her apartment at all hours of the day and night. And Alistair looked exactly like him when he was little. Though he grew out of that and started to take more after his mother's side as he got older. But I don't know how you could have a soul and treat a child that way. I can't imagine what it does. To be rejected by your father and then hounded by the press."

"I think it'd cause a whole heaping lot of trauma with a side order of trust issues," I say. "Why didn't the king acknowledge him, do you think?"

"The focus was supposed to be on him and his shiny new fiancée. How expensive and over-the-top their wedding would be. Their entire existence is about clinging to outdated traditions. I think they're fighting a losing battle with the modern world, and that poor little boy got caught in the cross fire," she says. "It always struck me as curious timing, though. How news of your friend's existence was leaked at just that moment."

"Yeah. I agree. They never did find out who did it. Or they never said publicly who did it."

"But the king reaped what he sowed. It's not like he and his missus look particularly happy when they're together these days, do they?" she asks. "I don't even think they share the same castle."

"No, they don't. Not according to the gossip sites, at least."

Cemeteries are kind of cool. I can't say that I've spent much time in one before. But in full daylight, they're not so spooky. There are lots of trees, and apart from the occasional person visiting a loved one's grave, it's peaceful and quiet. I could get used to this. Guess we all do in the end.

"I hope you'll come and visit me and tell me all the news when I'm dead," I say without thinking.

Mom laughs. "I'll be gone long before you and buried just over there."

"You bought a plot?"

"Your father and I did a while back."

"Huh." I run the palm of my hand back and forth over a dandelion. "I didn't know that."

"It's not a secret." She sits back on her haunches. "I might have been a little upset when your grandfather announced he wished to be buried next to his second wife. But I understand. Or I try to. It's been a while since Mom passed, and he's moved on with his life, but…"

"You don't want to leave Grandma on her own."

"No. Your father believes the spirit world doesn't exist and there is no great beyond. But on the off chance there is, I hate the thought that she's waiting. Hoping for someone who will never come."

"Love sucks."

"Sometimes," she agrees. "But not all the time."

"I don't have any strong feelings on final resting places. Can they just throw me in with you?"

Mom smiles. "The more, the merrier."

"Make sure they play 'Someone You Loved' by Lewis Capaldi at my funeral. That'll get everyone crying for sure."

Mom's smile is bemused. "A very important consideration."

"And don't bake anything nice for them to eat at the wake either. The day should be one of complete and utter misery."

"Got it," says Mom. "I'll give them stale sandwiches and that awful tasteless meat loaf your uncle insists on making. I gave him a spice rack for Christmas and everything. You would think he'd take a hint."

I try to smile, but it slips straight off my face. Hard not to wonder if this is another last moment right here and now. A bit morbid that my final conversation with my mother might take place in a cemetery. But oh well. My father has this method of coping with difficult situations. He decides what the logical and rational worst scenario looks like and makes peace with it. He prepares himself for possible failure or whatever. (This inclination of his might explain where my own occasional pessimism stems from.) So, if the worst possible option is me dying and being buried here, is that so bad?

Hmm. Yeah. That still sucks.

A shiver works down my spine as if the sun has disappeared and left me in shade. Only there are no clouds today. The sky is as clear and calm as it has ever been. And yet I feel cold suddenly, like maybe someone stepped on my grave.

"Mom, are you scared of dying?"

"No." She shakes her head. "Not really. The way I see it, we're either stardust to be scattered across the universe and returned to nothing. Or we get to go on and be with the people we've loved and lost."

"That's a nice way to look at it."

"Or worm food. There's that too."

I just frown.

"Whatever happens to us, wasting energy worrying won't change a single thing," she says. "We all have to die someday."

Despite her making a solid point, my anxiety is still slowly mounting. I can feel it building beneath my skin. Talking about death probably isn't helpful. Same goes for visiting graveyards. It's nice to hang out with Mom, though. What I should do is focus on the upcoming sex fest with Alistair. A much brighter topic. But not one I will be sharing with my mother anytime soon.

"Are you going to tell your grandmother and me about the beard rash on your cheek that you didn't quite manage to cover with concealer?" she asks like she's reading my mind.

"Shit." I carefully feel my face. There's a definite tender patch. "Stupid stubble."

"But they're just friends," she says to Inge. "Friends who kiss, apparently. He's who you were with last night, right? Or have you met someone else?" Mom doesn't wait for an answer. Instead telling Grandma's grave, "Your granddaughter has not been slow about moving on from Josh."

"Oof. Feel that judgment, Grandma?"

"I just think it wouldn't hurt to take a while to think through what happened and work out what you want. Rushing into something new with someone different might not be the best course of action."

She assumes I have time. But I am not getting into all that with her. Good Witch Willow can stay far away from this conversation. And she's wrong about Alistair and me. We're not soulmates. If we were, he would have offered me more than orgasms and good company. Not that there's anything wrong with orgasms and good company. Given the time pressures with my possible upcoming death, it's really all I have time for anyway.

"I'm not rushing into anything," I say.

She gives me a long look.

"Believe what you want. But I've thought about what's best and have decided we're just going to stay friends, Mother."

"She calls me *Mother* in that tone of voice when she gets irritated," says Mom, resting her hand on top of the headstone. "Usually when I'm treading a little too close to the truth. You might recall I used to do a similar thing with you. But I used your name. Inge. *You don't know what you're talking about, Inge. Stay out of my business, Inge.* See? The tone of voice is the same. This is how you can tell that she's mine."

I snort. Such a genteel noise.

"Inge always knew what was right. Always had something to say about everything." Mom's smile is bittersweet. "Then you were gone, and I would love to have you back so you could stick your nose in where it doesn't belong just one more time. But such is life. So...it seems like 'just friends' covers a lot of situations these days."

"Yeah." I sigh. "You ever like someone too much?"

"Our hearts can be rampaging idiots at times," says my very wise mother.

"Our loins aren't any better."

Mom laughs. "Loins. You're not a cut of meat. But no, they're generally worse. Are you going to be able to keep your heart and loins safe from this man?"

"I doubt it." I lie down on the green grass beside Grandma's grave. Just stretch out and close my eyes. Call it a practice run. "How did you know Dad was the one? I know you met him at a dance and dumped the loser you were with. But why him?"

"You're going to get grass in your hair. And the loser I was with went on to play for the 49ers." Mom was and is a proud blonde bombshell. She has definitely made people weak in the knees. "But I could talk to your father. He was so creative and knew such interesting things. I'd never met anyone quite like him. We used to talk for hours and hours on the phone. It drove Inge wild that I was tying up the line all the time."

I just lie there, play dead, and listen.

"You need to challenge each other. Make each other want to be better. But you have to feel safe with each other too," she says. "Does your prince do that for you?"

"I don't know. But we're not in the process of falling in love and making a commitment, so it doesn't necessarily matter."

Mom cocks her head. "You two seem to be spending a lot of time together lately. Are you sure about that? Have you asked him how he feels?"

"You don't just ask someone how they feel."

"Why not?"

"To answer your initial question, somewhere between 'Sort of' and 'Hell no.' Let's settle on 'It's complicated.'"

"Lilah." She clicks her tongue in displeasure. "Talk to the man. Don't be afraid."

"Easy for you to say."

Given my decision to be more daring, not asking him directly how he feels about me does come across as cowardly. But he only just admitted to wanting to be more than friends. For a bang or two. Doesn't that basically cover things?

"And for my final piece of advice—always try before you buy," she says. "If you don't work in bed, then sooner or later, you won't work outside of it either."

"Such scandalous advice."

"I'm a realist."

"You're a realist?" I laugh. "Mother, you're here to commune with the dead."

She shrugs and smiles serenely. "People are complicated, honey. What can I say?"

Me: How do you feel about me? If you don't mind sharing. Please use precise words.

Alistair: I'm not texting about that. Let's meet later.

Me: OK

Alistair: Was about to call. Where are you?

Me: Heading home.

Alistair: Today has gotten hectic. Can you pick something up for me and bring it over tonight?

Me: Sure. Where from?

Alistair: Not far. I'll send you the address.

Me: OK

Alistair: It needs to be right now.

Me: Yes, sir.

Alistair: I like the sound of that.

Me: It was meant to be read in a sarcastic tone of voice. You're doing it wrong.

Rodeo Drive is packed with tourists and pretty people. The luxury department store he sends me to is shiny beyond belief. I tend not to step foot in such places for various reasons. The top one being funds. However, it makes sense Alistair would shop here. The personal stylist area is on the top floor behind an expanse of frosted glass, and the woman at the reception desk is not impressed with me. I can tell from the slow once-over she gives me from head to toe. From my worn sneakers to my baggy light blue jeans with a rip in one knee and the oversize faded hoodie. I'm wearing it with the hood up because I am almost certain there's still some grass in my hair.

"My name is Lilah Goodluck. I'm here to pick up something for Alistair Lennox," I say without a smile. Being polite has its limits, and sometimes you have to give to get.

Her demeanor instantly changes. A brilliant smile is plastered on her face as she leads me toward a room at the back. "Of course. We've been expecting you. This way, please. Can I get you a coffee or water or perhaps a glass of wine or bubbly?"

"No. Thanks."

She holds the door open for me. Inside is an even more extravagant room. It is white with gold touches from the potted orchids to the giant gilt-framed mirrors and small crystal chandelier. A changing area waits behind some curtains, and several racks of clothing hang nearby. And lounging on a velvet chaise longue with a laptop is the man himself. The one who did the kissing. At the sight of me, Alistair rises and crosses the room. I could watch him do this forever, just striding toward me in his dapper black suit. He shouldn't still have this strong an effect on me. But he does.

"There you are," he says with a brief smile.

"Ali, what's going on? I thought we were meeting tonight."

"Why do you have grass in your hair?" he asks, picking out one piece and then another. We have reached the preening each other stage, apparently. It's a pity I don't hate it. Not even a little.

"I was lying on the ground beside my grandmother's grave practicing being dead and chatting with my mom."

He nods like this makes total sense. Then he pushes back my hood. "This is hideous, Lilah. Take it off. Why are you hiding beneath this thing?"

"It's my emotional-support hoodie. Leave it alone." I slap at his hands. "Did they teach you how to be bossy in that castle in Scotland you grew up in?"

"No. I learned that at boarding school. They were do-or-die climates, packed to the rafters with obnoxious rich little shits. But if you projected strength, they usually left you alone."

All I can do is stare. The man just gave me actual private information about his life. Without me pushing and prodding. He just answered a question in a reasonable manner like a normal person. Amazing.

His gaze is amused. "Better shut your mouth before you catch another insect."

My lips slam shut. Then open again. "Why do I keep seeing you in suits? I thought tech bros wore sneakers?"

"It depends on who I'm meeting with. Some people expect the suit, given who I am and all. It helps to facilitate certain situations."

"Huh."

"Lilah, I'd like you to meet Carolina," he says, stepping aside.

"Hello, Lilah," says a woman in a white pantsuit. No wonder I didn't notice her. She blends perfectly with the decor. That and I am a little overwhelmed. And this perfectly coiffed woman with a golden tan saw us bickering over my old sweats with plant life in my hair. Wonderful.

"Hello," I say with an awkward-as-fuck smile.

Alistair retrieves his wallet from the inner pocket of his suit jacket. And from this he extracts his black Amex. "This is for you."

"For me?"

"I know the line is something about salespeople only being nice to credit cards. But I think you'll find Carolina to be friendly and helpful," he says. "I've got some work to do. I'll be over there if you need me."

"Wait. We're doing the *Pretty Woman* thing? Now? For real?"

"Yes," he says. "You're a little slow today. Didn't you get any sleep last night?"

"I had a lot on my mind." I take the card and look it over with interest and no small amount of excitement. "Wow. Okay. What's my limit?"

"There isn't one."

"Ali," I say with no small amount of awe, "you do realize, if you put me in this situation and give me your credit card, I am going to do some damage? There will be no polite pair of shoes and a dress. I will live out my dream to the fullest. You know this, right?"

"Do your worst, Leannan." He sits once more on the fancy couch. "I dare you."

Huh.

I know what *leannan* means. The Gaelic word is in plenty of romance novels and TV shows. However, there's no need to lose my shit over him saying it to me. He's just playing, after all. This moment, though—this particular addition to the wish list—it's perfect. Or almost perfect. "What you're supposed to say is, do you have anything in this shop as beautiful as she is?"

"Asking questions I already know the answer to is a waste of time." He doesn't even look up from his laptop. Just takes out his cell, makes a call, and starts arguing with Gael, by the sound of things.

"Lilah," says Carolina. "Can I show you some outfits?"

It turns out it's hard to speak with your heart stuck in your throat. I smile and nod and hand over his credit card.

15

Alistair works in the corner while I play dress-up. A pair of designer jeans with a red tank and matching Saint Laurent flat mules gets a disinterested glance from him. While the blue floor-length seventies-style V-neck gown with balloon sleeves receives the high praise of a distracted nod. His full attention isn't garnered until the black pencil skirt with white silk top and Louboutin slingback sandals with a four-inch heel. Top-tier sexy librarian.

"She'll take that," he says to Carolina before returning to his laptop.

"She can make her own choices," I reply. "But you were nice enough to give me your credit card, so I'll allow you a small say in the matter."

He smiles, but nothing is said.

There's lots of nice stuff on the rack, but I settle on just the three outfits. More than enough to make me feel indulged. Not so much that if I die in the next few days, it will go to waste. With the shoes and purses, it must add up to four or five figures. Which is mind-blowing. But Carolina saved the truly interesting items for last. Chemises and camisoles and corsets made of the finest lace, embroidered tulle, and smoothest silk. I always thought if I had money, I'd spend it on lingerie and books. Luxury for the butt and the brain—a perfect balance. And these pieces of intimate apparel are breathtaking. But despite my brave words about credit card usage, a wee smidgen of guilt is happening.

"It's beautiful." I turn this way and that, admiring the black bodysuit with lace edging. "But I think I have enough for now."

Carolina says nothing to me. She does, however, step out of the changing room and announce, "Alistair, if you'd like to take over?"

"That time, is it?" I hear him say. "If we could have the room, please."

"Of course."

The door quietly opens and closes. We're alone.

"Lilah, can I come in?"

It's not that all the salient parts of me aren't covered. I look amazing in the overpriced intimate apparel, and he better appreciate it. It's also not like he wasn't going to see a whole lot more sooner or later. Any adverse reaction to the cellulite on my thighs can be dealt with here and now. This is a good thing. "Sure. Why not?"

He wanders on into the changing room area without a word, pushes aside the curtain, and grinds to a halt. "Fuck."

"Just out of curiosity, is that a good expletive or a bad expletive?"

"Good. Very good." He cocks his head and circles me like a shark. All hunger and intent. Heat curls through me in response. Everything low in my body drawing tight. His dark gaze is nothing less than thrilling. "The way it pushes up your tits is amazing. Does this come in other colors?"

"No idea."

"I definitely think you should have several of these. You know...for emergencies."

"What sort of emergency would that be?"

He leans against the wall and crosses his arms. Totally at his ease in this situation. "You wanted to know how I feel about you. I thought it best we discuss it face-to-face."

"You want to talk about that now?"

"Yes."

Standing around in silk and lace in front of him has me feeling all sorts of exposed. The ogling doesn't need to be one-sided, however. He ditched the suit jacket and tie and rolled up the sleeves of his white shirt. Such man porn. His forearms are a thing of beauty. It's the couple of buttons undone revealing his throat and a patch of his chest that get me, however. Something about his muscular neck just does it for me. Makes me want to use my tongue and teeth on him.

"You do realize I know you're thinking about sex when you look at me that way," he says in a calm voice. "I have a sneaking suspicion you do it more often than you realize."

My mouth opens. Then it closes again because sometimes saying nothing is best. Take now, for instance.

"If I could have your full attention, please," he says. "My eyes are up here, so stop staring at my chest."

I do not blush. "Get on with it."

"I don't want there to be any miscommunication between us," he says. His eyebrows are drawn together just a little. Just enough to let me know he is serious. "Before I address any-one's feelings, let's cover the basics. I can't make the press leave you alone, and you don't want to deal with them, which is fair enough. Those dickheads are a nightmare. Being famous is a part of my life I can't control. But us being friends we can attempt to keep secret so that aspect of my life isn't disrupting your life any more than necessary."

"You're not a disruption, Ali."

"Kind of you to say so. As for my feelings for you?"

"Yes?"

"They're exceptionally warm and friendly." He takes a deep breath and steps closer instead. Because of course he does. "And sometimes, like now, they're a lot more."

"You're talking about feelings in your pants region."

"Yes, I am," he agrees. "But you do know you're safe with me, don't you? I would never deliberately hurt you. You know that, right?"

I nod.

"As for this situation here… You tried to tap out. Said you didn't want to shop anymore. What's that about?"

"You had Carolina tell on me?"

"Why else do you think I've been sitting out there for the last hour?"

"Guess I thought you were guarding your card," I say. "I can't believe she snitched. And she seemed like such a nice person."

"She works on commission. What do you expect?"

"Valid point."

"Do you think Julia Roberts would walk out before seeing everything? Just give up after only an hour and go home?" he asks with mock outrage. "Is that really the sort of quitter mentality you're embracing? What happened to being bold?"

"I may only need a few days' worth of clothing."

This time his scowl is real. "I'm going to do you a favor and pretend you didn't say that. There will be no mention of bullshit predictions when you're meant to be having fun. Am I understood?"

"So bossy. You're very lucky it works for you. But I think you're underestimating how much of your money I've already spent."

He shakes his head slowly. Never ever has someone been so disappointed. I am officially the worst. "And you threatened to do my credit card some damage. What a liar you are, Leannan."

"You do realize I know what that word means."

"Do you?" he asks with a smile in his eyes. "It's just a term of affection. There's no need to get carried away."

"You use it often, then?"

"No," he says, scratching at his stubble. No idea if he's won an award for the most confusing man in the past. But wow is he right up there in the running this year. A definite candidate for top three. "What are your feelings for me, just out of curiosity?"

"I'm hardly going to admit to anything more than friendship with the occasional side of lust now, am I?"

He pauses. "Did you want to? Before I said what I said?"

"I don't know," I say, because even bravery has its limits.

"If it makes you feel any better, a relationship between us wouldn't likely work. As Gael made a point of noting, my success rate is dire."

I snort. "Everyone's success rate is dire until it's not or they decide they'd rather be alone. Not every relationship ends in disaster."

"Beside the point. I haven't even considered the idea of

us dating because paparazzi hiding in your front garden is a nonstarter."

"Wait a minute. You would—what?—have to sit down and make your own list to decide whether you wanted to date me? Isn't that just the sort of thing you know?"

"No. It's a serious question. I would need time to consider all aspects of the situation," he repeats. But his gaze drops to the neckline of my bodysuit again and stays there a second or two. Important relationship issues aren't the only thing on his mind, apparently.

"Hey. My eyes are also up here. You just told me off for playing it safe," I say. "The hypocrisy."

"I was talking about you wisely investing in some high-quality lingerie. I'll have you know I take relationships seriously. So I suppose I could say my feelings for you are unresolved at present."

The ability to read minds or auras or something would be so useful. Because apart from admiring my cleavage, I have no idea what's on his mind. Not a fucking clue. "Is this about the soulmate thing? Is that why you're reluctant to say more?"

"No." He snorts. "I know you have your concerns, but Winnie the Witch and her predictions are nothing more than a couple of coincidences and a big pile of bullshit."

"Good Witch Willow," I correct. "Let me see if I understand what you're asking. You want me to put myself out there and say I have feelings for you with no guarantee of you reciprocating?"

"Taking risks is part of life. Or you can play it safe. I know that's more your thing. But I thought you were trying to kick that habit." He's taunting me. It's obvious in the way he steps closer with a hint of a smile. "What do you say? Am I wrong about you only wanting great sex?"

"You still haven't proven you can deliver. Let's not get ahead of ourselves."

"This again," he says with disgust.

"A solid love of research is at the heart of every librarian. And information-wise, you're giving me nothing. Zip. Zilch."

Him and his ego will never cease to amaze me. His gaze goes hard, and his lips are a thin unimpressed line. But he doesn't say anything. Is it wrong that his mean face thrills me? We must buy the bodysuit now. He and his general hotness have made me soak through my thong.

"Let's deal with this once and for all, shall we?" he asks with the fakest smile. The curve of his mouth is a facade and more than a touch malicious. He grips my hips and turns me to face the nearest mirror. Then, with him pressed hard against my back, he walks me closer. "If you would stand over here, please."

"What are you doing?"

He sniffs the curve of my neck, taking me in with a deep breath. "Fixing your lack of faith."

"As fun as it is to get you all riled up, we can't do this here."

"Carolina won't come back in until one of us calls for her. There are no security cameras. No one will know what we do."

"Ali…"

His hands slide up my sides, fingers trailing down, tracing the edge of the lace to between my breasts. And I watch their path in the mirror. There's something hypnotizing about standing passive in his arms while he explores me. How his fingers follow the edge of lace back up to my shoulders. And there, they stop.

He inserts a fingertip beneath one thin strap and drags it slowly over the slope of my rounded shoulder. But the bodice of the bodysuit defies gravity and stays put. He grunts in dismay and gently tugs the strap down a little lower. Nope. Too much for me, apparently. I slap my hand over my breast and hold the thin material in place.

"Well, that's not helpful," he chides.

"This is really not the place for this."

"Nonsense. We're fine. I think we look good together," he says, meeting my gaze in the mirror. "Don't you?"

The palm of his hand slides over the back of mine in a tantalizingly light caress. He strokes my skin as if I need settling or soothing. I suppose I do. Then he rubs his cheek against my hair as if he's scenting me. All I can do is feel him…the fine cotton of his shirt against my back and his hardening cock against my ass. The restrained strength in his arms as he holds me against him. My breath doesn't stutter, however, until he wraps his fingers around my neck. Just holds me in place, his hand a brand against my skin. I can breathe, but his grip is good and firm. And all the time, he keeps watching me in the mirror, gauging my reactions.

"Should have known you were a control freak," I say, attempting a little levity.

His grin is sharp and sudden. "Don't act like you don't love it."

"Ali…"

"Put your hand down, please."

And I do. *Shit.*

"Thank you. You're such a good girl, Leannan."

The words send shivers up my spine. Though it's more than just the words. It's him and the position he's holding me in and everything. This is... I don't know what the fuck this is. But he has my full and complete attention. I don't think I could be more in the moment.

My pointed nipples are obvious to one and all beneath the thin material. The situation only gets worse when he trails his knuckles back and forth over them. Something inside me coils hotter and tighter with each touch. It's a unique sort of torture, and I wouldn't stop it if I could. The tips of his fingers slide over the smooth material. Over my belly and teasingly lower before heading back up to cup the weight of one of my breasts.

"I like your body," he says casually. Just making conversation. "Very much."

"I like yours too."

He slips his hand beneath the fabric of the bodysuit to continue cupping my breast. That side still has the strap in place. Though with all the maneuvering, the other is slowly sliding down, about to expose me. The pad of his thumb toys with my nipple. It kind of kills me the way he takes his time. How he builds me up higher and higher. I am a raw nerve on the edge. Each sensation takes me over. The heat of his hand and the calluses on his fingers. His hand tenses around my neck, tightening for a moment. As if I had forgotten he was the one in charge of this situation. Not likely.

By the time he slides his hand out of the bodice of my bodysuit and makes his way south, I am almost shaking. The tension building at the base of my spine, deep inside of me, is so intense. It might have been years since someone touched me. That's how it feels. His sure touch and heated gaze are everything. He cups me between the legs. Just covers my sex over the top of the silky material.

"Are you watching?" he whispers. "Do I have your full attention?"

"Yes, but...Ali..."

"It's just you and me. You're safe with me, Lilah. You know that, don't you?"

I worry over it for a moment. But he's right and I nod.

"That's lucky," he says. "Because there was no way I was going to stop now. I've been wanting to get my hand between your legs for a while now."

I don't know about that. But his fingers tighten around my neck again. A warning or a reminder. No idea which. Then he starts gently grazing the heel of his hand against my mound. But it doesn't stay easy for long. His big hands make short work of me. Everything in me responds to him. A sheen of sweat breaks out across my body. One hand holds me immobile while the other rubs and coaxes until I come. Until the tension inside me grows too great. My thighs squeeze his hand tight and my insides spasm as I clench on nothing. The orgasm shakes me, radiating out from my core. And he holds me all the while, his dick hard against the small of my back.

"Fortunate you're not a shouter," he whispers, his breath warm against my ear. "But we will work on that for future reference. As a woman in today's society, it's important to make yourself heard."

"Fuck," I gasp, working on catching my breath.

"Now, that would be going too far. We can't do that here, Leannan. Show some decorum." He fixes the fallen strap and watches me in the mirror. "To think I got you off over the top of your clothes too. Below the waist, at least. No more doubting my ability to give you good sex. You'll have to think of something else to give me shit about. I have every faith in you and look forward to finding out what it will be." He stops and takes a deep breath. "Right. I need to go look at spreadsheets for a while to calm me down. You let Carolina know she can come back inside when you're ready. Do find out if that comes in other colors, please."

"Ali," I say, still catching my breath.

He settles himself carefully back on the couch. There is wincing involved. "Yes?"

"It was never about the press. I mean, they wouldn't bother me. Or I would learn to get used to them if... You know."

He turns statue still. "No. I don't know. Why don't you tell me?"

Attempting to think after an orgasm of this magnitude is tricky. Same goes for laying my heart on the line. But I do my best. "It's not fair on my neighbors to have paparazzi hanging around. There's no security at my building, so we would have to find a way around that. If we decided to do the dating thing. If that's something we wanted to do."

I don't say it would only be an issue for a couple of days. It would only make him upset. But the fact that there's a limit on our time together is foremost in my mind. I am an idiot for not jumping him last night. Anxiety and body issues and everything else be damned.

Meanwhile, he just sits there staring at me.

Which doesn't ramp up my nerves at all. "What I'm trying to say is you're worth any hassle or disruption. Of course you are. Please don't think otherwise."

For a moment, we just stare at each other.

His smile is slow and beautiful and lights up my whole

damn world. The emotion in his careful expression can't be concealed. He needed to hear this just as much as I needed to say it. "All right, Lilah. I won't think that. Thank you."

I smile back at him, and the moment is perfect. It's like something out of a book. One with a guaranteed happy-ever-after. Something I don't have in this situation, sadly. But protecting my heart from him isn't going to work. I don't know why I thought it would. Fuck it. There's a chance I'll be dead soon. We all die sometime. Why not make my time count? If he decides against us getting together, it will hurt. But everything hurts now and then—it's how you know you're alive.

He raises an eyebrow in query. "What does that look mean?"

"Nothing."

"Come home with me after this," he says, his gaze back on his laptop screen.

"Aren't you sick of me yet?"

"No," he says. "And if you're with me, I don't have to worry about you suddenly deciding to go storm-chasing or snake-charming or I don't know what."

"There are so many rude jokes I could make right now about snake-charming, but I won't. I would, however, like to point out it was only one skateboarding class and a very small tattoo. Hardly living-on-the-edge type stuff," I say. "Are you sure you don't need alone time to think about whether you want to date me or not?"

"It seems to me, Leannan, that the best way to see if we should spend more time exploring our feelings is by going on an actual date. Dinner, drinks, the usual. Then tomorrow we'll take the convertible for a drive. I know a place that does mud baths an hour outside the city. It wasn't on your list, but

I thought it seemed like your sort of thing. You can slather yourself in the stuff, and I'll watch and generally be supportive because the idea of covering myself in wet dirt doesn't appeal. What do you say?"

My heart bangs against my breastbone. Like there isn't enough room for everything he inspires inside of me. The last thing Josh planned for me was to pick up his laundry. But here Alistair is, going above and beyond on the regular. And the things he does... They're a lot.

"That sounds great," I say, definitely not getting all emotional. "But I thought you only borrowed the convertible?"

His gaze returns to the laptop, and there it stays. "You liked it, so I decided to keep it. Had a feeling we might want to use it again."

"You kept the car? But you were so pissed at me that day. And most of the one after."

"It's not a big deal," he says briskly. "That reminds me, we should talk about what you're going to get to replace the Prius. I was thinking something like a G Wagon. Big, boxy, extremely safe. Did you know you can even get those armored?"

"There's no way I'm spending that much on a vehicle. I'll also have you know I am usually an excellent driver." Not that it's likely I'll even need another vehicle. But again with the not saying the part that upsets him out loud.

"Of course you are," he says, smooth as can be. "We can talk about it later. What's your answer on the date—yes or no?"

"Yes."

"Good." He smiles at his spreadsheets. "Make sure you buy everything you'll need for an overnight stay."

16

"Isn't that your mother's Rolls-Royce?"

We're driving down Alistair's street after my shopping spree. The Aston Martin wasn't big enough to handle all the packages. How wild that (a) I shopped that hard and (b) the trunk on his vehicle is so small. I took too long to decide what I wanted to take with me versus what I wanted delivered to my apartment, so Alistair arranged for all of it to be sent to his house. Guess he'd had enough of shopping.

"Yes," he says with a frown for the luxe car. "That's her."

"You weren't expecting a visit?"

"No, I was not."

I sense something has gone down between him and his mom, but I have no idea what or when. Family can be complicated. But there's the distinct feeling Alistair would rather have it out with her in the street than let her into his sanctuary. The problem is you never know when paparazzi might be lurking. As soon as the gate slides open, the Rolls heads inside followed by a shiny new Cadillac Escalade. A man and a woman dressed in sharp black suits step out of the Escalade once it parks. I may not have much experience around the rich and famous; however, these people all but scream security detail. This fact is confirmed when a petite white woman with silver hair wearing a brown tweed skirt suit steps out behind them. A woman I have seen a time or two on the gossip sites.

Whoa. Royalty has come to call. It's a good thing I swapped my old jeans and emotional-support hoodie for a nice new outfit of black pants, a white silk blouse, and black combat ankle boots by Jimmy Choo. Faking rich is fun.

Alistair swears profusely. The array of languages is impressive. French, Italian, and Spanish are all in there. I recognize *scheisse* as being German. Not sure about the rest. He is seriously unhappy.

"I take it visits don't happen often," I say. "How do you want to handle it?"

He sits slumped over the wheel. "It's not too late for us to buy a private island. Just a small one. Nothing too extravagant. We could disappear and never be seen again. Live out our days sipping cocktails on the beach. I'd be more than happy to rub suntan lotion on your back. I'm useful like that."

"It does sound tempting."

Lady Helena and Dougal stand waiting by the front door. Judging by the set of her chin, she's no happier about the situation than her son. Though Dougal seems unperturbed as he whistles a tune while surveying the property.

Alistair sighs. "Guess we better get it over with."

"Should I wait out here?"

"No" is all he says, opening the driver's-side door.

"Okay, then."

We climb out of the car, and the only noise is the crunch of gravel beneath our feet. The silence filling the spaces between is deafening. Why does this feel like an ambush?

"Those hedges need trimming." Dougal points to the offending shrubbery. "They're out of control, lad."

"I like them that high." Alistair turns to the stranger in our midst and nods his head. It's a brief show of deference. "Your Royal Highness, what brings you by?"

Princess Alexandra, the king's sister, gives us all a sour look and says, "We'll talk inside."

As soon as the front door is open and the security alarm dealt with, one of her people ventures inside. No doubt to search for any hidden anti-monarchists. The princess doesn't wait for the all clear, however, striding into the house with her nose held high. Although the remaining security person isn't happy, she doesn't seem surprised. And there's a job you could not pay me enough money to do. Following them inside isn't particularly appealing. A feeling shared by more than me. Alistair, Lady Helena, and Dougal all linger in the open air.

Lady Helena presents her cheek to her son for a kiss. "Hello, sweetheart."

"Mother," Alistair greets her.

"I was notified by a friend when her private jet landed. Had a feeling she might be headed your way. I tried to call, but you were apparently doing something very important and had your phone switched off."

Nothing from her son.

"I'm sure that's what it was. You wouldn't be avoiding my calls, would you? Of course not. How silly of me to even think that." Her diamond bracelets clatter as she pats me on the cheek. "Good to see you're still with us, Lilah."

"Thank you, Your Ladyship," I say. "Am I supposed to curtsy to the princess or what?"

Lady Helena's response is a maudlin sigh. "It's been years since I've been around anybody that outranks me."

"There, there," says Dougal, ushering her inside.

Alistair's face is blank. Never a good sign. "The king likes to send someone to lecture me once a year or so. But this is only the second time an actual member of the family has seen fit to visit."

"I suggest we be exactly as polite to her as she is to us."

His answering smile is all sharp teeth.

Princess Alexandra stands rigid with her back to the room, staring out at the garden. Her security people hover nearby. So much tension.

"We'll talk alone, Alistair," she says without turning.

He directs me into the corner of the sofa and stands at my side. "No. We won't."

The princess turns and sniffs with derision in our general direction. "Very well. I'm sure you know who sent me."

"Can you name names?" Lady Helena sits beside me on the sofa. "It would be awfully helpful. My memory isn't what it used to be, and you know subtext was never my strong suit."

"Your recent behavior has been the cause of much concern. The photos of you in the media, particularly," she continues, ignoring Helena.

"You mean the ones of him in public with a couple of different female friends? The ones where everyone was fully clothed?" I ask. "How the hell could they be seen as scandalous?"

The princess ignores me too and carries on. "We'd hoped

you would have settled down by now. It's not as if suitable candidates weren't made available."

"Do you mean that awful girl you had the audacity to send chasing after him the second he turned eighteen?" asks Lady Helena. "You remember, sweetie—" she turns to Alistair "—her father was some billionaire. Of course, it turned out that he was a close friend of a certain monarch. We had to find out about the connection through other means. It was all rather distasteful, as I recall."

Alistair just grunts and sits on the arm of the sofa beside me. He apparently feels the need to hover. As for me, I feel the need to protect him from these assholes.

"Then there was that supposedly chance meeting with His Royal Highness's goddaughter," continues Her Ladyship. "She transferred to your college for a semester. Not the least bit subtle. Next came the young, widowed countess who tried to climb into your bed in Bali. And the rather fetching equerry's daughter who tailed you around town for a while. I was also highly dubious about the one from the Royal Ballet. What was her name again?"

"How the hell did you hear about Bali?" asks Alistair.

Her Ladyship winks. "Never you mind."

"That's enough." The princess's gaze is cold and hard. "The point is you've had numerous opportunities to find yourself a suitable match. At least previously you were always seen with women of worth."

"Oh, dear. I never could fault your bravery, Lexi, just your wisdom. Safe to say that hasn't changed. Whatever it is you want from him, let me assure you that attacking his friend is not the way to get it." Lady Helena raises her hand. "A drink, please, Dougal."

"Yes, Your Ladyship."

"Best get one for Lilah as well."

"Aye."

"Women of worth?" repeats Alistair with a blank face. "Are you fucking with me?"

"How dare you use such language." The princess's lips are a thin line. "I suppose it was too much to hope that you had been raised correctly."

"He went to all the best schools, as you well know," says Lady Helena in a cool tone. "Received training in etiquette, has a working knowledge of the Constitution…all that nonsense. We even had regular formal meals to ensure he was comfortable in such a setting. All on the off chance that his father might one day deign to acknowledge his existence. When news of my son was made public, we received no support from you or your family. And still Alistair did his best to make his father proud. He even served in the military."

"For the wrong bloody country."

"For the country that wanted him."

"This is all beside the point," says the princess. "His latest dalliance is ill-advised and cannot continue."

Before Alistair can lose his shit, I ask, "What's so awful about me? Just out of curiosity."

"Nothing. You are perfectly ordinary in every way. You are the very epitome of unremarkable. And for someone of Alistair's pedigree, that is simply unacceptable."

"You would know all about conduct and pedigree," says Lady Helena. "I once saw you so drunk you were spinning in circles with the skirt of your ball gown held high above your head. That was a good night. We were at Kensington Palace with that bartender you were seeing on the sly... What was his name?"

Nothing from the princess.

"Ordinary how, exactly?" I press.

More sniffing from the princess. The lady needs a tissue. "Your upbringing, education, appearance, social circles... Everything about you is objectionable."

"That's enough," growls Alistair. "I've never heard such utter shite."

To which I respond, "I want to hear what she has to say."

Which is just as well since the princess shows no signs of stopping. "Not to mention how erratic your recent behavior has been. Getting tattoos and such."

"Wait a minute. How do you know about that? I haven't posted on social media since last Saturday." And then it hits me. "Huh. You have someone following me, don't you?"

"You've had someone following Lilah?" Alistair's jaw is an angry jagged line. "Are you kidding me?"

"Alistair, you are not in a position to simply do as you please," says the princess.

"Watch me."

"You actually hired someone to stalk me," I say again in surprise. "What the hell is wrong with you people?"

"A basic background check is standard protocol." The princess returns my glare with one of her own. "Alistair has a connection to the crown. Of course we had to know who you were."

I just shake my head.

Lady Helena jumps to her feet. "I am outraged—outraged, I say—that you would treat my soon-to-be daughter-in-law this way!"

Alistair's brows are pinched. "Mother…"

"My darling baby boy finally finds happiness, and this is how you behave. I can believe it of your brother. He was always a self-absorbed twat. But in all honesty, Lexi, I'd hoped for better from you."

"They're engaged?" asks the princess with no small amount of horror.

"Yes, they most certainly are, and I, for one, could not be happier. The tears of joy I wept when they told me the good news. I couldn't stop howling with happiness for hours. Hours, I say!"

Dougal makes a noise in the back of his throat. It sounds vaguely like him trying to choke down laughter.

I have nothing.

The princess turns to Alistair and demands, "Is this the truth?"

But he's busy doing the blank-expression thing again. However, if his mother wants to mess with these people…it's okay with me. They actually paid someone to follow me around and report on my doings. Paparazzi are an invasion of privacy. This, though, feels like taking it to a whole new level.

"Go on, darling." Lady Helena smiles encouragingly. "You might as well tell her."

"Right." Alistair clears his throat. "Lilah and I are… Yes… we, um…"

"We're thinking of a July wedding," I say. "Just something small and intimate."

"Absolutely no more than a few hundred of their closest family and friends." Lady Helena plays with her pearls. "And of course, an exclusive will be sold to a respectable media outlet. Photos and a tell-all interview. Merchandise will of course be on sale once we get their official website up and running. Coffee cups and tea towels and suchlike. All of good make. It wouldn't do to be stingy."

The princess falls into a nearby chair as if she might faint. Though even that is done elegantly. "He'll have my head for this."

"I'm reasonably certain that's no longer legal," says Alistair, barely hiding a smile. "But don't quote me on it."

"He was hoping you might take an interest in a distant cousin. She's quite a nice girl. A little horsey for me, but not everyone minds that."

"That's not going to happen," says Alistair.

"You don't understand. The king is finally willing to acknowledge you. So long as you agree to certain caveats, of course."

The blood drains from Lady Helena's face. "He's willing to what? What did you say?"

"You will never be in line for the throne," says the princess. "But the king is willing to acknowledge you, and you would no longer be persona non grata."

Alistair blinks repeatedly. As if he too is taken aback.

Dougal hands me a glass of ice water, and I down a mouthful. And immediately start coughing because the clear liquid is vodka. What a rookie mistake. How embarrassing. Alistair smothers a smile and rubs my back. Always nice to know someone finds me entertaining. How unfortunate that it's my new fake fiancé who might be about to dump me in favor of finally having a relationship with his father and some strange girl.

"Why now?" asks Alistair. "What's changed?"

"It's an offer that won't be repeated," says the princess, not answering his question.

Lady Helena sighs. "Lexi, he won't consider the proposal without the appropriate information. Be sensible. I didn't raise a fool."

"In front of her?" The princess gives me serious side-eye.

"Lilah knows how to keep her mouth shut. Come on. Out with it."

"I have missed you, Hel. Your directness was refreshing… up to a point." The princess turns away for a moment, staring at the sterile gray wall. "The political climate is more lenient at present."

"It has nothing to do with the current negative public opinion of him, does it?" asks Alistair.

"There's also his rumored separation from the queen consort to consider. You would make a wonderful distraction from all that, darling," says Lady Helena. "You're rather popular. The dashing Scotsman of royal descent who found success on his own terms. Embracing you now would breathe some life back into him and make him seem more human. It would also help drag the monarchy into the modern age. Something which is direly needed."

The princess's gaze is guarded. "These are all just suppositions. What's your answer?"

"Why should Alistair help you? What have any of you ever done for him?" asks Lady Helena. "Your brother pays me handsomely to keep my mouth shut and stay on my side of the Atlantic. That, however, is a business arrangement. He's yet to show his firstborn a single kindness. Given time, several great artworks, an estate or two, and a lot of jewelry, I could perhaps forgive him for hurting me. But not my child."

A line appears between Alistair's brows.

Dougal hands the princess a drink. You can be certain Her Royal Highness doesn't cough or choke. She cocks her head. "If they're engaged, where's her ring?"

"Oh. I knew I forgot something. How silly of me." Lady Helena wrestles with one of the many rings on her fingers. "Shit. It seems to be stuck. Dougal!"

"Coming," says the Scotsman. "Been a while since you've taken that one off. Let me just... Oof. There we go."

The princess gasps. "You're not giving her the Lennox diamond."

"Of course I am. It's the pride of our family. A cherished heirloom that's worth a small fortune. Here, Lilah, catch." And Lady Helena tosses the ring.

I lunge for the ring with my usual sporting finesse. But Alistair plucks it out of the air with ease. It's an obscenely large emerald-cut diamond in a platinum setting. His smile is bemused as he slides it on my finger. He stares into my eyes, and I know this is all just a joke, but it's hard not to get all up in my feelings. And those feelings have nothing to do with amusement and everything to do with him. Then he gives my fingers a squeeze and turns away, which is for the best. My ability to keep a straight face is at an all-time low. At least I can go to the grave saying I was engaged. Sort of. That's something new, unexpected, and quite daring. What I really want to know, however, is if I am about to be dumped by my friend in favor of his father.

"Thank you, Mother," he says eventually. "I couldn't have done better myself."

"I'd hope not, sweetheart. Nice to see family come in handy now and then, isn't it?" Lady Helena takes a sip of her drink and turns back to our royal guest. "Lexi, why did he send you and not one of the firm's flunkies?"

"I daresay, given the topic of conversation, he knew none of them would get past the front door," answers Her Royal Highness. "I don't know. Ask him when he calls you again tonight."

Alistair frowns at his mother. "You're talking to him that often?"

"I have been lately. The king is in a rare state of agitation. It had been a while since we butted heads. I don't think I'd heard from him since you dislocated your shoulder surfing a few years back. *Tell him there's to be no more extreme sports. I forbid it.* He truly is hilarious. But he enjoys yelling at me and I enjoy yelling at him. It's a win for everyone, really." Lady Helena frowns at her empty glass. "This conversation requires further refreshments. Sweetheart, you wouldn't happen to have a decent bottle of champagne on hand, would you?"

"No," says Alistair. "Sorry."

"Time for us to depart, then," says Lady Helena. "My place or yours, Lexi?"

The princess gets to her feet. "Yours, I suppose. But we can't be seen together. And you mustn't tell him I told you these things."

"No one's going to tattle. Do stop fussing, old girl."

They head for the door with Dougal and the security guards in tow.

As soon as they're gone, Alistair rises and paces the room. Back and forth he strides with a frown on his face. The man is obviously thinking deep thoughts.

"That was a lot," I say. "A whole wide lot."

He grunts.

Not knowing where I stand with him sucks. How has this conversation changed things? My family is important to me. The thought of not having a healthy relationship with my parents is horrible. I rub my sweaty palms on the side of my nice new black pants. "I just want you to know, whatever decision you make, you have my support."

He stops and stares at me.

"You've wanted a chance to get to know your father your whole life. This is it. It's finally here."

"What are you saying, Lilah?"

"We've only known each other a week. Not even that exactly."

"And?"

"Like the princess said, this might be your only opportunity to make peace with that side of your family. To get to know them. Losing me is obviously one of the conditions. I don't know why I bother them that badly. But it's not a big deal... We're not even really dating." With each word, my heart and hopes sink further. He's not stopping me. He's not saying anything. "Ali, you should take this chance if that's what you want to do. What I'm trying to say is, it's okay with me."

He blinks. "It's okay with you if we never see each other again?"

"I, um... Yeah. If that's what you want."

"Are you breaking up with me?"

"Were we ever really together?" I ask with a wince. "I thought that was still up for debate."

He holds out a hand and pulls me to my feet. But he doesn't take a step back, he doesn't give me any room. I am stuck between him and the sofa. "That's very self-sacrificing of you, Leannan. Throwing yourself on the sword like that so I can have a relationship with the man who has done nothing but regret my existence since the day I was born. That's when he wasn't of a mind to try and manipulate me and meddle in my life, of course."

I remain silent, not sure how to respond.

"Are you rethinking your very generous offer?" he asks.

"A little. Yes."

He nods.

I place my hands against his chest and say, "Let me rephrase all of that. Ali, what do you want to do?"

"I've already told you what I want to do in the immediate future. My thoughts on the matter haven't changed."

"Dinner and drinks. Okay." I take a deep breath. "Do you have a bottle of good champagne?"

"Several. But I bought them for you. And the last thing we need is Mother and the princess hanging around here getting pissed and reminiscing about the good old days." He leans down, putting his face close to mine. "It's the middle of the night in London, but I'll try to get a message to him. Tell him and his people to back off and leave you alone."

"The king doesn't scare me."

The edge of his mouth rises. "He does a little."

"Maybe a little," I admit. "But he's not going to stop me."

"That's my girl."

17

Alistair's bedroom is amazing. Floor-to-ceiling French doors lead out to a balcony overlooking the back garden. More of the high ceilings and gray walls like downstairs, but the effect is softened by the furniture. Both the bed and side tables are solid wooden pieces matched with another large white lounge. He obviously spends most of his time up here. There's evidence of his presence. The huge unmade bed with white linens, bedside tables piled high with books, and an empty teacup and saucer. Because of course he drinks tea. A discarded T-shirt lies on the blanket box at the foot of the bed. I definitely do not sniff it, because that would be weird and wrong. Like it's my fault the man smells divine.

He had my shopping bags brought upstairs to his walk-in closet. So many packages. But I refuse to feel guilty for spending his cash. He goaded me into going hard. He knew what he was doing. None of this, however, explains why he finds me barefoot and bewildered. Just surrounded by stuff. An overwhelming number of new things.

"I got through to his personal secretary," says Alistair, appearing in the doorway, phone in hand. Judging by the set of his jaw, his mood is set to unhappy. "Told him to call off the private investigator or else."

"Or else what?"

"I haven't quite decided," he admits. "But he seemed to take the threat seriously. I can't protect you from the paparazzi. Not really. But I won't have you being followed by a private fucking investigator."

"Thank you. Though why they would require someone to continue reporting on me if I am so boring and subpar would be nice to know."

He leans against the door frame and crosses his arms. "Lilah, what are you doing?"

"Cataloging. I organized them by color, then by outfit, and now by vibe."

"I thought you'd be getting ready for tonight."

I nod and turn back to the assortment of clothing and accessories spread across the room. "That was definitely the direction I was going in, and then…"

"Then what?"

"There are so many options. I mean, do I go with a dress? If I do, should it be short, long, or midi? And what level of fancy are we talking? Because I now own several evening gowns," I say. "Not something I thought I would ever say. One may even qualify as a ball gown."

"Hmm."

"But wait, because then there's the shoes to consider. And bags and jewelry, and the list goes on and on." I take a breath, not that it helps. "Your face is very serious, Ali. What's on your mind apart from my failure to get my act together for dinner?"

His gaze jumps to the ring on my finger and his brow furrows. Which is telling.

"Here." I wiggle the diamond off my finger. "You should put this somewhere safe."

He takes the ring and slips it into his pocket without comment. "We don't have to go out."

"Don't you want to go out?"

He just shrugs. As if it means nothing. A heck of a change in attitude.

"Talk to me."

"This is just… It's all happening rather quickly."

Not going to lie. His words hurt. But on the other hand, he has a point. It's almost a week since we met, and here I am, making myself at home. "Do you need some breathing room?"

"No," he says with no hesitation.

This is a tricky situation. I have a sneaking suspicion his abandonment issues are butting heads with his whole lone-wolf/man-of-few-words aesthetic. Usually at this point I might spiral into a one-girl pity party. But the clock is ticking. I don't have time for that shit. Not when it does me no good.

I lean against the door frame opposite him and give him my best supportive smile. "We're not really engaged. That was just some nonsense spun by your mother to mess with the princess, right?"

"Right."

"And you want me here, but you're not used to having people all up in your personal space, are you? The question is, which side is going to win?"

His lips flatline.

"We never did get around to discussing your rules for dating. You know, the ones Shane mentioned," I say. "Care to give me a brief rundown?"

"I'd prefer not."

I just wait.

He turns away for a moment. "I don't usually encourage the people I'm seeing to hang out here."

"It's more of a come-and-go situation, huh? How do you get them to leave?" I ask, curious. "What do you say?"

"Lilah…"

"Tell me."

"I don't know. I tell them I have work to do," he finally admits. "It's usually the truth."

"But you want me here because you're worried I'll do something stupid. Like go swimming with sharks or tap-dance on the highway."

"Yes," he says in a low and reluctant voice. "But it's more than that."

"Is it?"

He licks his lips and sighs. "You know I enjoy your company, Leannan. Where are you going with this?"

"Kind of wondering if you're going to turn tail and run."

"That's not going to happen."

"Guess we'll see," I say. "How often do people try to use you in the hope of getting close to your father or some such bullshit?"

"Often enough."

"Protecting yourself makes sense. Controlling your little corner of the world. It's just self-preservation."

"I'll ask again, where are you going with this?"

"Just thinking out loud," I say. "Your anxieties and my insecurities are bound to keep things interesting between us, that's for sure. But back to the topic of your previous relationships. So, you've actually dated people for months or even years at a time while maintaining these strict boundaries?"

He huffs out a "Yes."

"No hanging out at your house and no meeting your friends for the first month?"

A stiff nod is the only response.

"They have their lives, and you have yours. It all sounds very... What's the word I'm looking for?"

He offers nothing.

"Neat. Contained. *Cautious*." I cover the short distance between us. The polish on his plain black oxford business shoes is flawless. His hands are stuffed in his pants pockets, and his face is back to the careful blank. His default setting. He hides from the world behind that handsome face. You might think he feels nothing at all. The only tell is the thin line of his lips. And the sight of it fucking thrills me. "None of those things are really me. At least, not these days."

He grunts.

"I kind of feel like you've been on at least part of that journey with me. But now I wonder if we've finally hit a wall now that I've made myself at home. Because you do not look comfortable."

A muscle in his perfect jawline pops. "It's not a problem."

"Are you sure you don't want to tell me you have work to do?"

"Lilah—"

"What's going to happen when I really start stepping on your toes? That's what I'm worrying about. And between you and me, it's bound to happen sooner or later. What do you think?" I ask, getting all up in his face. "Should I just go ahead and do it and see what happens? Put us both out of our misery?"

The man is whip-fast when he moves. Hands fist in my hair and his mouth slams down on mine. This is absolutely what I want. No holding back. I've finally shredded his control, and it's a beautiful thing. His tongue in my mouth as he kisses me senseless. My fingers fumbling over the buttons of his shirt. There's no teasing in him now. No clever talk or power play. The hem of my shirt is ripped out of the waistband of my pants. Then he tears the two sides of my top apart caveman style, buttons spilling across the floor.

His own shirt is given similar rough treatment. Just wrenched off over his head. How I love touching him, feeling the heat of his smooth skin. My palms travel up and over his thick shoulders. I am an endorphin-soaked mess. And all the while, he's moving us in the direction of the bed. He toes off his shoes, tears off his socks, and dismisses his pants in short fashion. *Holy shit*. The sight of him in nothing but a pair of black boxer briefs is sublime. And I am not above staring at the outline of his cock. While I'm lost in wonder, he's dealing with my pants, and we're both in our underwear in no time. He's already seen me in lingerie. Though the way he stops to appreciate the sight is sweet. He slowly trails his fingers over the lace edging of my bra. He caresses the curve of my stomach and the thickness of my thighs. I couldn't be more seduced by the man.

"On the bed," he says, his voice rough.

There's something hypnotizing about his dark eyes. His pupils are dilated and his focus on me complete. I do as I'm asked and he follows, looming over me like a predator. My back hits the mattress and he hooks a finger on either side of my nice new panties. Going, going, gone. I don't recall anyone stopping and staring at my sex in this manner. But Alistair plays by his own rules. His cheekbones stand out in stark relief, and the hunger in his eyes is… *Shit.* I don't know. My mind is mush.

Oral is often hit-and-miss for me. Josh had an attention span of less than a minute. And that's being generous. The one before him would only go down on special occasions. You can imagine how upset I was when we broke up mere days before my birthday. The sad truth is, in my experience, a sex toy is generally more reliable than a man. I hate to be harsh, but—

Teeth deliver a sting to my mound. Alistair bites me just hard enough to ensure he has my full fucking attention. There is no easing into things. No slow getting to know you and your private parts. He licks and sucks and bites as he pleases. With an arm wrapped around each thigh, he holds my legs wide open. He suckles on my labia and nibbles on my inner thigh. His breath warms me as he runs his tongue back and forth along my seam. No part of me is neglected. From drawing circles around my clit with the tip of his tongue to teasing my back entrance. I swear, when he groans, it goes right through me. Same with his snarl. The noises he makes light me up from inside.

Each move he makes amps me higher and higher. So much pressure low in my body, gathering at the base of my spine. When he settles in to suck on my clit, it's all over. The orgasm crashes into me like a supernova. I am darkness and stardust, scattered throughout space and time. At least, that's what it feels like when he blows my damn mind.

While I catch my breath, he wipes off his mouth, retrieves a condom from the bedside drawer, and loses the boxer briefs. His dick is sizable. A little longer than average length and a bit thicker too. On goes the protection as his gaze wanders over the flush that's coloring my neck and chest.

"I like that shade," he says. "Why is your bra still on?"

I have removed brassieres daily since the age of twelve. Nearly twenty years' worth of dealing with hooks and straps. But sex addled as I am, my fingers blunder about. The man's mouth is dangerous, his tongue a hazard, and as for those teeth… There are no words. I almost high-five myself when I finally manage to remove the damn thing.

All the while he watches with amusement. "Well done, Leannan."

"Shut up."

"Such language." He crawls up my body, taking a breast in hand and sucking on the nipple. "And not even a thank-you. Your manners are appalling. See if I eat your sweet cunt again."

"I take it back and thank you."

"Hmm." He gives the same attention to the other breast. "To be honest, I had my fingers crossed. I will definitely eat you again soon. Now be a good girl and wrap your legs around me."

Being no fool, the man doesn't need to ask me twice. What he does do is take his dick in hand and line it up with my opening. Then his hips kick, and with one hard thrust, he's buried inside of me. Such an overwhelming feeling of full-ness. I gasp and he moans. The way he stretches me leaves room for nothing else. No thoughts. No worries. There is only him and me and now. My fingers knot in his hair and this is just a whole lot of him. His heat and scent and everything. It would be safe to say the "great sex" thing can be crossed off the wish list.

Teeth scrape over the soft skin of my neck and his whispered breath warms my ear. "We're definitely missing dinner. Do you mind?"

"No."

"Good."

And with that, he proceeds to fuck me into the bed. My back must leave a permanent outline in the mattress. His hands hold me tight as he pumps into me fast and hard. First with a firm grip on my thigh, before inching all the way up to encircle my throat. How he gives me just enough pressure. A hint of a threat. A tease of control. He stares at me, and I stare back at him. Nothing else matters. We are one feverish sweaty mess. My hips rise to meet him, and my legs stay locked around him. The scent of sex fills the room. He swivels his hips and alters his angle, watching me all the while. When my mouth pops open, he gives me a manic grin. And he proceeds to hit the same spot over and over.

I rarely come once, let alone twice in a day, with hope for a third. But with his dick moving deep inside of me, stroking everything good and right, sensation spirals through me. The only things I can hear are the slap of skin against skin and the blood beating behind my ears. His hand tightens around my throat and it's too much. The orgasm slams into me, making me gasp. My back bows and my limbs lock, holding him to me. Like I might never let him go. His hips buck against me. Then he buries himself deep and comes with a groan.

There's this perfect moment. An instance when we're one. Our hearts beat in time the same as our breaths. Then he carefully draws himself free and collapses at my side. The rise and fall of his chest are the only signs of life. I've never seen him so replete. He just seems serene for once.

He opens one eyelid and looks me over. "Sex hair becomes you, Leannan."

"Thanks."

"You're very welcome." The eyelid closes. "You haven't changed your mind about dinner, have you?"

"No. Though you will have to feed me at some stage."

"We can order whatever whenever you like. I'm extremely easygoing after great sex."

"Great sex. You just had to slip that in there, didn't you?" I stare at the ceiling, thinking deep thoughts. "Ali?"

"Hmm?"

"How many times in a night would you say you can do that?"

"Do what?"

For some reason, I can't get the words past my lips. Maybe it's because I'm naked. Maybe it's because we just had sex. I don't know. However, the only thing that matters right now is my hormones and getting more of him.

Both eyes open and his head turns my way. "Are you asking how many times in one night I can fuck you?"

I nod.

He smiles. "Why don't we find out?"

Saturday

Something wakes me. No idea what. Alistair is in the big spoon position, meaning he has a face full of my hair. I, on the other hand, have his morning boner poking into my lower back. Like that morning at the hotel. Only this time it's not an accident, and we're both as naked as the day we were born. My smile is satiated. A great word to be using the morning after. All in all, the world this morning feels…peaceful.

Which is damn nice. There is nowhere else I would rather be. Not even the Royal Portuguese Cabinet of Reading in Brazil and that library looks amazing. This might just be the best Saturday ever.

The only possible problem with this morning is my view of my new Hermès watch ticking away on my wrist. Its second hand makes precise motions around and around. Marking the minutes of my life slipping away. And this could be my almost last day on Earth. It's like there's a waiting pit of doom and gloom inside me. A yawning abyss of fear and misery.

No. I refuse to think about that. Not today. Or not right now, at least.

"Go back to sleep," Alistair mumbles in my ear. Then he grumbles something else I can't make out.

I shuffle about and roll onto my back instead. All the better to see him and ignore my watch. He really is ridiculously attractive. And rich. Though I choose not to hold that against him. It's his heart that gets me—so guarded and yet so giving. Feeling so much about someone so quickly should make me worry. There's a lot on the line. More of me is invested in him and making this work than is safe. But I couldn't stop now if I tried. My heart is all sorts of hung up on him, and it's much too late to gird my loins. That country was successfully conquered and then some.

So I happy sigh and stare at him some more. On the off chance my demise is at hand, at least we had this time together. No one can take these memories of waking up beside Alistair Lennox after a wonderful night. And not even the cloudy day could diminish my general feeling of joy.

Speaking of which, the likelihood of my dying sooner rather than later has now increased. Given the past day's events and all.

I can no longer award the soulmate prediction only half a point due to us meeting. There are now feelings to be considered. This takes the prophecy tally up to a solid three-quarters. I still don't know if we're soulmates. But what even is a soulmate, really?

At any rate, there's now a 3.5 or 70 percent chance of me dying. Which sucks. I need to make my last days count. Go out with a bang. Or more banging. Which works for me.

He opens one eye and says, "What are you doing?"

"Being present and appreciating the moment."

"Mmm."

"And thinking."

"About what?" he asks with a yawn.

"I just want you to know that there doesn't need to be any hasty revisiting of people's feelings. I am perfectly happy as things are now."

Lines fill his forehead. "We're getting straight into it, are we? Okay. Let me ask you, Lilah, do you see dating as a type of commitment?"

"Did we actually get around to confirming the dating thing?"

"Aye."

I frown in confusion. "When?"

"Last night."

"So you saw it as just a sort of bang-it-out situation?"

"Bang it out. Please." He sniffs. "I wooed you properly. Made an eloquent speech on the subject and all."

"Oh. That sounds nice. Remind me again when you did that?"

"Let me think." He scratches his stubble. "It was around two p.m. After the third time. If you slept through it, that's on you. I just assumed you were overjoyed to be my significant other but too overcome with emotion to respond."

"Sounds plausible."

He gives me a flash of a smile. "That's what I thought. So there's no need for us to talk about our feelings again. It's all sorted."

"I'm significant, huh?"

"Damn right you are."

"That's nice to hear."

"I have to admit, I was a little worried you might have changed your mind. That you might have decided you'd had your fill of this circus after yesterday. You know, it's still not too late. Though I'd be very hurt, Leannan," he says. "You might have noticed I've grown somewhat fond of you."

Whoa. The warmth that fills my chest at his words.

A buzzing noise comes from the bedside table. "Ugh. Is that my phone?"

"No. Mine."

"Are you going to answer it?"

"Not yet," he says, stretching his neck. Then he stops and stares at me. "You're still worried about something. What's wrong?"

"Nothing."

"Are you sure about that?"

"I'm really glad we got this time together. It means a lot to me."

His gaze narrows and he scowls. "You're thinking about that damn death prediction again."

"It's hard not to. Seeing the lotto money appear in my account yesterday makes it more real somehow. But how many people win the lotto each year? Hundreds?"

"Thousands."

"Thousands." I cover the worry lines on my forehead with the palm of my hand. Like it helps. "Right."

"Please hear me when I say that fucking prediction isn't real. You're not dying on me anytime soon. It's rude and unnecessary and I won't allow it," he declares. "I think it's time I had a talk with this Great Witch Willa face-to-face. Get this sorted out once and for all."

"You want to meet Good Witch Willow?"

"Yes. As soon as possible." His cell buzzes again. With a groan, Alistair stretches to reach for his cell, and the sheet slides down. And down some more. He really is incredibly distracting. I don't mean to objectify the man, but oh well. With a frown at the screen he says, "What the fuck?"

"What the fuck, what?"

"Just a minute."

I wait while he focuses on sliding his finger across the screen. He has such elegant hands. Both strong and dexterous. As he showed me time and again last night. There's every chance my thoughts regarding this man are going to be purely physical and in the gutter for the next few days to come.

"My apologies, but I'm going to have to retract that last bit," he finally announces. "It seems it is in fact too late for you to change your mind about us. There's a horde of paparazzi and news vans at the gate. I'm sorry, Lilah. But news of our fake nuptials has been leaked."

My eyes all but fall out of my head. "The world thinks we're engaged?"

"Yes."

"The whole wide world?"

He just nods.

"Shit," I say. "Why? How?"

"That's what I plan on finding out." His cell buzzes and his gaze jumps to the screen. His lips thin as he puts the call on speaker. "Mother, what did you do?"

"How hurtful. I didn't do anything, darling," she says. "Unless you're talking about the small fire at your grandfather's hunting lodge that time. Someone really should have told me that serving flammable cocktails at my sweet sixteen was a bad idea. But it's not like they weren't able to rebuild. Still. You wouldn't believe how Daddy carried on about it. Of course, Mummy didn't care, but—"

"Mother, I'm not talking about that."

"No? Oh, no. Of course not. You're talking about today's big news—your engagement! So exciting, my sweet boy. I see the news is everywhere!"

"Did you have anything to do with that?"

"No."

"Are you sure about that?"

Lady Helena's sigh is epic. "I suppose I *did* tell the princess in the first place. But how was I to know she'd tell them and they'd decide to leak it to the press? Though of course I knew she'd report back to them. Any idiot would know that. But telling reporters…how déclassé. My point is, I'm a mostly innocent party in all of this!"

"It definitely wasn't you that told the media?"

"No. Absolutely not."

"Why would the palace leak it?" I ask. "What do they hope to gain?"

"Good question, sweetie," says Her Ladyship. "As I was

opening the second magnum of champagne last night, the princess happened to mention that the heir apparent is less than happy with his new fiancée. In fact, she said he's close to calling the whole thing off. You can imagine the commotion such an announcement would cause. Which explains why the king has been calling me to work off some stress."

"They're using us to distract the media?" asks Alistair.

"I imagine the press were about to run a report the crown didn't like. So they offered up you two instead. It's not the first time we've lost control of the narrative," says Her Lady-ship. "But does it necessarily have to be a bad thing? Does it really matter if people know you're engaged?"

Which is when I join in on the frowning. "But we're not engaged."

"Aren't you?"

"Yes. I mean, no. I mean... Oh, God, I don't know." I drop my voice to a whisper. "Make her stop, Ali. I love your mother, I really do. But it's too early in the morning for this. The world thinks we're getting married, and I haven't even had coffee yet. Let alone talked to my parents."

"It's not as if you haven't always yearned for some stability, my darling boy," continues Her Ladyship, blissfully unaware. "And any fool can see you have feelings for each other."

Alistair squeezes his eyelids shut tight and shakes his head. As if he's in actual pain. "Mother. No."

"You two are so sweet together and you've already got the ring. And you can be certain I wouldn't hand over the Len-nox diamond to just anyone. As I told the princess yesterday, it's a treasured family heirloom."

"You lost it for most of the early 2000s."

"But I found it again. That's what's important."

Her son does not look convinced.

"You and Lilah make such a charming couple. Odds are you were bound to take the leap sooner or later, don't you think? And I don't mean to be harsh, but you're not getting any younger, darling. It takes a certain amount of energy to run around after children, and to make them in the first place," she says with much raunch. "Just think about it... You could have the ceremony and reception here at the beach. The house is big enough for a few hundred guests at least."

"I'm hanging up now."

"But, darling—"

I reach for my cell. Things have calmed down since I turned off notifications. But I still have a bunch of texts, several from Rebecca.

THIS IS YOUR MAID OF HONOR TEXTING. Are you really getting married?

Definitely not getting married, I reply. Long story. TTYL

There are also many messages from my mother, whose name starts flashing on my screen as the cell vibrates again.

"Mom?"

"How could you not tell me you were engaged?"

"Oh."

"*Oh.* Is that all you have to say? I had to find out about it from Otto at the bakery on my morning walk."

"Otto from the bakery told you Alistair and I were getting married?"

"And Minh and Jackie across the road. They were out watering their garden!" exclaims Mom. "Nadine yelled out something as she rode past on her moped, but she was going too fast for me to hear. The point is, everybody knew except me!"

"That's really only three people that we can be sure of. Not exactly everybody."

"Lilah!"

I wince at the ringing in my ear. Mom always did have a great set of lungs on her. "Um. Yes, Mom. You're upset. But the thing is—"

"I know we've had our issues over the years, but this is very disappointing, not to mention reckless behavior. You've barely known him a week. How could you be so foolish?"

"I know. But if you'd just listen—"

"You've hurt your father's feelings."

"My feelings are fine," my father calls out in the background.

Oh my God. "Mom, please let me explain."

"We haven't even met this man."

"May I?" Alistair holds out a hand. Hell yes, he can take the call if he wants. He clears his throat and says, "Ma'am, this is...Yes...If I could just...I would always try to be worthy of your daughter, of course, but...Sorry...Yes...I understand and...Hello?"

I accept the phone back without comment.

"We're expected for lunch at one," he says. "Probably best not to be late."

"Okay."

"She hung up on me," he says in surprise. "I can't remember the last time someone hung up on me."

"It would seem my mother is experiencing a lot of big feelings right now. Try not to take it personally."

"She didn't even give me a chance to explain. To tell her the engagement isn't real."

"I'm not entirely sure that would have stopped the yelling.

But never mind. We'll break it to her at lunch." And then something occurs to me. "How do we even get out of here without a swarm of media following us?"

His smile is almost childlike with glee. "Don't worry. I have a plan."

18

Saturday

"I'm not sure this is a good idea," I say, staring at Good Witch Willow's apartment door.

Alistair just picks another leaf out of my hair. This is my week for incorporating random greenery in my hairdos, apparently. His plan for escaping the media worked and then some. We made it all the way downtown without a single paparazzo on our tail. It turns out there's a hidden wooden door in the hedge behind his house. Very *Secret Garden*. The neighboring property houses a rustic (but sprawling) wood cabin, with the biggest hot tub in creation, owned by a retired music producer. He was good friends with the original owner of Alistair's house. They used to play cards several nights a week while taking turns working their way through each other's wine cellar, hence the gate. But now it provides a discreet exit for either party.

Kevin, the previously mentioned music producer, didn't seem surprised to find us standing on his back deck this morning, disheveled from fighting the overgrown shrubbery. He just tossed Alistair the keys to a vintage cherry-red Cadillac with a nod.

Now here we are. All the way up in the old elevator, Alistair was agitated. The toe of his boot wouldn't stop tap-tap-tapping. But now he's back to his usual take-charge self. "It's going to be fine. I contacted Willow through her website, and she agreed to see us. We're just going to have a little talk."

"That's the first time you've gotten her name right. How much is she charging you for this emergency witching session?"

"It doesn't matter. Your peace of mind is worth it."

"What exactly are you going to ask her?" I say. "Just out of curiosity..."

He gives me a wink and knocks on the door.

As pleasant as the idea of him magically sorting all of this out is, I don't see him succeeding. Though his determination to try is admirable. Heartwarming.

Willow opens the door wearing a patchwork silk robe, and her long silver hair is flowing down her back. "If it isn't bonny Prince Charming."

"Not really a prince," says Alistair smoothly. "It's a pleasure to meet you."

Willow snorts. "Get that smile off your face. Don't bother to lie to me, boy. Come in before my neighbors get nosy."

Willow is a maximalist. Her apartment is small and colorful and packed to the ceiling with crystals and dried flowers, old black-and-white photos and books, ceramic animals, and an upright piano. It's the sort of space you could spend a day just poking around, never knowing what you might find.

"This is amazing," I say in awe.

Willow watches me with a faint frown. "Thank you, Lilah. I don't know that it's good to see you again."

"Right back at you, Willow."

"Where do we start?" Alistair asks, all business.

"You could pay me," she says. "That's one way to break the ice."

Out of his jeans pocket comes a wad of money. "I believe you said the fee for an emergency reading was one thousand dollars."

"Yes. For you, it is." Willow doesn't count the cash. Just slips it into the pocket of her robe and takes a seat at a small round wooden table. "Go on, then. The clock is ticking. Ask your questions."

"I can ask whatever I want?"

"Within reason."

"How did you get into this?" Alistair sits opposite her, the picture of cool, calm, and confident. As if he's interviewing Willow or something. "Being a witch?"

"That's what you want to ask?"

"I'm interested in your story. I'd also like to know what credentials you have exactly to tell people they're about to die."

"Hmm. I inherited the gift from my grandmother. She had a talent for knowing things."

"It skipped a generation."

Willow just nods.

"What sort of things could she predict?"

"If the biscuits would burn or when her neighbor would go into labor or if her father was going to lose his job." Willow shrugs. "Things of a domestic nature mostly, since that was her world. Messages can be both big and small."

"And yourself?"

"The times had changed. I grew up in the city and often traveled with my mother. So the things I saw were of a different nature." And that is all she says.

"At about what age did it start?" asks Alistair.

"With the onset of puberty."

"Seeing the future at such a young age must have been terrifying."

"There were often times when I didn't understand the message. As a child, I simply lacked the maturity or the knowledge." Willow gives him a long look. "You learn to keep quiet after scaring and alienating people. Growing up is hard. However, being alone and misunderstood is its own special sort of hell. As you well know."

He ignores her last remark and asks, "How did you handle it?"

"I was fortunate—I had my gran. But knowing things isn't always nice, as your fiancée can attest to."

"Talking of my fiancée, how do I save her?"

"Her heart will stop soon," says Willow. "There's no getting around that."

I freeze in my seat as if my heart has stopped already. Hearing it said out loud in this manner is a whole new world of awfulness. Not even him referring to me as his fiancée can soften the blow. Though I sure like the sound of those words coming from his lips. I know it's nonsense, but still. Why not enjoy it?

"Are you sure you can't sell us a protection spell or something?" he asks.

"I can sell you as many protection spells as you like. There are also amulets, potions, and talismans I could recommend. If you like, for another thousand dollars, I could pull out my cauldron and wand and get busy," she says. "But the fact is, none of these things can fight fate."

"So they're pointless."

"Everyone has to die someday," says Willow in a gentler tone of voice.

"Not her," insists Alistair in a stern voice. "Not right now."

Willow sighs.

"How often are you wrong?" he asks, his head cocked. "Things like Lilah's idiot of an ex cheating on her and missing out on the promotion seem pretty standard life events. Horrible, but nothing out of the ordinary. They could happen to just about anyone at one time or another. Though the lotto numbers were impressive."

"Thanks," says Willow dryly, flicking her silver hair over her shoulder.

"As for her and me meeting...it's a hell of a coincidence. But you must guess incorrectly sometimes. Nobody's right all the time, are they?"

"But I'm not guessing."

"Let's agree to disagree."

Willow's gaze moves to me. "Look at you, standing over there, quiet as can be. Are you going to let him do all the talking, Lilah? Is that who you are now?"

"*No.* I'm standing over here and staying out of it because I feel like we said everything we needed to the other day in the garden."

"True enough."

"But if I think of anything new, I'll be sure to ask."

"Glad to see you haven't lost your voice. It happens so often to women in relationships with, shall we say, alpha types?" Willow's answering smile is amused as she turns back to Alistair. "So, Prince Not-So-Charming, you want me to prove myself?"

Alistair's gaze is arctic. "If it wouldn't be too much trouble…"

"Not at all. Lay your hands on the table." Willow shifts in her chair, getting closer. "Palms up."

"You're going to perform some palmistry?"

"If you shut up long enough to let me."

Alistair closes his mouth, though his expression remains conflicted. Half amused and half worried. Like he can't quite believe this is happening. As if he hates how he's not in control of the situation. How exactly had his choices in life led him here? And that makes two of us. He flinches when Willow's hands touch his. Then he falls back on his usual frown, the one he definitely got from his father.

"No surprise," says Good Witch Willow. "You're a fire sign. That means you're confident, ambitious, and passionate. But you can also be an asshole…thoughtless and tactless and so on. You might want to watch out for such behaviors."

"That doesn't sound like me at all," says Alistair, giving me a brief smile. "What do you think, Leannan?"

I smile back.

"Your heart line is broken. Life hasn't always been easy for you, has it?" Willow peers at him from above her glasses. "They shouldn't have locked you in that cupboard. Children can be unspeakably cruel."

Alistair's lips part, but no words come out. And the emotion in his eyes isn't one I've seen before. Not on him.

"And you were just a wee little thing. You were in there for hours, scared and alone. Nothing but the rank stench of old sporting gear to keep you company."

"How do you know about that?" he asks, each word deliberate. As if he's forcing them out, shoving each and every one past his clenched teeth. "I've never discussed it with anyone."

"As I mentioned, I have gifts, Your Highness. An image appears in my head accompanied by feelings. Emotions that are not my own."

Alistair swallows. "Keep going."

"Quite an interesting fate line. Being born into those two families wasn't helpful to your peace of mind or general happiness. But you've done your best to stay out of trouble. Within reason." Willow glances at me. "Shall we jump to the juicy stuff?"

I am now throttling the strap of my purse. And it's Gucci. "Sure."

Willow snorts. "Let's see… Alistair, you'll marry once and have one child."

No idea where the weird choking noise comes from. It couldn't possibly have been me. But it definitely needs to never happen again, please and thank you. Because if I am about to shuffle off this mortal coil, then of course I want him to be happy. After he mourns me for a suitable period. Say a decade or so. Keeping a small shrine dedication to me in his bedroom for the rest of his life is also not out of the question.

Alistair's frown intensifies, the little line between his brows deepening. He does not, however, look my way. He's lost in his thoughts.

"Your career will continue to be successful. No financial woes for you. But watch out for your left knee. The one you hurt in the service. Might be best to swap running for some lower-impact sport like swimming now that you're getting older," says Willow, peering at the air around Alistair's head. Guess she's reading his aura or something.

"You could have gotten that off Wikipedia."

"Could I? Hmm. What else is there," she muses. "Oh. I don't much like the look of this. You're not averse to holding a grudge, are you? But, Alistair, you're wrong about your mother, and you need to let that old bitterness go before she's gone and it's too late."

"I don't know what you mean," says Alistair in a tone both flat and unfriendly.

"Yes, you do. As you said before, we all make mistakes, and you've made one with her. Be adult enough to admit to it."

"Is Lady Helena going to die soon?" I ask nervously.

Alistair just shakes his head.

"It's a little while off yet." Willow sits back in her seat. "But she's more the type to be here for a good time rather than a long time, isn't she?"

It's a valid point.

"How much?" asks Alistair in a flat, unfriendly tone.

Willow turns back to him. "How much what?"

"How much money to tell Lilah it's all bullshit and she's not going to die?"

Willow just sighs. "Not everything is for sale."

"You're a charlatan," continues Alistair. "Just another fraudster conning people out of cash. I've seen plenty of your type over the years."

"I understand that you're scared. But that's no excuse to be rude. However, the main fault in your accusation is I just refused more of your money, didn't I? How do you explain that, boyo?"

"Enough. You won't help Lilah is what you're saying." Alistair pushes back his chair in a rush and gets to his feet. "You won't admit that this is all rubbish and she's going to be perfectly fucking fine. Even though you know this is hurting her."

"It would be nice, wouldn't it? If I said those things and pacified you both?" asks Willow. "But I won't tell pretty lies for any amount of money, Your Highness. And I cannot help your fiancée."

Alistair grabs my hand and heads for the door. "We're done here."

Now we're back out in the hallway waiting for the elevator. Alistair's hackles have been well and truly raised. It's not like I haven't seen him upset before. But this is something else. He keeps a tight hold of my hand, but stares straight ahead. The bell dings and the elevator doors slide open. It's a small and battered space. At a guess, the building is about a hundred years old and has seen better days. There's scratched wood paneling and a mirrored ceiling. And the vibe inside the box is not good. He punches the button for the ground floor.

"Hey," I say, putting my hand on his chest. "I appreciate you trying to help. But, Ali, this might be the sort of situation where we just have to wait and see."

He stares down at me unhappily. "I don't like waiting and I don't like you worrying."

"You can't fix everything. You can't control it either."

A grunt.

"Everything will be fine," I say, even though I don't particularly believe it.

"I hate seeing you upset."

"I appreciate that. But being with you makes things better."

"Even though your name and face are splashed over every fucking gossip site in the world again?"

A grinding noise precedes the elevator coming to a stop.

Somewhere between the second and third floor. Then the overhead light flickers and dims. His hold on my hand instantly ramps up to bone grinding, and I let out a yelp.

"Shit." He releases my hand with a panicked face. "I'm so sorry, Leannan. Are you all right?"

I carefully flex my fingers. "It's okay. All good."

But the angst doesn't disappear from his eyes. His harried gaze sweeps the control panel, and he pushes the button to call for help. And he just keeps pressing that sucker as if it's his job. The accompanying ringing noise is deafening. No one in the building could be unaware of our situation. Which is when I remember what Willow said about him being locked in the cupboard.

"Alistair, look at me," I say. "Someone will be getting help."

His hand falls back to his side without comment. Both sets of fingers curl into fists.

"You really don't like small spaces, huh?"

"No."

"Guess it goes back to when you were a child. But we'll be out of here soon," I say. "An old building like this, they're probably used to it stopping and starting all the time."

His nod is more a jerk of the chin than anything else.

"Do breathing exercises work or—"

"No."

"Okay. Can you tell me what might help?"

He says nothing. Nor does he meet my eyes. There's a general air of misery about him, and I desperately want to make it all better. *Shit.* He wouldn't even be in this situation if it weren't for me. Though he is also an adult who made his own choices. But yeah.

"You know, plenty of people have phobias," I say. "It's not a moral failing. No one is asking you to be perfect."

His laughter is wholly without humor.

"Let me amend that to no one who matters."

A muscle jumps in his jaw. "You can just imagine what the fucking media would make of this if they knew. That I lose my mind over something as basic as a fucking elevator. I should have outgrown it by now."

"Who said our brains made sense and do what we want? Because that is a lie. Big. Huge. Just an enormous fucking fabrication."

"Is that so?" He gives me a glance. "I don't like being vulnerable."

"How can I take your mind off this?"

"It's fine. I'm fine."

"Damn right you are. Have you seen your ass?" I ask with a smile. "Because I was watching when you got out of bed this morning and whoa. The thirst is real."

"Thanks."

"You're very welcome."

The air inside the elevator has warmed some. It is a seriously small space. I don't even have an issue with being confined, and I am not loving this. Not even a little. I stare up at my hazy reflection in the mirrored ceiling.

"Have you ever thought about putting a mirror above your bed?" I ask. "Just a thought."

He too looks up, and the rigid set of his shoulders eases at the distraction. "I can almost see down the front of your top."

"Can you?"

"You really do have the most amazing breasts."

"Bountiful cleavage is my burden in life."

"It's one I'm happy to help you with whenever you like." A corner of his mouth twitches. Like he almost had a happy thought, but not quite. "Though it's more of a gift you've got, when you think about it. And I do think about your tits often."

"You say the sweetest things. And you do have decent-sized hands."

"They're at your disposal."

I smile at him, but he hesitates. His gaze returns to the elevator walls and doors. All is still. There's no sign or sound of our rescue and his fists are opening and closing, opening and closing.

He might be used to handling everything himself. He's had to from a young age. What with boarding schools and news of his parentage and the general chaos that is his life at times. That he didn't get to go home at the end of the school day must have sucked. I know it's life for a lot of children, to be away from their family. But still. He doesn't have to handle it all alone now, at least.

"Ali, have you ever had sex in an elevator?"

His nervous gaze jumps to me. "They're not really the kind of place I associate with good things."

"It's just that if my cleavage managed to distract you for a minute…"

"That's a kind offer, Leannan. But as much as I enjoy getting you off, I don't know that now is the right time."

"I was thinking more of a me-getting-you-off type of situation," I clarify. "What if I attempted to get you in the mood? Would that be okay with you? Or not so much?"

He thinks it over for a moment. "It would be churlish of me not to at least let you try. Especially since you seem to have your heart set on the idea."

"That's kind of you, considering it's the summation of all my hopes and dreams."

"Hmm. I thought as much." His hands haven't stopped the curling-into-fists thing. But they have slowed down. A promising sight. "Are you sure, Lilah?"

"I can't see a security camera in here. Can you?"

"No. It's an old building."

I drop to my knees with all due decorum and set my purse aside. Thank goodness I'm wearing denim, though the elevator floor doesn't seem dirty. Some things are definitely more important than getting dust on your clothes. Alistair's eyes darken as he watches me undo his belt before moving on to the button and zipper of his jeans. Navy boxer briefs wait beneath. There's something about revealing the metaphorical soft underbelly. His has a dark trail of hair leading down to where I want to go. Guess a distraction is good because his cock is already growing hard. I slide his underwear and jeans down to midthigh, getting them out of the way. It hits me how lucky I am that I get to be this close to him. To be the one who shares these intimacies with him.

"I trust you," he says quietly. Though he seems to be talking to himself more than me.

His breath hitches when I take hold of him in a firm grip. Holding his cock aside, I press my lips against his torso. Soft skin and firm body beneath. The scent of soap and him. It makes my mouth water. I could breathe him in forever, no questions asked. And the man is no longer fixated on the walls. He watches my every move with absolute focus. Strange how things take on different meanings with different people. Sex seemed more transactional with Josh. But with Alistair it's like love in motion.

Wait. Did I just use the *L* word? Because it's way too soon to be throwing that around. Affection or tenderness or adoration… they all work great. There's no need to get carried away.

"What's wrong?" he asks, watching me with a worried gaze.

"Nothing. Absolutely nothing."

"Are you sure?"

The best way to soothe him is soft and easy. At least to start. I trace the tip of my tongue up the underside of his shaft, teasing the raised veins and velvet skin. Touching and smelling and tasting him is a treat to be savored. In an ideal world, I would never take my hands off him. We would always be within reach of each other. And these thoughts are edging dangerously close to the *L*-word territory again. I'm usually so sensible. Sort of. My heart and mind need to calm the heck down.

Taking the head of his cock into my mouth distracts us both. The salt and musk and heat of him. He widens his stance and lets me have my way. I suck on him hard before teasing the crown with my tongue. My right hand massages his balls while my left holds him steady. Firm stroking motions with my fingers. I really give this blow job my all, a 110 percent commitment to the cause. Nothing matters but him. He makes a noise in the back of his throat, and I take him as deep as possible. Deep enough to make my eyes water. My lips stretch wide around his thick shaft, and his hands find my hair. Which is a much better way to keep them occupied than his previous anxiety.

I suck and stroke my heart out. The way he swells against my tongue is… I don't know. It's good and satisfying and *yeah*. This man can have my mouth when he wants it, and I know he will give back in kind.

"Leannan," he groans. "Look at you, on your knees for me. Such a good girl and such a clever fucking mouth."

My hands creep around to his ass and my nails dig in just a little. His hips flex, and his hands tighten in my hair. Every nerve ending in my scalp wakes up at the pinch of pain. Which is nice. And he can pretend he's in control all he likes, but I'm the one giving him this. We could be anywhere now. He doesn't care. Or doesn't seem to mind. His hips rock, pushing his dick deeper, and his eyelids slam shut. Only to open a moment later in panic. "Lilah. Shit. I'm going to come."

Like that wasn't the point of the exercise. When he tries to withdraw from my mouth, my nails dig into his ass cheeks. Guess the message is received. Because he comes with an animalistic growl. One I would pay good money to hear on the regular. I swallow over and over. How his face goes slack as his head falls back. A moment of pure peace. In the long term, oral sex is no replacement for therapy. But it works just fine for the here and now.

His chest continues to rise and fall with swift motions. I place a parting kiss on his still-half-hard cock and put his clothing back in place. Without a word, he watches me grab the water bottle out of my bag and take a drink. I can't read the look in his eyes. Then the overhead light flickers, a grinding sound shakes the elevator, and we resume our descent to the ground floor. Alistair's jaw is set in place once more, but he doesn't seem as wired as before.

He offers me his hand and helps me to my feet just in time for the doors to open. We don't waste any time stepping into the foyer, where a man is waiting. He's older, has a shaved head and a hefty ring of keys. At the sight of us, he nods once before wandering off down a back hallway. The ring of keys jangles in his hand the whole way.

"I think we should go," I say in a low voice.

"Yes." Alistair straightens his clothes. "That seems like an excellent idea. And if we ever come back here, let's take the stairs."

I take a step in the direction of the front door.

He grabs my elbow and steps closer. "One thing first."

"What?"

His hand slides around the back of my neck and his mouth meets mine and he's kissing me. Using his tongue and taking me over. A rush of hormones hits my bloodstream, but it's more than that. It's the heat in my heart as well. The passion between us and how he shows me. What he's feeling and thinking and everything.

He breaks the kiss and presses the pad of his thumb to the side of my mouth. "I mucked up your lipstick."

"I don't care."

The smile he gives me is beautiful. "Thank you for coming to my rescue, Lilah."

"Anytime."

19

Saturday

My father stands waiting in the driveway to usher us straight into the garage. We're still without the media on our tail, and it would be handy to have the Cadillac hidden from view. The car is not exactly subtle, though it hasn't been linked to us so far as I'm aware. Better safe than sorry. It's wild to think this might be my life now (however much life I have left), dating an unofficial prince and avoiding the paparazzi. Meanwhile, my insides feel light and buoyant for some reason (Alistair). And I don't hate it.

For the second time today, the man himself seems nervous. Not the panic from earlier in the claustrophobic confines of the elevator. It's more manageable than that. But he keeps nodding grimly at me. Like we're going to war or something. Though he's also been affectionate, or comfortable even, resting his hand on my thigh during the drive over when it wasn't needed for such important tasks as steering and changing gears. Last night seems to have settled things between us in a nice way.

It's tempting to ask if he's like this with the other women he's dated. Touchy-feely. But I'm not sure I want to know. Never ask a question you don't want the answer to—Mom taught me that. And I worry that if I mention his sweet behavior, he'll feel self-conscious and shut it down. Which would be sad.

Never has holding hands with someone been so over-thought.

As soon as we climb out of the car, he approaches my dad with his hand outstretched. "It's a pleasure to meet you, sir."

Dad shakes his hand with a bemused smile. "You should have told him it's your mother he needs to beware of. I'm the nice one."

"Right." An impending sense of doom settles in my middle. And I was having such a nice time. "What did she make for lunch?"

"Meatballs."

"Oh."

"Oh what? What does 'meatballs' mean?" asks Alistair in a worried tone. "Why did your eyebrows just do a thing?"

"Meatballs means we haven't earned any of her special-occasion dishes," I say. "But it is the everyday meal that she makes best. So it's sort of a fuck you with a side order of you better be impressed."

"That about sums it up. Hearing about your wedding plans via the neighborhood gossips rubbed her the wrong way." Dad scratches at his short beard. "But she does make amazing meatballs."

"I was hoping she might have had a little time to calm down," says Alistair as the hope fades from his eyes.

"Nope," answers Dad.

I just shrug. Mom has always been a force of nature. I come by my dramatic tendencies and general anxiety honestly.

"Okay." Alistair swallows hard. "I'll just have to win her over."

"Good luck with that," says Dad cheerfully, opening the door. "Honey, did I ever tell you about the time your mother accidentally kneed me in the groin on our first date? At least, she said it was an accident."

"He's joking," I say quickly as Dad disappears from view. "I'm like 55 percent certain that never happened. Forty-nine at worst."

Alistair's smile is closer to a wince. "Those aren't great odds."

"Hey," I say. "I have every faith in you. You're the most charming man I've ever met. Why, you charmed the pants off me just last night!"

"I do note that as one of the greatest accomplishments of my life."

"You should. But also, it's important to remember that it's not my mom who decides who I date."

"Thank you, Leannan."

"We'll just go in there and explain that it was all a mistake and we're not actually getting married," I say. "She might be a tad perplexed, but then she'll be fine. Who knows...she might even think it's funny."

All he does is frown. Guess we're not ready to think this is funny ourselves.

We head around to the backyard, where a riot of colorful flowers fills the garden beds. A fat drop of water falls on my head, making me look to the sky. Sunshine filters through the clouds like beams of light sent from heaven. Some days LA is just like that—a movie set come to life. And sometimes, if you're really lucky, the movie in question is a romance with a happy-ever-after. More raindrops land on the cracked old walkway beneath our feet. The same one I played on as a child. It was a road for my toy cars and a canvas for my chalk pictures.

The warning drops turn into a sun shower, and Alistair takes hold of my hand. His skin is warm and his grip sure. Standing beside him forever would be fine with me. Just fine. The scent of petrichor fills the air and the world smells clean and new. Full of possibilities. Like magic, as a rainbow appears in the distance. It's another one of those everyday enchantments. But then life gets busy, and you forget to stop and stare at the wonder. Warmth fills my chest as I reflect on how right things are in this moment. I am the fairy-tale princess holding the prince's hand.

"You wanted to dance in the rain," he says with all due seriousness. "It was on your wish list, wasn't it?"

"Yes."

"Well?"

"Do you really want to do that now, with my mother waiting?"

He just nods and draws me closer. "This is more important. We might not get another chance for a while."

"With no music?"

"I can sing if you like."

I smother a smile. "I heard you singing Rihanna in the shower this morning."

"And I was brilliant?"

"That is exactly what I was about to say. How did you know?"

"Just a guess. 'Bitch Better Have My Money' is one of my

favorites. Anyway," he says with a small smile. "Who needs music? Where's your imagination?"

Dad chuckles and wanders toward the back door, where my mother is no doubt watching from the kitchen. They might as well be on the other side of the world, because when Alistair slides an arm around my waist, nothing else matters. He gazes down at me and *wow*. The feel of him and the scent of him and just everything. How does he keep doing this with such ease? We assume a waltz type position and, oh, God, I do not know what I am doing. Not dance-wise or heart-wise—which is beating double time. It's amazing previous me was able to turn down his offer of sex the other night. I doubt I could say no to him about almost anything now.

"I never had dance lessons," I say. "Tell me if I step on your toes."

He spins me around with a small smile. "That's all right. I had enough for both of us. You can tread where you like—my feet will be just fine."

We dance in the rain with no music playing. Our own best intentions lead the way. He moves with ease and confidence, and he holds me tight. Tight enough that nothing else matters.

"Have I ever told you that your eyes are the exact same color as the California sky this time of year?" I ask.

His smile increases ever so slightly. "Are they?"

I just nod.

He looks around the yard. "So, this is where you grew up?"

"Yeah."

"It's nice."

"It's just your regular normal chunk of suburbia."

"Yeah." His gaze is thoughtful. "I think that's what I like best about it."

"Do you ever miss where you grew up in Scotland?"

He sighs. "Quite often, actually. But not enough to go back."

Because being that close to his father's side of the family would be horrible. Because the UK press would be unbearable. The media are bad enough here. I've seen more than enough to reach that conclusion. Now there's a new item for my wish list: to be his knight in shining armor. To rescue him from the fuckery of his birth. But neither a long sword nor a faithful steed will help the situation. When it comes to privacy and his right to live his life, what his mother said was right. Alistair never had a choice, and he never stood a chance. The best I can do is stand with him. To not leave him to face it alone. As long as I don't die tomorrow and he wants to keep dating me. Fingers crossed on both counts.

"What are you thinking about?" he asks.

"How much I appreciate you doing this."

The edge of his mouth eases up. "It's not a hardship. I'll dance in the rain with you whenever you like. Just say the word."

We don't talk anymore. Our clothes are damp and my hair hangs in tendrils. I had hoped to impress my parents with my put-togetherness and not look like trash if or when the paparazzi catch up with us. But oh well. I'm sure I resemble a drowned rat while he has more in common with a dashing, debonair hero facing down the eye of the storm. I can just picture him on the cover of a romance novel wearing a kilt and a rakish grin. His shirt clings to the cut of his shoulders. His cheekbones slick with rain stand out in stark relief. He is, however, so much more than his looks. So much more than his money and fame. The online gossip sites don't know a thing about the real him.

Alistair smiles at me and I smile back. A cool breeze blows through the garden, but there's enough warmth in his eyes for both of us. Oh, God, this man makes me giddy. Spin in circles and giggle like an idiot...the whole thing. My delicate little feelings are in such danger and I cannot make myself care. Not when he looks at me the way he does. Forget the contents of my wish list. Being with him is everything. And if I press my ear against his chest, I can hear his heart beat strong and steady, which is officially one of my new favorite things.

Which is when my mother opens the back door, throws a towel at us, and says, "That's enough. Get in here, you two lovebirds, and explain yourselves."

"Harsh," I mutter, patting myself dry.

"Why do I suddenly feel as if I'm six years old getting caught stealing sweets from the pantry?" he asks in a low voice.

"Did you do that often?"

"Now and then." He gives me a wink. "I was a growing lad."

Inside, the kitchen table is set with the everyday silverware and plain beige dishes that have been around forever. Further evidence of my mother's foul mood. There's no sign of Grandma's good vintage Furnival dishes with the pretty blue design. Nope. Not for this lunch. Though the familiar scent of Mom's cooking makes my tummy rumble. And regardless of the arctic welcome, it's nice to visit. To show Alistair this place and introduce him to my parents.

"Handsome, isn't he?" Mom is not impressed. She also doesn't allow a word to escape her intended prey. He has no sooner pasted on his most winning smile than she asks, "Why do you think you're good enough for my daughter?"

"Ah," he says with much wisdom. "I don't think that I'm good enough, ma'am. I don't know that anyone could be."

"Then why should I give you my blessing?" asks Mom. "Hmm?"

"We need your blessing?" I cock my head. "What is this, the Victorian era? Should I go and put on a bustle and fetch my needlework? A gentleman has come to call!"

Dad smothers a smile.

"Alistair, I give you my word I'm a virgin." I put my hand on my heart. "We're an honest family. We wouldn't sell you dodgy goods."

"Thank goodness," he says dourly. "I did have my concerns."

Thunder crosses Mother's face. "Very funny."

"Mom, I'm sorry," I say. "I know you're upset. But listen, about the engagement—"

"The engagement is exactly what I wish to discuss. But not with you. Not if you're not going to take it seriously!"

"Wait a minute," I say.

But Mom just sniffs in disdain and takes another swing. "Alistair, my daughter is a bright and beautiful young woman. Most of the time. She only just escaped the clutches of an imbecile who couldn't keep it in his pants. How are you any better?"

"Oh, he's definitely better," I say. "Take my word for it. Sooo much better."

A faint red hue appears high on Alistair's cheeks. The man is blushing. Hilarious.

Dad calmly takes a seat at the table. Like this is a dinner show or something. And honestly, it is giving off those vibes.

Someone needs to start serving cocktails with smutty names or selling tees to commemorate the occasion.

Mom shushes me. "This is between me and Alistair. We'll have the conversation without you if you can't behave."

Sweet baby Jesus.

There's a definite flash of fear in Alistair's eyes. I do not think less of him for it. My mother can be mildly terrifying, and I wouldn't want to face her alone either. With her hands on her hips and her chin set sky-high, the woman is vexed as fuck. "Well? What do you say? Are you going to treat her better than that cheating butthead?"

"Yes, ma'am," says Alistair with a ruler-straight spine. "I will definitely treat her better than that butthead. But as Lilah was trying to say, our engagement is—"

"I looked you up online. You've dated at least forty women that I could see. Some of them were very fancy."

I put up my hand. "Ask me how many I've dated. Because I can assure you that thanks to online dating apps, I too have also been out with at least that many people. And some of the people I dated were also quite fancy, I'll have you know. There was this one guy who said he was a poet and insisted on wearing a beret everywhere we went."

Mom shushes me with more fervor than even a librarian could manage. It's quite impressive.

"Dad, say something," I plead. "Be the voice of reason here. Please."

He shakes his head. "Hell no. Not even for all the money in the world. I'm staying out of it."

"Coward."

"What if you get tired of her?" asks my mother. "She's not a countess or an Olympic cross-country skier or a famous

Hollywood actress. She's just herself and there's nothing wrong with that. But you do get my point."

"I don't get your point. Please explain it to me, oh Mother dearest," I say. "Ali, you never told me you dated an Olympic cross-country skier."

"We dated for a few months about thirteen or so years ago. I would have mentioned it had it ever come up in conversation," he says before turning to my mother with a pained expression. "Ma'am...um, no. I honestly never know what's going to come out of Lilah's mouth next. What she's about to do. I don't see being bored of her ever becoming an issue."

Mom's gaze narrows suspiciously. "She can be very stubborn too. Even difficult."

"That's true," says my father.

"Oh, now you have something to say, do you?" I ask with much ire. "Turncoat."

Dad mimes zipping his lips shut. As he should.

"Many others have disappointed and hurt her when they realized she was sometimes hard work." Mom sighs. "They didn't want to be with her badly enough to put in the effort. She didn't mean enough to them."

"You're making me sound like a used car with a year's worth of fast-food wrappers in the back," I say. "Not a good look."

"Is there a question in there somewhere, ma'am?" Alistair asks somewhat cagily.

Mom nods. "Do you want to be with her badly enough?"

"I believe so."

"Credit where credit's due," says Dad. "He's still standing here answering your questions."

"Hmm," answers Mom. "And are you so certain you can handle her, Alistair?"

"Yes, ma'am," he says with all due seriousness. "I believe I have already proven myself adept at handling her."

I try not to snort and fail dismally.

"I didn't mean it like that," says Alistair disapprovingly.

"My bad. Sorry."

But back to Mom. "She's independent, but that doesn't mean she won't need help now and then. And she's not always good at admitting when she's wrong. Certainly not something she got from my side of the family. But goodness can she be stubborn."

"Are you just going to let her get away with that?" I ask, outraged. "Father?"

Alistair continues to ignore me in favor of my mother. Dad just shrugs. Which goes to show you really can't depend on anyone these days.

"I am aware that your daughter can upon occasion be wrong." Alistair continues to stand at attention. "Very, very occasionally."

"Name one time," I challenge. "Go on. You can't, can you?"

"But I will always have your daughter's back," he says. "Whatever may happen and whether she likes it or not."

"That sounds like a threat."

He glances at me. "It was meant as a promise."

"Then there's your use of the word *always*…" I say.

"What about it?" he asks. And he doesn't back down.

Thus begins a staring competition of which I am not the winner. Not even a little. None of this is what I was expecting. "This isn't what we came here for, Ali."

"Is that necessarily a bad thing?" he asks, cocking his head.

I give him my very best *What the fuck?* look. The one I save for especially perplexing occasions. He remains undaunted and I do not understand.

None of this seems real. Not a word or a gesture. When Alice fell down the rabbit hole, she probably felt the way I do now. Tumbling head over ass without a clue. Because promises from this man make my world turn upside down. As if gravity has been given the afternoon off. The last person who made a commitment to me broke it while also setting a new land record speed for how fast they could exit my life. And we'd known each other longer than a week. I don't want to hear these sorts of things out of Alistair's mouth if he doesn't mean them—if he's only saying them to pacify my mother. Which of course he is. He has to be.

"Can we take a break?" I ask, my voice high and tight. Stress will do that to you. "Why don't we sit down and have a strong alcoholic beverage and give this whole interrogation scene a rest for a second?"

Alistair looks at me.

"You have money and fame," continues Mom in rapid-fire fashion, "but, from what I've seen, those things can cause trouble as easily as they can cure it. It's all fine and well to be able to buy her nice things. But will she have your time and attention?"

"Yes," he says without hesitation.

"Relationships are hard enough without rushing into it this way. What makes you so sure of your feelings?"

"Honestly, ma'am, your husband is right. I wouldn't be standing here doing this for anyone other than your daughter. That's how I know."

Dad chuckles.

Mom does not. Her gaze narrows more, zeroing in on the man standing at my side. While it's nice that she cares, at the end of the day, this is unnecessary and ridiculous. This would all be funny if not for the fact that I want it with all my heart and soul. But Alistair's professed love and devotion are a deception. A falsehood, a fib, and a fabrication. I hate the way his words are a barb in my throat. Because no one has ever said these sorts of things about me. No one has ever even pretended to care this much. There he stands with his serious face, and it scares me how much I wish his words were true.

I clear my throat. "Mom, like I was trying to say at the start, the engagement—"

"Is wonderful news that you should have heard directly from us," Alistair finishes for me. Though that most definitely is not what I was going to say. Not even a little. "I sincerely apologize you didn't. With the media's interest in my life, this sort of thing unfortunately happens."

Which is when I see the look in his eyes. The yearning for my family and this home and all that it means. For the normal humdrum life that we live. A life that he was never allowed to have. But this runaway train needs to be stopped. Fast. And yet I sit there in stunned silence.

The fire has gone out of my mother. She stares at us in silence for a moment before saying, "I can see that you have our girl's heart, and I understand why. She's always been a romantic. Even if she does try to hide it with sarcasm. But what I need to hear from you, and be sure that you're being honest with me when you answer…"

He nods.

"Does she have your heart, Alistair?"

Blinks and takes a breath. Then he says nothing at all. And I'm just about to butt in and tell her how the whole engagement is a mistake. How everything we've uttered since entering the building is bullshit. But Alistair is already saying something. Just a word. Only the one. "Yes."

"Wh-what?" I stammer. "What did you say?"

He turns to me and brushes a strand of damp hair off my forehead. He's so careful about how he touches me. As if someone stamped Handle with Care on my forehead. "You heard me, Leannan."

"I'm satisfied. You have my blessing." My mom nods sagely. "Take a seat and let's eat."

"Thank goodness for that," mumbles Dad.

"You're satisfied. Okay." An awkward high-pitched laugh bubbles out of me. One of those *What the fuck is happening?* type noises. Then I ask in a whisper hiss, "Holy shit. What are you doing?"

"Let's talk about it later."

"You let them believe the engagement is real. Why would you do that?"

Alistair pulls out a chair, waiting for me to sit before taking his own seat at the table and announcing to the room, "Of course, it's probably going to be a long engagement. Give us time to get to know each other better. To give Lilah the chance to plan whatever kind of wedding she wants. Or to dump me if she decides that's what she should do."

"She's not going to dump you. Not unless you do something terrible. I've never seen her so besotted." Mom laughs and starts loading plates with meatballs, potato salad, and pickles. "There's no rush, of course. Though a June wedding is always lovely."

"It's entirely up to your daughter," says Alistair, giving my shoulder a squeeze.

"Something wrong, honey?" asks my father.

Alistair says nothing. But his smile is as calm as can be. He sits back in his seat and watches me, waiting to see if I am going to back him up or blow him and our fake engagement right out of the water. Though I've already blown him today. Another word would be better.

"No, Dad." I take a sip of water. "Everything is fine."

"My own daughter marrying someone with royal blood," says Mom with no small amount of delight. "Who would have thought?"

"Not me," I answer. "Definitely not me."

20

It's dark by the time I drag Alistair out of the house and away from my parents' adoring clutches. Safe to say they like him. There was a discussion on Nietzsche with my dad, a heated debate on the rejection of the euro by Denmark in the year 2000 with my mom, the swapping of stories regarding trips to the white cliffs of Møns Klint with both, and the perusal of many photo albums. Given that he told them we were engaged, I made no effort to save him from this dire fate.

From baby photos to my college years, he has seen it all. He didn't even mock the unicorn costume I made myself for Halloween when I was five, which was basically just an empty toilet roll attached to my forehead and some sparkles stuck to my face. Maybe he is the perfect man after all. He even backed me up when Mom tried to get me to try on her heavily beaded wedding dress with organza ruffles. Of course, he did this by saying I wasn't wearing any underwear.

We wave one last time at my parents, step into the garage, and close the door. Moonlight shines through the mottled glass window in the door. There's enough light to see.

"Explain it to me, Ali." I push him against the side of the Cadillac. "And use really small words, because my mind is worn out from chasing itself in circles for the last five hours trying to figure out what the hell you were thinking."

"Why didn't you stop me?"

"I asked you a question first," I say. "Answer it."

"Won't they be wondering why we're taking so long in here?"

"Don't change the subject," I order. "Why did you lie to them and tell them we were engaged?"

"Is it really a lie?"

"Yes."

"You don't want to marry me, then?" he asks. "Do you think maybe you didn't stop me because you secretly like the idea?"

I make a growling sound low in my throat. "Ali."

"Sorry," he says. "But you saw your mother's eyes. They were full of the hope and worry and love for you and I just couldn't let her down. Telling her it was all bullshit would have hurt her more than finding out the way she did."

"Oh, really?"

"She wants you to be happy so badly. And between you and me, I actually quite enjoy making you happy."

"Don't be cute. We haven't even been dating for twenty-four hours!"

"But you can't say they haven't been the best almost twenty-four hours of your life," he says. "Right? Lilah? I'm waiting for your answer. Still waiting."

"How to put this… They've certainly been the most inter-esting twenty-four hours of my life."

"That'll do for now. Furthermore, in my defense, what was it you told my mother? That time is just a construct?"

"I don't remember saying that."

"You had been drinking absinthe."

"That explains it. Don't quote me to me." I poke him in the ribs.

"Your parents are great, and they care about you so much. This house and the life they've built are all wonderful. I didn't want to tell them I dragged your name into the media again and that assholes online are picking you apart and it's all my fault."

"Fuck what random strangers online think of me. It's not your fault."

He frowns. "It wouldn't be happening if you weren't with me."

"Are you aware that we both have a habit of worrying in common?"

"Can't say it comes as a surprise."

"Ali, we talked about this. Several times, in fact. I am fully aware that there are consequences to dating you. But telling them we're getting married... What were you thinking? Please help me make it make sense!"

"As I mentioned previously, I think if you're honest, you'll admit that part of you really likes the idea of us getting hitched and that's why you didn't stop me." He sighs. "Look at it this way. You can always call off the engagement later. Tell them I snore or smell funny or something."

"Because we're not really getting married, right? I mean, that would be ridiculous, right?"

"What would Good Witch Willow say?" His mouth skews to one side. "I lack her supposed powers of prediction. But I feel like it would be something along the lines of 'Who knows what the future may bring?'"

I just groan.

He cocks his head. "Why did *you* go along with it, for that matter? Come on. Tell me the truth."

"I don't know. Your general hotness lulled me into a false state of calm regarding the topic of our fake nuptials. It's not my fault you're a walking, talking thirst trap. And we were all having such a good time. I guess I didn't want to burst their bubble."

"You didn't want to let them down either. They did seem really excited about it all, didn't they?"

"Yeah. You're the first man I brought home that they actually liked instead of just pretending to. Now that I've seen the difference, it seems so obvious."

"I'm honored." His cell buzzes in his pocket and he pulls it out. "It's my mother. I'll talk to her later."

"No. You should answer it. It might be important."

He does as told, putting the call on speaker. "Yes?"

"Thank goodness you picked up, my sweet boy. Your father is on his way," says Lady Helena in a harried voice. "I just heard from his people. It's an unofficial thing. Top secret. No firm ETA given, but we're to expect him within the next two to twenty-four hours. We need to plan our defense or attack or whatever the hell it is we're going to do. How quickly can you two get here?"

"He's coming to see you?"

"No, my darling. He's coming to see *you*."

Alistair gazes into the shadows of the garage in shock. "Shit."

"Indeed," she says. "I suggested this would be the perfect

time for us to all disappear and avoid him entirely. Tanzania is lovely this time of year for a family vacation. I have a friend with a beach house in Zanzibar. Such a great spot for a wedding. But Dougal said no. Then he made some long-winded speech about how you deserved the chance to meet your father and settle things between you once and for all. At least, I think that's what it was about. I tuned out halfway through. You know how he can go on."

Alistair says nothing. He just keeps blinking.

"Lady Helena, we're on our way," I jump in, and hang up the call. "I think it would be best if I drive."

Nothing from him.

"Ali?"

This time, he blinks in my direction. "Lilah. Sorry, I…"

"I know. It's okay. I've got you. Get in the car."

It's weird to be making the drive up the Pacific Coast Highway again under these conditions. And in a different prestige vehicle. A lot has changed since Monday. Just about everything.

Alistair doesn't speak again until we can see the sea. All the charm and clever talking from the last few hours with my folks have disappeared without a trace. He is an entirely different man. The blank face that hides every last one of his feelings reappears for the first time in a while. "I met him once…the king. Though to say I met him is misleading. There was no introduction or anything like that."

"When was that?"

"I was about six or seven. He and my mother were arguing in the billiard room. She always hated that room, said the glass eyes of Grandfather's hunting trophies followed her around."

He smiles briefly. "The king wanted me sent out of the country for schooling, and she refused. Said that I was too little to be sent away just because he wanted to hide his dirty secret. She told him he could fuck right off."

"I do like your mother."

He grunts.

"Did he say anything to you?"

"He told me to move," says Alistair, his brogue thickening. "I'd been standing in the doorway listening. I was in his way, and he wanted to leave."

"That's all he said to you? 'Move'?"

"Aye."

"What an asshole."

"He just seemed so tall and angry. I didn't even know who he was until the housekeeper curtsied and a groundskeeper called him *Your Highness*." He sighs. "I'll never forget the look on Helena's face when she saw me there... She hadn't meant for me to hear her call me that. His 'dirty secret.' For years, she'd been telling me I didn't have a father and I didn't need one. That we were better off on our own. She felt so bad about it she drove us to an ice cream parlor two towns over and let me order whatever I wanted."

"Did you make yourself sick?"

"You bet I did," he says. "Then she told me the same thing she always did. That we don't need him. But also that he didn't deserve us. I believed her that time."

I steer the Cadillac through the nighttime traffic. It's a heck of a vehicle. Huge and stately.

Out of nowhere, he says, "I'll tell your parents the engagement isn't real. Say that I just got carried away or something."

"Decided you don't want to marry me after all?" I ask,

glancing at him. "That's disappointing. I've been mentally shopping for my wedding dress for the past hour."

He gives me a long look but says nothing. Then he fiddles with the radio until he finds some music. Then we sit in silence.

The tall gates swing open as we approach the beach shack. The palms and olive trees are lit to perfection from below, and a cool salty wind is blowing. The sprawling midcentury mansion is as impressive as last time.

There are a lot of differences between Alistair and me, with our families and lifestyles and finances. But I'm not sure much of it matters. Maybe it's like Mom said: either you care enough to be there and do the hard work or not.

Lady Helena and Dougal stand waiting by the door. Her tousled hair is piled atop her head as always, and she's wearing an ornate floaty cream silk evening dress with diamonds around her neck and a pair of flip-flops on her feet. Because of course she is. "Hello, darlings!"

Alistair nods.

"We've received an update. There was some sort of holdup and he'll now be here in time for breakfast. I believe the menu will consist of lumpy porridge, tepid weak tea that's been strained through an unwashed sock, and cold burnt toast with no butter. What do you think?"

"You're in a right state all wound up, aren't you, lad?" asks Dougal, placing a hand on Alistair's shoulder. "Come on. Let's get you sorted and give you a chance to clear your head."

The two men head off to one of the two smaller buildings at the back of the property.

Lady Helena frowns. "I wanted to talk to my son. Am I allowed to come?"

Dougal looks back and says "No" over his shoulder.

"How rude." Her Ladyship turns to me with an unperturbed grin. "What will you have, Lilah? Gin and tonic, brandy, a glass of red, perhaps?"

"Do you have any coffee?"

She clicks her tongue. "You Americans. Honestly."

"Tea is also fine."

"I should hope so," she says. "There's plenty of crab wontons and lobster left over from the dinner delivery if you're hungry. A lovely wedge salad too with blue cheese and bacon and walnuts. That is one thing this country actually does well. Though the first time I was served a half a head of lettuce, I wondered what the hell was going on."

"There's only one thing we do well?"

"There might be more. I just haven't found them. But you never know."

I snort.

She smiles. Then her expression turns serious. "How is he taking the news of his father's visit?"

I don't know what to say. Or if I should say anything. Their mother-son relationship is complicated enough without me getting involved.

"Never mind. Dougal knows how to handle him," she says, staring at the stone path leading through the gardens. "When I found out I was with child, it was Dougal who saw me through the pregnancy. He even held my hand and let me yell at him while I was giving birth. And some of the things I called him... Oof. A lesser man would have been brought to his knees. It would have been funny had I not been quite so preoccupied with pushing out a baby. He had such a large head. But I digress. When the press descended on us, it was

Dougal who helped us move and settle here. I never would have thought he'd leave Scotland, but he's never left my side. Apart from that time I stayed at a nudist beach resort in the Caribbean. Such a shame. Between you and me, I wouldn't mind a look at what he's been hiding under that kilt all these years. You can usually tell, can't you? Some men just have a strut about them. A certain way of walking. I believe they call it *big-dick energy* these days?"

Her smile is knowing. Mine is the opposite. "I don't know what to say."

"Probably for the best." She smiles some more. "Come along. I have a bottle of a century-old port my father was hoarding. This feels like just the occasion to finally open it."

"I thought we were having tea."

"You are endlessly amusing, Lilah. Just a constant delight to have around."

"Oh, good," I say, following Lady Helena into the house.

I hang out with Her Ladyship for an hour or so. Then I go looking for Alistair. The first building I see, half hidden behind trees, is a smaller version of the main house, a midcentury wooden construct with lots of floor-to-ceiling windows. The sliding glass door opens onto a large central room with an open lounge/kitchen/dining area, though the only furniture is a punching bag hanging from a rafter and some weights and a surfboard discarded on the other side of the room.

Dougal is bracing the bag while Alistair does his best to pound it into pieces. He's like a machine, slamming his fists into it over and over again. The only sounds in the room are his labored breathing and the thwack of each impact. And the only item of clothing on him is a pair of basketball shorts. His skin glistens with sweat beneath the low lighting.

It's Dougal who notices my presence first. "That'll do," he says, stepping back from the bag. "Hit the shower. You stink worse than a rank goat in summer."

Alistair nods and cracks his neck. Then he picks up a water bottle and chugs down half of its contents.

"Where is Her Ladyship?" asks Dougal. "Asleep on the settee?"

"No. She said she felt like baking some shortbread. Though it took her a minute to remember where the kitchen was located."

"Shit." Dougal heads for the door in an almighty rush. "We'll be lucky if she doesn't accidentally burn down the house. Good night."

"How are you?" I ask Alistair.

Alistair unwinds the tape or whatever it is from his hands. "As rank as a goat, apparently."

"I've never actually sniffed a goat, so I can't compare. But I guess you better get in the shower."

"Good idea. How is she?"

"Your mother? She's worried about you."

He just frowns. "Talk to me while I clean up."

"Okay." I follow him down a short hallway. There are two other rooms, one set up as a bedroom. The other is a sort of lounge, with an old game console and screen sitting on the ground, a beanbag chair and some surfing magazines nearby. Connecting the two rooms is a large bathroom with a walk-in shower and ginormous tub. "What is this place, a guesthouse?"

"Yeah," he says. "I moved out here soon after we arrived. Wanted my own space."

"Understandable."

He turns on the shower and tests the water with his hand. Then down go his shorts and boxer briefs as he steps beneath the spray. The man is a work of art, and I would be more than happy to wash his back or any other part of his anatomy for him. Or to just give him a hug. But he specified he wanted to talk, so I keep my hands to myself. He rubs a bar of soap briskly over his skin. I don't think I've ever watched someone bathe before. Not without me being naked and wet as well. He handles himself in such a matter-of-fact manner. There's none of the care I take with his dick.

It's a privilege to be given access to these private moments. To be permitted to be a part of his everyday life when he guards his privacy so carefully. One I don't take for granted.

"Dougal lives in the other cottage," he continues. "It's not like I was all alone out here."

"How did your mom take it?"

"She hated it. We fought about it constantly at first." He washes his hair, then stands beneath the showerhead, letting the spray pound his back. "But she's not the sort to try and force you to do something. That's how I wound up living on only fish and chips for a week when I was a wee lad. Then my gran visited and insisted I eat some fruit and vegetables. Anyway, eventually Mom got used to me being out here, and her mind turned to other matters. Like where we could go on the next holiday and who was her latest famous friend."

"Dougal might have been nearby, but you were all alone."

"Back then, I wanted to be." His blue eyes watch me thoughtfully. "But I'm not alone anymore. You're here."

My smile is weak. It's been a long day. And then there's the clock ticking down to tomorrow that I am trying so damn hard not to think about. "We should get some sleep. Who knows what time the royal cavalcade will appear? Have you decided what you're going to say?"

"That'll depend on why he's here. I'd rather not get ahead of myself and start guessing." He turns off the water, and the sudden silence fills the humid air. "Tell me, Lilah. What are you going to do when you find yourself still alive on Monday?"

"I honestly don't know."

"Because you will be." With the same brisk motions, he dries himself off with a plush white towel. "I've been meaning to ask, that wallpaper on your phone... It's the Bibliothèque in Paris, isn't it?"

I nod. "I change it every month or so to a different library I'd like to visit."

"Another wish-list item."

"You could say that," I agree.

"Cold in France this time of year. You'll need a good coat, gloves, and scarf. Some decent boots too."

"Is that your way of suggesting we take a trip?"

"Is that your way of saying yes?" He wraps the towel around his hips and stares down at me.

It's an effort to keep my arms by my sides. My hands get grabby around him. What can I say? He gets to me. But the man needs his sleep, what with his father turning up tomorrow morning.

"What are you thinking?" he asks, stepping closer.

"That we should get some sleep."

"We should go to bed. You're right about that."

The bedroom has a large king-size bed made up in navy linens. And the wardrobe door is half-open, showing various items of clothing, tees, and jeans he left behind way back when. But there's no sign of dust or the scent of stale air in here. Everything is pristine, as if he only left yesterday.

"Your mother keeps this room ready for you?" I ask.

Evidence of a younger version of Alistair is hidden here and there. A skateboard lying forgotten at the bottom of the wardrobe and a Foo Fighters poster on the back of the bed-room door.

"Yeah. Just in case." He gazes at my face. "You look like you want to say something."

"I don't know the full story of what happened between you two. Therefore, I am keeping my mouth shut."

"That's a pity. You have such a lovely mouth. Why, I like your mouth almost as much as I admire your—"

I slap a hand over his lips to smother what he might have said. What he definitely said. With a laugh, I ask, "That's not very princely language, is it?"

"As I told you at the start, I'm not really a prince. And thank goodness for that. I never wanted my life mapped out for me. For the whole world to feel they have a right to know everything about me. As if being born to that family means I have no choice. My privacy is sold to the highest bidder as is—and now yours is too," he says, cupping my face. "Not that it wouldn't be fun to call you *princess* and fuck you wear-ing only a tiara."

"I think you'd look very fetching in a tiara."

"I meant you, smart-ass." And he backs up the statement with a sharp slap to my butt cheek.

"Ouch."

"Give me your mouth."

"Say 'please.'"

With a feral grin, he presses his lips hard against mine.

Each time we kiss, there's this flood of happy hormones. He has fast become my addiction. His hands on my body and the way he doesn't hold back. I know how much he wants me. It's impossible to ignore in the way his tongue sweeps into my mouth and the taste of him hits me. Then he gentles the kiss to something sweet and sincere.

"Did you really want to just go to sleep?" he asks in a harsh whisper. "Because it's okay if that's what you want."

In response, I push the towel off his hips and toe off my fancy new red flats. He shows how helpful he can be by lifting the hem of my top and carefully taking it off me. We both fumble for the button and zipper of my jeans until he's sidetracked by my boobs.

"This is new," he says, inspecting the lace of my bra as he fills his hands with my breasts. "I approve, Leannan."

"The lingerie alone cost you a small fortune. I should hope you like it."

His thumbs toy with my nipples, the fine fabric an intriguing sensation against sensitive skin. Because whenever he touches me, my whole body lights up. In no time at all, I'm panting and he's groaning about what a good girl I am, and we're heading for the bed. Removing my underwear while stroking his thick cock along the way is a challenge. But I am 100 percent here for it. He smells like soap and shampoo and himself. A scent I cannot define but could find in the dark if necessary.

Maybe it's the looming threat of my doomsday tomorrow. I don't know. But we're frenzied. Both of us feel the urgency. His hands grasping and groping. My teeth nipping at the cushion of his bottom lip. We seem to want to mark our territory tonight. To be more than a little possessive. I am not usually rough like this. As much as I want to touch him with all the tenderness in the world, to treasure him, this moment calls for more.

He allows me to push him back onto the mattress. And his strong hands are there, urging me to straddle him. To hold the blunt head of his cock in position and sink down and take all of him in one brutal move. Oh my God. Forget about tomorrow. I am dead and gone tonight. How his wide cock stretches me. It is sweet and sharp and so damn necessary. With this much emotion involved, with the way he gets me, sex with this man is on another level. I did not have a damn clue what I was missing up until now. There's every chance I could forgo my next breath. But not him and not this. Not ever.

He hisses and bares his teeth. "The feel of you... Fuck."

I just nod. With my synapses firing the way they are, words are way out of reach.

His fingers dig into my hips, holding me down on his hard length. But suddenly his gaze clears and his face blanks and *oh, shit*. I know exactly what he's thinking. "We forgot to use any protection."

"Yeah."

"Okay. Wait," he says, still holding me in place. A bead of sweat slips down the side of his face. "Fuck, it's hard to think, what with being inside you bare. But I get tested regularly. Haven't had unprotected sex in the meantime. How about you?"

"I, um..."

"Think, Lilah. Have you been tested?"

I squeeze my eyelids shut. "Yes to testing. No to unprotected sex. I'm also on birth control."

"Okay. What do you want to do?"

"You…" I lick my lips and try not to rock. Holding still has never been this hard. "You feel so good. This is a hell of a time to be having this conversation."

"Do we stop and suit up or stay as we are? What do you want?"

"You're fine with bare?"

"Yes," he says with no hesitation. "It's your choice."

With my palms flat against his chest for purchase, I finally give in and gyrate my hips. His eyes roll back in his head. It's gratifying to see. His grip on my thighs tightens, and then he moves his hands higher. All the better to lift me and slam me back down. And I am more than happy to go along with it. Heck. I'm happy to ride him all on my own. Having him between my thighs is always a guaranteed good time. And feeling how hot he is, the ridges in his cock, the way he grunts like a caveman as he urges me on. Faster. Harder.

The thick length of him rubs me just the right way. Every nerve ending in me is paying attention to what we're doing. It's an elemental combination of heat and electricity. A thrilling magical thing. That's how it feels to have him inside me and beneath me and grabbing hold of me.

"Fuck, this is going to be fast. Eyes here, Lilah," he says, and grabs hold of my throat. His hand is like a brand against my skin. And he looks at me like he never wants to let go. I know exactly how he feels. Sheer sensation spreads out from my sex and takes me over. From my flesh and skin right down to my bones. I'd like this to last longer. But my orgasm races through me like there's no time to lose. Like every second matters.

My whole body spasms. All those inner muscles tighten on him, milking him dry. Watching him coming would have been nice. But I am lost to the stars and some deep inner or outer space. I don't know. Orgasms don't usually send me interstellar. It's like my world got spun around and around, leaving me with no idea of up or down. All I can do is cling to him, to hold on tight. And he does the same.

His hand soothes up and down my back for I don't know how long. I stay collapsed on his chest where I landed. It's all his fault anyway. I don't know how to think or feel or anything. How dare sex with him be this good.

"About the soulmates idea," he says eventually.

"Ali," I mumble, "don't even go there."

"I'm just saying, it's an interesting thought. It would certainly explain how we got so entangled so quickly."

"We're entangled?"

"Amongst other things." He wraps a strand of my hair carefully around his finger. "If it wasn't tied to the bollocks prediction about you dying tomorrow, which is still absolutely not fucking happening—thank you very much—it might be worth looking into."

"That's a big change of attitude coming from you."

He just grunts.

"Is that your way of saying you like me?" I joke.

"You could take it that way, Leannan. Though I would have thought telling your parents we were engaged would have given that away."

"Guess I'm slow sometimes."

"Great sex will do that to you." He presses a kiss to my head. "Go to sleep, Lilah. You're safe with me. You know that, don't you?"

"I know that." I climb off him and collapse onto the bed at his side. "Do you think they leaked the engagement story to the press to try and scare me off? Then when that didn't immediately work, your father decided to visit?"

"I honestly have no idea," he says. "But whatever happens tomorrow, we'll deal with it. Together."

21

Sunday

"Leannan," a voice whispers in my ear. "Wake up."

My eyes open to find Alistair staring down at me. What a wonderful sight to see first thing in the morning. He carefully brushes my hair out of my face with a distracted smile. No idea how long he's been up for, but he's already dressed. The warm scent of his cologne and rumpled sheets beneath me make for a great morning. At least, they would under normal circumstances. But today is not normal in the least. The red in his eyes from lack of sleep attest to that. Like it or not—and I definitely do not—this could very well be my last day on Earth. *Fuck.* I don't even know what to think about that. It's an existential type of terror. From the time we're old enough to understand death and dying, the idea of our life being over follows us around. It's an ominous shadow with as big or as little a role to play as we allow. And right now, for me, it is a big enough stain to block out the sun.

"Hey," I say with my best fake smile. "Is your father here?"

"About to arrive."

"Okay." I take a deep breath and sit up, covering my breasts with the sheet. Sunlight streams through the gap in the curtains. "What do you want me to do? Stay here or come to the main house or what?"

"Given everything, I think I'd like to keep you close today."

"I thought you weren't interested in the death-and-doom prediction."

He frowns. "As much as it irks me to admit it, now that the day is here, I might be just a tiny bit concerned."

"Okay."

"Nothing is going to happen to you, Lilah. I won't allow it. It took me a long time to find you. I refuse to lose you now."

I do my best to keep my smile steady, but the urge to burst into tears of fear or happiness or I don't know what is immense. "How long do I have to get ready?"

He winces. "Five minutes?"

"Shit."

"I wanted to give you as much of a lie-in as I could."

I make for the edge of the mattress as he moves aside. Mornings aren't really my thing. But never mind. No time to wallow in bed and ponder the meaning of life and death. And honestly, I've had a week to do that, and it hasn't helped.

"Hurry but be careful," he says. "Those tiles in the bathroom can be a little slippery when wet. We don't want you falling."

"I'm fine."

"And go easy with your hairbrush and toothbrush and so on."

"I'm not going to choke on my own toothbrush, Ali. Calm down, please."

"Maybe I should come with you…"

Which is about when I close the bathroom door to get a moment's peace to pull myself together. I hand-washed my underwear with soap last night and left it hanging over a towel rack. Yesterday's top and jeans are okay for another round. I tie back my hair in a ponytail and brush my teeth. Meeting royalty should be a bigger deal, necessitating a trip to the salon and actual fresh and pressed clothing. On the other hand, it's just another jerk who has treated Alistair like crap. Lip gloss and mascara will do.

"Ready?" he asks with his blank face back on and his hand held out to me. His fingers close around mine and hold on tight. "Let's get this over and done with so I can get you some breakfast."

"That sounds like a great plan. I really need coffee."

"So," he says. "Last night when I couldn't sleep, I did some thinking. Whether I believe in the validity of predictions or not, the others have come true. I was therefore thinking it wouldn't be imprudent of us to take some precautions today."

"I'm listening."

"What if after this we spend the day holed up in the guest-house? Just you and me."

"You mean stay off the road in case of any crashes, away from the general public in case of I don't know what, and generally keep me close so you can keep an eye on me?"

"Yes," he says. "That about sums up my plan. Are you amenable?"

"Sounds good." As if I would not want to spend my possible last day with the person I have big feelings for. Really big. Like, huge. "But if a toilet seat from a space station plummets to Earth and kills both of us on impact, it's not my fault that you die too just because you were with me."

He gives me a long look.

"It's a plot point from an old TV show."

"Okay."

"You have to admit, it would make for an interesting death."

He gives me another of those looks.

"Then there's getting stoned by the townsfolk like in 'The Lottery' by Shirley Jackson. Or pulled into the sewer by a monster like Georgie in *It* by Stephen King," I say, the words flowing faster and faster from my mouth. "And how about when—"

"Stop," orders Alistair. "Breathe."

I do as I'm told and suck in a deep breath, letting it out slowly. "Sorry. I was getting panicky and babbling, wasn't I?"

"Just a little. Which is not a problem. But perhaps you could choose a friendlier topic to discuss? One that won't send us both into a meltdown."

"Right. Yeah."

He just waits.

"I'm good," I say with a grim smile. "Nothing dire is going to happen. Everything will be fine."

"Are you just saying that to pacify me?"

"Both of us, really." I pull myself up tall. "Let's do this."

The road to the main house is cluttered with shiny vehicles of all shapes and sizes, including a limousine. Traveling incognito obviously isn't His Highness's specialty. Makes me wonder if there'll soon be media waiting at the gate. It can't be easy keeping a trip like this secret. Security people in their universal uniform of chinos and polos watch us from behind their sunglasses. Talk about the feeling of having eyes on you.

They've taken over the property, apparently. I am happy to be holding Alistair's hand because it's all intimidating as heck. I do not, however, let it show on my face. Not a chance. We don't rush past them toward the house, but we don't dawdle either. It wouldn't do to keep His Highness waiting too long.

Silence fills the inside of the house. Lady Helena is perched on the arm of the lounge wearing a hot-pink dress with a poufy skirt and spaghetti straps. A floppy black bow sits in the center of the low neckline, and this dress is a lot, but she pulls it off just fine. Her makeup is just so, and her heels are sky-high. If this is her revenge dress, then I approve. Meanwhile, Dougal stands behind her with his arms crossed over his chest. Such an expression of disapproval on his craggy face and it is all directed at the man standing opposite.

Lady Helena beams as we walk in. "There you are, my darlings."

"You look amazing," I say.

"What? This old thing?" She gives me a wink. "It's just a Christian Lacroix I picked up in the eighties. Thought it was fitting for today."

The king's demeanor is highly unimpressed. Regardless of having just stepped off a plane, his shirt and slacks appear freshly pressed. As if a wrinkle would dare mar such a personage. Not fucking likely. The outfit is rounded off with a blazer. His mouth is a flat line and his eyes are unhappy. No idea exactly what I was expecting, but he could be anyone's uptight uncle. Sort of stuffy and vaguely commanding. But also ordinary in a way. The family resemblance is more obvious in the flesh. How the high forehead and deep set of his eyes have been passed down to his son. His gaze locks on to

Alistair and his jaw goes rigid. Another thing the father and son have in common.

"Go on, then," Lady Helena says to him. "Say what you came all this way to say. Or would you like a formal introduction first?"

Nothing from the king as he stares at his son silently. And Alistair returns the stare as calm as can be.

Lady Helena stands and executes a perfect curtsy. This is not her first time dealing with the high and mighty. "Your Royal Highness, may I present to you your firstborn child, Alistair George Arthur Lennox. Accompanying him is his delightful fiancée, Lilah."

His Royal Highness doesn't even spare me a glance. Talk about being put in your place.

"My apologies for the lack of middle and surname, Lilah," says Her Ladyship. "I don't actually know them yet."

I give her a discreet thumbs-up.

Alistair jerks his chin. "Why are you here, sir?"

The king blinks at the harsh tone of voice. "We met once before a long time ago. I don't suppose you remember."

"I remember perfectly. I was in your way. You told me to move."

Dougal snorts. "That's all you had to say to your son? And he was a wee lad and all. What the hell is wrong with you?"

"I don't recall your opinion being asked for," snaps the king. "Who even are you? Why are you here?"

"Dougal lives here and is part of our family. He belongs here. But why are you here, sir?" asks Alistair again. And there's something about the way he says *sir*. It makes his feelings on the matter of this veritable stranger known to one and all.

Lady Helena sighs. "That's what we all want to know. If you'd be so kind as to answer?"

"What I'm about to say cannot go beyond this room," orders the king. "Is that understood?"

No one says a thing. So much tension. You would need a sword at least to cut it—a knife would be insufficient. An axe is not out of the question.

In an ever so slightly more conciliatory tone, he asks again. "Do I have your word?"

"None of us have any interest in being caught up in any of your nonsense." Lady Helena shakes her head tiredly. "Out with it already."

The king pulls on the cuffs of his shirt and says, "I need to know if you've seen your brother."

"Wait. What?" asks Lady Helena with much confusion. "You mean James, the Prince of Wales? The one who's supposed to be about to get married?"

"Yes. He's currently not communicating with his office nor any family members nor friends. None that I am aware of, at least." The king's gaze returns to his son. "He's always been curious about you. I hoped he might have sought you out."

"*Hoped* is the wrong word," says Her Ladyship. "Or it's correct only inasmuch as you hoped coming here would mean you could stop chasing after your wayward second son, right?"

"Just answer the question."

"*That's* why you leaked news about Alistair and Lilah's engagement. You're desperately trying to divert attention that your heir has disappeared. What a disaster."

"You could enjoy this a little less," snaps the king.

A bitter smile curves Helena's lips. "The way you lot throw people under the bus whenever it's convenient. Just like when your sister announced my young son's presence to the world. All because she was jealous of the attention your pretty bride was receiving and wanted to tarnish your image. Though she told me recently that she was under the influence at the time. Said she was quite sorry about all the trouble it caused us. Which goes to show, people can change. Sort of."

Alistair's eyebrows rise halfway up his forehead. "Alexandra did that? She told the media?"

"Yes, my darling. I always suspected, of course, but never knew for sure. Not until her visit the other day. You don't think I was pouring magnums of champagne down her neck for the fun of it?"

The king grinds his teeth. "I do not have time to revisit ancient history."

"But I thought it was you," says Alistair with emotion.

"Me?" Lady Helena's eyes go wide. "No, my sweetheart. Having the world find out about you upended our rather nice, quiet little country life. It was a simple sort of existence, but I quite enjoyed those years."

"You were still living in a castle," says Dougal. "Not that simple."

"Oh, hush, old man." Helena turns back to her son. "Is that what you've been upset about all this time?"

"Yes," says Alistair.

"Huh. How about that. I thought you were just going through a stage."

"For thirty years?" asks Dougal.

Her Ladyship shrugs. "Relationships between mothers and sons can be tense for all sorts of reasons. Candy, my psychic when we first moved here, told me that. Said to just give you space and the situation would resolve itself eventually. And here we are! She was right!"

"Don't look at me, lad," says Dougal. "I've been telling her to sit down with you and sort it out forever."

"That's true. He has."

"If you don't mind," says the king in his outside voice. "Has anyone seen my son?"

"Your other son, you mean?" asks Her Ladyship. "Your second-born?"

"Helena, now is not the time!"

"Do not raise your voice at her," says Alistair in warning. "No one's seen him. Was there anything else you wanted, or will you be on your way?"

The king's mouth opens, but nothing comes out. He must have thought better about whatever he was going to say. Which goes to show he's not a complete idiot.

"Foolish of me to think you'd have anything of value to say to me," continues Alistair. "But you're only here because of your real son. The one whose birth meets your archaic bullshit standards."

"That isn't true." His Highness's gaze warms the smallest amount. "I was hoping we could have a word in private."

"About your generous offer to be seen in public with me?"

"Amongst other things."

"I'd like to say something first," says Lady Helena, waving a hand in the air. "Now seems like as good a time as ever. If I could have everyone's attention, please?"

His Highness sucks on his teeth with pure irritation. "What is it?"

"You and I have been each other's bad habit for many years. I think it's time for that to stop." Her smile gentles. "I'm going to be blocking your number. All your numbers. And all the numbers of all the lackeys who work for you. I would ask that you respect my decision and not attempt to contact me. There will be no more moaning to me about your marriage or duties or anything else. And no more funny stuff over the phone either. We're finished. For good this time."

The king pauses. "You can't mean that, Hel."

"But I do," she says calmly. "I don't blame you for not believing me. There have been so many occasions when I should have ended things once and for all. But the reality is you chose not to choose me a long time ago. Then you kept on choosing to turn your back on me and our child so long as our existence didn't suit you. I don't know why I kept forgiving you. Well... I do... The heart is an exceptionally stupid organ. However, this time I really am done, and I'm going to make the smart choice. The one I should have made a long time ago."

"Hel..."

Then Lady Helena turns to Dougal and asks, "Feel like eloping with me?"

Dougal ponders the question for a moment. "Well, I don't know. Where were you thinking?"

"Venice or maybe Lake Como? I feel like pasta and red wine for some reason. We could have gelato instead of wedding cake. Doesn't that sound like fun?"

Dougal scrunches up his nose. "Not Europe at this time of year. The damp will play havoc with my knees."

"Fine," says Lady Helena under much duress. "How about... oh, I don't know, Cairns?"

"Australia? Aye. That'll do."

Alistair's mouth just hangs open. So does the king's.

"Just to be certain we're both on the same page," says Her Ladyship. "We are getting married, old man?"

"That's right." Dougal nods. "Thought you'd never come to your senses and ask."

"I'm a slow learner. What can I say?" Lady Helena shrugs. "How about a glass of champagne for everyone to celebrate?"

"At this hour of the morning?"

"Mimosas, then," she says decidedly. "Don't bother buying me a ring. I have more than enough of them already."

"If I did, you'd just lose it anyway."

Lady Helena's smile is huge. "That's true."

"B-but you can't," splutters the king. "He's your gardener or butler or whatever the hell he's supposed to be."

Dougal raises one brow. "Aye. I am. And I'll be sure to do a fine job of being her husband as well. She's a high-needs woman, to be sure. But then, I'm a very giving man."

"Yes, you are. Which way is the kitchen again?" Lady Helena asks, heading for the hallway. "We're going to need juice and maybe some little snacky things. I can't decide between sweet and savory. What do you think would suit?"

"Not sure. But there's bound to be something that'll do." Dougal follows his fiancée. "Let's see what's in the fridge."

Father and son both seem to be somewhat stupefied. At least, they're both staring at the newly betrothed couple as they leave the room. The expressions of disbelief for Alistair and horror for the king are rather comic.

"I just want to say right now, we are not having a double wedding." I also head for the exit. "Do not let her talk you into it."

"No," agrees Alistair. "Where are you going, if you don't mind me asking?"

"To give you two some privacy."

A line appears embedded between his brows. "You could wait with Mother and Dougal."

"I'm not standing there watching those two make out. Don't ask me to do that. It's too much."

"Fair point." He holds out his hand. "Stay with me. Please. I trust you. There's nothing we're going to say that you can't hear."

The king opens his mouth to no doubt disagree, but Alistair repeats, "Nothing."

"You're serious about her," his father says. Though it's strange to think of him that way. He's been a grim face in magazines and online gossip sites my whole life.

"You know, you've been this distant disapproving figure since I was born. That's the only contribution you've made to my life. So you'll understand when I say your opinion regarding my fiancée is not required."

I hold Alistair's hand and keep my mouth shut. For now, at least.

The king tugs on his cuffs and stands up straight. "I understand my sister shared the details regarding the opportunity for you to attend some smaller official events this spring. To be introduced to the public and to meet more of the family in a somewhat formal setting. It would be a chance for you to be recognized to a certain degree."

"Listen to you," drawls Alistair.

"I'm being as forthright as I can be."

"Which is not much. The optics aren't great, are they?" he asks. "Your heir doing a runner and all. Those rumors about your own marriage falling apart."

The king's lips are a fine line. "That's none of your concern."

"Of course not. Because we're not really family. Family are the people who care for you, and that has never been you."

"It would be foolish of you to be pining for some emotional outpouring from me."

"But when you use me to deflect attention with the media, you put Lilah in the frame as well. I don't like that."

"The world knows who you are, Alistair. There's nothing I can do to remedy that."

"There've been many things you could have done over the years to try and ease the way for me. Whether it be encouraging your pet paparazzi to give me space or to send a simple message of support and fatherly affection. But you chose to do none of those things." Alistair's fingers tighten around mine. I give his hand a squeeze. Just to let him know I am with him. And his grip eases some. "Now you decide I can be useful."

The king's nostrils flare like a pissed-off stallion. There's every chance Alistair gets his temper from that side of the family. Though he generally hides it better.

"I have no interest in attending your garden party, Father. Nor will I be marrying someone you choose for me. What I *will* be doing is spending time with my fiancée and working on my relationship with my mother. Someone who I can now see I have been a complete dick to for no good reason."

"You should be with someone suitable," the king argues. "Someone who could handle the public demands of your position."

"I should be with someone I love who makes me happy."

"As if that lasts…" The king scoffs. "You have a position to uphold. Like it or not, you come from bloodlines that require things of you."

"I don't owe you a fucking thing."

"Marrying this woman would be a mistake. She is—"

"It would not be wise of you to finish that sentence," Alistair says in a low tone.

It would also be fair to say I have had enough of being insulted by royal assholes this week. "Time for some fresh air. I'm going to go stand out by the pool. Right there where you can see me, okay?"

Alistair frowns. "Keep the glass door open, please."

I nod and give his hand another squeeze before heading out the front of the beach house. The king doesn't deserve any sort of acknowledgment from me. Let them look down on me all they like. I refuse to care what they think. Life is too short to worry about the opinions of assholes.

Between the house and the beach is a large lagoon-style pool surrounded by assorted lounges and umbrellas. All the space Lady Helena could desire to loll about with a drink in hand. Lots of decorative rocks and seaside daisies with a neat row of hedges to maintain a boundary between her and the outside world. To try to protect her privacy without blocking too much of the view.

It's warm today in the sun. I take off my shoes and wander onto the first step to get my toes wet. The pool is of course kept at a civilized temperature. My reflection wavers in the water surrounding my feet. Out here, I can breathe better already. What a morning. The idea of cuddling up in the guesthouse with Ali for the rest of the day is growing more appealing by the moment. Just lock out the world and enjoy the peace.

As promised, I stand where he can see me. By the pool with my back to the house, staring out at the ocean. On the off chance I don't die, I am due back at work tomorrow. I've missed the books and stacks and all the avid readers. It would almost be a relief to return to a normal daily routine again. Nothing has been ordinary since I crossed paths with Good Witch Willow. Though the lotto money gives me the luxury of choice. To think of all those libraries out there I've always wanted to see, like the Strahov Library in Prague and the Starfield Library in Seoul. Ali mentioned something about wanting to travel. We could go together.

A flock of seagulls takes flight from down on the sand, and I turn my head to track them. One bird swoops in the general direction of the house before returning to the rest. Imagine owning a house with such a view. Lady Helena was right—it would be a nice place for a wedding. The way my heart squeezes tight in excitement at the thought. It makes a nice change from the ongoing angst. The man is going to give me arrhythmia. Perhaps that's how I die—due to excessive swooning over a certain Scot. Not a bad way to go. To do such a death justice, I would really need a velvet chaise longue to genteelly collapse upon (while wearing some billowy white gown) and then expire with much Gothic romance drama.

Which is the absolute nonsense I am thinking when the seagull circles back and does another dive. And this time it's aimed straight at my head. It all happens so fast. I wave my arms in the air to ward off the bird. It screeches and flaps its wings, coming at me yet again. You would think I was Tippi Hedren or a French fry or something. All of this fucks my balance, and my feet slip on the pool's smooth ceramic tiles. I am falling before I even know what's going on. The stone edge of the pool rises to meet my face and everything goes black.

When I come to, my throat is burning and my chest feels much the same. The world above me is a shapeless blaze of light that I don't understand. Hands roll me onto my side and pool water gushes out of my mouth and nose. A Niagara Falls amount of the stuff. I do my best to choke down some air. It's like oxygen has become a solid and my lungs have forgotten how to operate. The way they seize and stop and start. Oh my fucking God. There isn't an inch of me that isn't water-logged and aching. But it's my face that pounds in time with the beat of my heart.

"That's it." Alistair rubs my back with much vigor. "Get it out."

"An ambulance is on its way," says Dougal somewhere close by.

"She's conscious. She's okay," answers Lady Helena. "Thank goodness!"

My vision swims and *oh, shit*. There is every chance I am about to black out. But I roll onto my back and those same strong hands are there to help me and hold me steady. I try to swallow and even that hurts.

"Take it easy, Leannan. Nice and slow."

The world stops wavering and rights itself at last. The shapes of people nearby and the world around us solidify into reality. I am lying by the pool with my head on Alistair's lap. He stares down at me with stark lines of worry embedded in his face. His clothes are dripping wet the same as mine.

"You scared the shit out of me," he breathes.

"What happened?" I ask weakly.

"I was about to ask you the same damn question. One minute you were standing there watching the beach. The next you were floating face down in the fucking pool. I've never… Please don't do that again."

"No."

"You weren't breathing," he says with all due horror. I reach up to touch my forehead to locate the exact spot of all the pain. But he catches my fingers and says, "You've got a bad gash there that's bleeding. Best not to touch it."

"Take this." The king steps forward and offers a handkerchief. He gives me a curt nod, like *Good work for not dying and making things even more awkward or whatever.*

Alistair holds the neatly folded-up cloth to my temple. "Lilah, did you hear me? You weren't breathing when I pulled you out of that pool. Do you understand?"

"You mean I was dead? I actually died?" *Ouch.* Frowning is a bad idea.

He just nods.

"Huh."

"One moment," says the king, sounding astonished. "You almost die and that's all you've got to say regarding the matter? 'Huh'?"

"It wasn't completely unexpected." Lady Helena sighs. "But that's a long story and none of your business."

The two bodyguards standing beside the king appear just as mystified by this statement as the man himself. Not that anyone is in a mood to explain. Weirding out royalty could be seen as an accomplishment. It wasn't on my original wish list, but I don't hate the addition.

"I am not officially here," the king announces with his usual stern expression back in place. "It's best if I leave before emergency services arrive. Alistair…"

"You should go," answers his son without hesitation.

Lady Helena wiggles her fingers at him in farewell.

Dougal grunts and gives him a sour look.

Without further ado, the king and his retinue leave the

scene. It sort of seemed as if he wanted to say more. To have more time with his firstborn child. But then, he's had forty years to say something.

"I can't believe it. I'm alive." The sense of relief is staggering. How the predictions have all come true and I am still here. Amazing.

Alistair just nods.

"A seagull dive-bombed me," I add in a harsh whisper. My throat still feels like it has been scraped raw. I do not recommend drowning. Not at all.

"What did you say?" asks Alistair.

"A seagull. I fell. Hit my head."

"A seagull attacked you?" His brows rise to all new heights at the news. "So, you lost your footing and hit your head falling into the pool? Is that what you mean?"

I nod and wince. Neither talking nor moving are great. "Willow was right."

"Yeah. Guess she was. You weren't breathing...didn't have a pulse. You actually died." He carefully dabs my forehead with the handkerchief. "No more of this shit, Leannan. I love you, and thinking you were gone took about a decade off my life."

"Wh-what did you say?"

"You heard me."

I am not going to cry. My eyes are just glitching or something. It's been a really big morning.

"Och." He presses a gentle kiss to the tip of my wet nose. "I've been following your fine ass around town for a week now. How could you not have suspected?"

"I love you too."

"Lucky for me," he says with a smile.

Off in the distance, the sound of an ambulance draws closer.

Lady Helena also sniffles somewhere nearby. "Oh, that was so beautiful. You two really are the cutest." Then she gasps. "You know what I just thought of? We could have a double wedding! Isn't that a great idea?"

EPILOGUE

"We could always try swimming to the mainland." Alistair rubs sunscreen onto my back. He's been doing it for the past half an hour or so. No idea what's taking him so long. But there's no way I am complaining. Any day with his hands on me is a great day.

"Aren't there meant to be sharks out there?" I ask, inspecting the stretch of blue over the top of my sunglasses.

Another high-pitched scream of delight followed by a feminine giggle comes from inside the house.

"Yes," he says with a wince. "But I am willing to take the risk if you are."

"Hmm." I take a sip of my mojito. "I could always ask Gael to send me the mermaid costume from his friend who owns the bar. Do you think that would help?"

"Probably not." He leans down and busses the lobe of my ear with his nose. "You're too tasty to let the sharks have you. I think I'll keep you to myself."

"A wise choice."

It was Lady Helena's idea for us to accompany her and her

new husband on this island getaway. Alistair is making up for years of misunderstanding and putting distance between him and his mom by having quality time with her now. Neither of us understood quite how small the private island in question was, however. There's a luxury beach hut with two bedrooms and bathrooms and a living space, a lush garden that wraps around it full of palms and plumeria, and a little stretch of white sand. It is absolutely beautiful and sits off the coast of Brazil. But it also leaves us with absolutely no chance of escaping the newlyweds.

"I asked her if they could perhaps be quieter in the bedroom, and she patted me on the head," says Alistair in a sorrowful tone. "Said I was old enough to understand the powerful nature of sex between new lovers. But if I wanted to discuss it further with her, she was open to having that conversation with me."

"Thinking of taking her up on the offer?"

"I was actually considering walking into the sea, never to be seen again."

I snort.

"It's not funny, Leannan. She's out of control."

"Has she ever actually been in control?"

"No. Fair point."

"Get back here, lass!" Dougal's voice carries just fine in the tropical quiet. "Ye've work to be doing!"

"That's it." Alistair stops rubbing my back and reaches for his phone. "I am booking us a boat ride out of here. Mother and Dougal will just have to understand. They'll be fine here without us. It won't hurt to get to London ahead of schedule. Sounds like James could do with the support."

"Whatever you say, dear." I snap a shot of me poking my

tongue out and text it to Rebecca. It's a suitable reply to her request to be knighted. Then I slowly rise with a smile on my face. "I'll go start packing my bag."

Why not smile? Life is great. As much as I love being a librarian, there's nothing like a close call with death to make you prioritize. Work can wait. For now. There's so much to see and experience. The mystery of the missing Prince of Wales has also been solved. He and Alistair had been quietly texting for years, working on their brotherly bond. James was hiding out at a boutique hotel in Romania with a certain supermodel. Apparently, his upcoming nuptials are more in the way of a business arrangement between him and an acquaintance. Someone the king was willing to approve. Only they can decide if they're happy to live that way.

The king has made an effort to reach out again to Alistair. To invite him to his brother's wedding with no strings attached this time. I don't know if they'll ever have a real functioning relationship. But we're going to London to visit with that side of his family. It's a good start.

As for what comes next… We have decided to wander the world for a while. To visit all the libraries I have only read about and bask in their bookish glory. And to hit all the great surf beaches he's been wanting to try. It's item number one on our combined wish list. We'll return to Los Angeles and real life and routine eventually. My family and friends are there and so are his. Our work is there. It's our home.

Whatever we do, we're going to make the most out of the time we have together. Whether that be one day or fifty years.

★ ★ ★ ★ ★

ACKNOWLEDGMENTS

With thanks to…Susan Swinwood and all of the team at Graydon House. Amy Tannenbaum, Jessica Errera, and everyone at Jane Rotrosen Agency. To my family and friends, Anna, Babette, Charlotte, Olivia, Mish, Ellie, Margarita, Andi, Lori, and everyone in Romancelandia.